"What about this one? 'Widower with six children seeks helpmate.'"

"Mr. White." Sarah put all the authority she'd ever used in the classroom into her voice, extending a trembling hand into the open stall door. How dare he make fun of her search for a husband.

"You really can't find anyone to marry in Lost Hollow?"

Had his childhood teachers had as much trouble with the man as she did now?

"Mr. White." She kept her hand outstretched, hoping against hope that he would give her the paper and leave her be.

"There's no one you like around here? I've heard some talk in the bunkhouse… There are a couple of cowpokes who'd come around if you'd give 'em a look."

"My private life is no business of yours, *Mr. White*, but I'm not interested in a cowboy."

Books by Lacy Williams

Love Inspired Historical

  Marrying Miss Marshal
  The Homesteader's Sweetheart
  Counterfeit Cowboy
*Roping the Wrangler

*Wyoming Legacy

LACY WILLIAMS

is a wife and mom from Oklahoma. Her first novel won ACFW's Genesis Award while it was still unpublished. She has loved romance books and movies from a young age and promises readers happy endings in all her stories. Lacy combines her love of dogs with her passion for literacy by volunteering with her therapy dog, Mr. Bingley, in a local Kids Reading to Dogs program.

Lacy loves to hear from readers. You can email her at lacyjwilliams@gmail.com. She also posts short stories and does giveaways at her website, www.lacywilliams.net, and you can follow her on Facebook (lacywilliamsbooks) or Twitter @lacy_williams.

Roping the Wrangler

LACY WILLIAMS

HARLEQUIN® LOVE INSPIRED® HISTORICAL

Recycling programs
for this product may
not exist in your area.

™ LOVE INSPIRED BOOKS

ISBN-13: 978-0-373-82977-4

ROPING THE WRANGLER

www.LoveInspiredBooks.com

Printed in U.S.A.

I will not leave you as orphans; I will come to you.
—*John* 14:18

With thanks to critique partners Mischelle and Regina, for keeping me and my characters in line, and all the babysitters who made this possible, as well as my family for your continued support.

Also thanks to my editor, Emily Rodmell, for her invaluable feedback and for suggesting this series of stories.

Chapter One

Wyoming, fall 1895

"They say if he whispers, the fillies cuddle right up to him."

"And that he's a wonder with a lasso...."

"Maybe Eric can get some pointers, if he wants to steal a kiss from—"

Sarah Hansen cleared her throat and the raucous laughter from the group of thirteen- and fourteen-year-old boys broke off.

"I rang the bell," she reminded them. "Please return to your desks."

Three of the four young men filed around the corner of the school with only a murmur of complaint. The fourth, Junior Allen, remained in place, arms crossed belligerently over his chest. "You gonna make me?"

She considered the strap her predecessor had left in the bottom drawer of the schoolteacher's desk. She'd never used it on a child before, had always been able to maintain order in the classroom with warnings or sometimes a rap with a ruler. But this particular student challenged her more than any other. His father was the head of the school board and Sarah's boss—and Junior would likely go running to him if she dared punish him.

"Please go inside," she said, putting as much authority in her voice as she could muster. Junior was tall for a fourteen-year-old, already a few inches above her height. Sarah knew she couldn't physically overpower him if he chose not to obey, but thankfully he backed down and followed his friends.

She paused at the building's corner as the boys tromped up the rickety wooden stairs, kept her eyes focused on the few remaining leaves clinging to the trees behind the schoolyard. She breathed in deeply of the crisp air and tried to find a shred of patience for the afternoon lessons.

She didn't have to ask who the boys had been talking about.

Oscar White. Legendary—ha!—horse trainer. The horseman, some called him.

A single schoolmarm, Sarah boarded at the Allen Ranch, and the entire spread had been buzzing for days over the man's impending arrival. Now the news had spread to the nearby town of Lost Hollow, in the northern part of the state, and to Sarah's schoolchildren, as well.

And it was all because of a horse. Sarah's employer, Paul Allen, had purchased a colt from an expensive race horse breeder and wanted the horseman to train it.

Sarah had known Oscar White back in the tiny town of Bear Creek, where she and her sisters had spent their growing-up years. He'd been sweet on Sarah's younger sister, but that had happened after Sarah had already begun attending the normal school in Cheyenne. Possibly he wouldn't even remember Sarah, as they'd only been in the schoolhouse together for a few months.

But Sarah would always remember the time he'd humiliated her in front of her classmates, calling her a shrew when she'd corrected the behavior of one of her sisters. He'd been right, but he hadn't known why she'd had no choice but to be that way. His and Sally's flirtation hadn't lasted, and Sarah had forgotten about him until recently.

Because she boarded at the Allen ranch, she supposed there was no way to avoid seeing Oscar around the place. She'd grit her teeth and endure it. And hope that his job training Paul Allen's horse went quickly.

She had plans to put in motion, plans for her future, and she didn't need the distraction of *this* man. But she had no choice but to bear his presence. How long could it take to train a horse? Weeks?

Inside the schoolroom, the children murmured and shuffled, but at least they remained at their desks. She called them to attention and began the after-lunch lessons.

The afternoon was coming to a close when two of the girls, sisters, began fidgeting in their seats and whispering.

Sarah nodded to the girl in the second row who was reading aloud and went to stand behind the two sisters, Cecilia and Susie Caldwell. They glanced up at her guiltily, and when she peered down at their shared desk, she noted that the afternoon's assignment hadn't been completed.

The girls' lack of attention was a surprise. These

two were usually attentive and well behaved. Before she could question them, one of the boys threw a pencil across the room, striking another child in the arm.

Moving to correct the rowdy child, she forgot all about the girls in the hullabaloo that ensued and didn't get a chance to speak to them after the day ended, as she had to rush off to join the so-called "welcoming committee" at her boss's behest.

The life of a schoolteacher was never boring, but there were some events she wished she could avoid. Greeting the horseman was one of them.

"They say he's magic with the long reins—"

"I saw him ride once in an exhibition down by Cheyenne...."

Sarah clutched the satchel with her schoolbooks until her knuckles turned white. The men of Lost Hollow were no better than little boys, excited over a wild cowboy! Unfortunately, her boss had insisted that as the schoolteacher and a prominent member of the town, she should come along as part of the welcoming committee. And because she'd known Oscar White in Bear Creek.

She just wanted to get this "welcome" over with. She needed to finish her plans for the basket auction social this weekend and to that end, her thoughts wandered until the train came to a hissing stop at the platform.

The man who strode off with a confident gait bore resemblance to the Oscar White she'd known, but *this man* was assuredly different. Stetson tilted back rakishly to reveal brown eyes his face no longer had the slight roundness of youth. No, those lean craggy features belonged to a man, without question. Broad shoulders easily parted the small crowd on the platform, and he headed straight for their group.

Sarah turned away, alarmed by the pulse pounding frantically in her temples. Why this reaction now, to *this man?*

Through the rhythmic beating in her ears—too fast!—she heard the men exchange greetings and then Mr. Allen cleared his throat.

"And I believe you already know our schoolteacher…"

Obediently, she turned and their gazes collided—his brown eyes curious until he glimpsed her face.

"…Miss Sarah Hansen."

His eyes instantly cooled and the handshake he gave her was perfunctory. He quickly looked back to the other men. "I've got to get my horses from the stock car. I'll catch up with you gentlemen in a moment. Miss Hansen." He tipped his hat before rushing off down the line of train cars.

Sarah found herself watching him and forced her eyes away. Obviously he remembered her, and perhaps what had passed between them seven years ago.

That was just fine with her. She had no use for reckless cowboys. She was looking for a responsible man for a husband.

Oscar strode toward the stock car, shaking his head slightly. Sarah Hansen. That old shrew. Who'd have known he would run into her here in Lost Hollow? She'd probably never married, since she was still the schoolteacher. He'd been friends with her sister Sally—sweet on her for a time—but had forgotten about Sarah's existence after she'd left his hometown of Bear Creek.

Well, he'd stay out of her way if she stayed out of his. He had a job to do. One last job, and he'd be able to purchase the stallion he wanted and start breeding the mares he'd spent years collecting. Breeding quality horses had been his dream for years, and after he'd built a little cabin just across the valley from his pa's place, he'd spent the past months riding in exhibitions and cattle drives, saving up all he could to purchase the fine stallion he wanted from a man his neighbor and family friend Poppy Walt had told him about over in Idaho.

One job, a few weeks, and then he could go home. Maybe by Christmas.

The flimsy boards that stretched from the ground to the stock car wobbled under his weight as he climbed in. He wasn't looking forward to bringing the new mare he'd bought down the incline. She was flighty as a cat in a roomful of dogs, and anything could spook her.

It was a fairly modern stock car, with the animals separated into stalls. He'd tucked both horses into one of the larger stalls, hoping that the presence of his gentle gelding, Pharaoh, would soothe the mare.

Oscar came to Pharaoh first, as he'd been the last animal on board, and began untying the rope that had been used to secure the horse.

A railroad employee stomped up behind Oscar, causing the mare to neigh and bob her head against the rope holding her.

"Got to get a move on, mister," the man said. "The train is pulling out now."

"I need a moment to get this boy down the ramp," Oscar explained with a winning smile. "The gal there is pretty skittish, so I'll need to take her down myself."

"Hurry it up, mister."

The gelding came easily, trusting Oscar without question even on the creaky ramp. They'd been together for years, and it showed.

Oscar was tying him off to the closest hitching post he could find when the train whistle blew and a high-pitched whinny broke out.

Racing back to the stock car, Oscar's boots pounded against the packed dirt that made up the unloading yard. The railroad employee fought with the mare, struggling with all his might to hold on to the lead rope while she thrashed and tossed her head at the top of the ramp.

Oscar pushed past a small group of folks—the men and schoolteacher, he realized absently—but didn't reach the stock car in time. The horse pulled away from the railroad man and galloped down the ramp, heading away from Oscar and straight for the small knot of people.

The men scattered, but Sarah Hansen stood frozen and wide-eyed, right in the mare's path.

Oscar shouted, but the mare was too far gone in her fright to stop.

At the last moment, Sarah jerked, her skirt swishing, and that saved her. The mare stopped her wild gallop, rearing instead.

Oscar moved toward the horse slowly, not wanting to scare her into running again.

Now Sarah found her feet, finally turning to flee, but the movement incensed the already-nervous horse, which reared again and stamped its front hooves, apparently attempting to drive the offending fabric away.

Sarah shrieked and that set off the horse even worse.

Oscar followed as the girl ran and horse chased, continuing to stamp and snort.

Sarah ducked into a narrow alley and the horse followed. Oscar paused at the opening, peering into the darkness, afraid of flying hooves if the horse kicked out.

Sarah had fallen midway down the shadowed alleyway, and the horse continued to follow. Afraid the woman would get trampled, Oscar braved the alley, taking care to stay close to the nearest building. If he could avoid those hooves flying his direction, he would.

As the horse neared her, he willed Sarah to stand up. To move. Anything. But she remained still on the ground, although she shrieked like a banshee.

Finally, he came even with the prancing, stamping horse and was able to catch her dangling lead rope. He spoke calmly to her and she began to settle, though her eyes remained wild and rolled in their sockets.

"I've got her steady," he told Sarah. "C'mon outta there."

With the narrow alley leaving no room to turn the horse, he was going to have to get Sarah out of the way and guide the horse forward. But the woman didn't move.

"I can't," she finally whispered.

"You hurt?"

She jerked her head.

That's when he looked past the surface. Sarah's entire body was shaking. Her breaths still came rapidly.

She wasn't scared of a wild horse on the loose. She was terrified.

Two fillies frightened out of their wits. What would his ma tell him to do?

Comfort the one who was worse off. Glancing from woman to horse, it was a toss-up. But if Sarah kept flailing and making noise, he'd never get the mare calm enough to get them out of there.

"All right," he said to the horse, patting its neck gently. He tied her off to a protruding nail on one of the walls, aware it might not hold if she jerked her head. The horse protested his movements with a gentle neigh, bobbing her head.

"It's all right," he said again.

He approached Sarah, aware of the pointy toes of her boots beneath those skirts and petticoats. If she got scared and kicked out... He scooted to one side, just like he'd done with the horse.

"Sarah," he said softly.

Her eyes darted to him, wide and frightened.

"Take it out. Get it away!" Her voice rose and he instinctively clasped her hand in his, instantly silencing her.

"I'm not gonna let anything happen to you," he promised.

Her eyes held on his. In this shadowy light between two buildings, the blue looked almost gray. His stomach clutched at the fear still there.

He squeezed her hand. "We can't move the horse until she calms down. There's no room to turn her in this narrow space and she won't back up when she's riled. You should've picked a better escape route."

Her eyes flashed once. "Are you saying this is *my fault?*" she asked.

One long strand of straight flax-colored hair had slipped free of its pins and fallen against her cheek, making her look much younger. Oscar knew she was at least his age, if not a year older, but at the moment she didn't look twenty-three. She looked about twelve.

"Why do you even have such an unpredictable animal?" The fire was returning to her tone, even as she continued to tremble.

"I found her a few weeks ago. She's got scars where someone used her hard— I've been working to earn her trust, but we're not there yet." He didn't mention the cash it had set him back, cash he could've used to get started on his breeding program. He blamed his nature. He couldn't let the animal continue to suffer.

Sarah's eyes narrowed on his face as if she didn't recognize him. She'd finally stopped shaking, and some color had returned to her cheeks.

"Miss Hansen!" a male voice called out, somewhere outside the periphery of this small enclosed area.

She glanced warily over Oscar's shoulder and shuddered.

"Sounds like they're looking for you. Think you can get up now?"

She didn't answer verbally, just struggled to stand. He kept a hand under her elbow to assist, but she pulled away as quickly as she'd gained her feet. "Just keep that beast away from me," she demanded softly, brushing at the dirt and debris from her skirt.

She swung around and bolted out of the alley, not waiting for him to check on or untie the mare. So much for catching up with an old friend.

Still shaken, Sarah walked slightly ahead of the men as they traversed the rutted dirt road that was the town's main thoroughfare. She kept one eye on Oscar White's horses at all times, but they appeared docile enough as he led them with loose reins.

Appearances could be deceiving. She needed to remember that, especially with the jolt of attraction that had surprised her upon seeing the horseman again after so many years. He might be handsome, and he might've shocked her with his kindness toward an abused animal, but he was still an irresponsible cowboy at heart.

She'd returned to the train yard and retrieved her schoolbooks, a little worse for wear after she'd dropped them in her haste to get away from the horse. Now she clutched them to her midsection, willing the men to hurry along so she could get in Mr. Allen's wagon and head for home.

"You'll want to steer clear of the schoolmarm," Mr. Piet, the local carpenter, said quietly, but not so quietly that Sarah couldn't hear him. She pretended to glance into one of the storefront windows, catching a glimpse of Oscar leaning close to him, listening earnestly.

"Everyone in town knows it, but she's on the hunt for a husband. Wouldn't do for you to get caught just because no one warned ya."

Sarah's face flamed. She kept her gaze on the street in front of her, unwilling to see laughter in the horseman's face. It was true she wanted to get married—wanted it more than anything—but she had *some* standards. Not a foolish man like her father, for one.

She wanted a caring, unassuming man for a husband. Possibly one who operated a business. Businessmen were safe, reliable. They didn't chase every whim and endanger themselves.

They wouldn't leave a family without its provider just for the sake of a thrill.

Cursing her fair skin, which she knew had turned the shade of a ripe tomato, she kept her face averted and waited for this torturous walk to end. There was Mr. Allen's wagon, parked near the end of the street. She'd have to bear the horseman's company on the way to Mr. Allen's spread outside town, but then she could escape to the room she shared with Mr. Allen's daughter.

"She's pretty enough," Mr. Piet went on, "but she's got some unusual notions about husbands and she's right bossy."

Now she was sure she heard Oscar cover a chuckle with a cough. "And a little long in the tooth," the horseman said under his breath.

She didn't care if it was rude. She refused to listen to the men poke fun at her. She hurried toward the wagon, leaving the men behind to their chuckles.

She didn't acknowledge the tears burning behind her eyes. She wouldn't let Oscar White know his jibes could still hurt her. She wasn't fifteen anymore, but a grown woman capable of keeping order in a classroom and providing for herself.

But that didn't mean she couldn't have someone, a husband, to take care of her. She just had to find him.

Chapter Two

"I've got fifty cents. Do I hear seventy-five?"

Sarah watched as the mayor, acting as auctioneer, peered over the crowd from his perch on the raised dais some of the townsmen had constructed at the picnic grounds near the church.

"Sixty cents. Come on, folks. Do I hear seventy-five?"

Sarah anxiously scanned the crowd, looking for interest in the faces of several men she'd greeted before the basket auction had begun. Where was Ty Kelly? Clara Allen, her boss's wife, had said her brother would bid on Sarah's basket, just as a precaution if no one else bid.

And Sarah's basket was next, one of two cloth-covered baskets left. The winning bidders would share lunch with the girl who cooked the food. Or in Sarah's case, packed the basket of food that Mrs. Allen had made.

Sarah hadn't planned on entering a basket in the auction until Mrs. Allen had insisted. She was too old for events like this. Most of the other girls participating were in their late teens or close to twenty. Sarah was twenty-four.

Very close to being considered a spinster.

She was ready to find a husband and start her own family, but was it necessary to subject herself to this? Surely several of the men she'd taken time to speak to in town lately would bid on her basket. The banker, or the liveryman. At least one of them must be interested. It was only a shared lunch.

The mayor called the bidding on the basket before Sarah's and her stomach swooped. Another frantic glance did not locate Ty. Where was he? Clara had promised, and if no one else bid…

Sarah adjusted the dark blue bonnet with a cluster of lighter blue flowers on its crown, flowers that matched the cloth on her basket, a little hint for the men as to which one was hers. Heat crept up her neck and into her cheeks. Here was the test. Would anyone bid?

"And now, a fine-looking basket. Smells like…" The mayor took an exaggerated sniff. "Potatoes…maybe some ham? And rolls, definitely rolls. Let's start the bidding at a quarter. Come on, gents. Who'll buy this one for a quarter?"

Silence. Not one whisper, not one raised hand.

Sarah craned her neck this time, face blazing, but still no sign of Ty. She'd known this was a bad idea. She'd never been to one of these events where a basket hadn't sold, but what if no one bid on hers?

"How about twenty cents? Remember it's for a worthy cause, folks. Church needs a new roof. Twenty cents."

How humiliating. Could things get any worse? She hung her head, wishing she dared just get up and leave.

"One dollar." A strong male voice rang out above the crowd and whispers quickly followed.

Sarah glanced behind her, but couldn't see who'd made the bid. The voice hadn't sounded like Ty at all.

"Sold! To the horseman. Come up here and collect your prize, sir."

Chuckles eddied through the crowd.

Noise roared in Sarah's ears as she stood on wobbly legs and made her way to the back of the dais, where Oscar White was handing over a dollar bill and collecting her basket.

He had bid on her basket? Why?

After the fiasco with his dangerous horse and his thoughtless words to the carpenter, she'd spent the past week avoiding him. It hadn't been hard since he'd moved into the bunkhouse with the rest of Mr. Allen's cowboys and spent his days in the barn or the corral, both places she circumvented unless she had no other choice.

And now she would have to face him for the noon meal. She clutched the folded blanket in her hands and straightened her shoulders. She wouldn't back out, even though today had turned into a disaster.

"Hello, Mr. White," she greeted coolly when he turned, basket in hand.

He grinned. "Sarah."

"Where would you like to sit?" She raised the blanket, almost using it as a shield between them.

"You choose. I'll follow."

Conscious of the many surreptitious glances they received, Sarah was careful of her steps as she picked her way through the edge of the crowd spilling across the prairie field. Was everyone interested because of the horseman and his rumored skill with horses? Or was Sarah the spectacle? The spinster schoolmarm with the pity bid on her basket.

Finally, she found a semiprivate place tucked between the edge of the crowd and the line of parked conveyances. She shook out the blanket, surprised when Oscar skirted around and took the other side, helping spread it evenly across the grass.

When he joined her, long legs stretching beside her, the blanket that had seemed plenty big before suddenly shrunk, and Sarah spent a moment adjusting her skirts, trying to gather herself.

"You're still mad at me, huh?" he asked, surprising her into raising her eyes. "For sayin' you were too old to be looking for a husband?" One corner of his mouth tilted up in an irrepressible grin.

Was he laughing at her again? She reached for the basket that held their lunch. Her hat slipped, the ribbon shifting beneath her chin, and she took a moment to adjust it, using the action as an excuse to keep her gaze away from his.

"I've been trying to apologize all week, but seems like you've been avoiding me."

She wouldn't grace that statement with an answer, even if it was true.

"I didn't mean to offend you the other day," he said. "You still looked so pale and I thought—" He shrugged. "I just wanted to tweak your tail a little. Actually, I expected you to turn around and tell me off. I knew you were listening."

She focused on keeping her hands from shaking as she flipped back the cloth cover and began unloading the bowls and platters of food. Finally she came to the two empty tin plates and the cutlery.

He caught her fingers in his large paw as she extended him a fork and knife, holding on to her until she lifted her eyes to his face. He wasn't smiling now, only considering her with intense brown eyes.

"I don't require an apology and I don't need your pity," she said through stiff lips. She jerked her hand away.

He held her gaze. When she couldn't hold his eyes any longer, she began dishing out the food, filling his plate first with thick slices of ham, mashed potatoes and two rolls. Her bonnet fell over her brow again, but this time she left it. It shielded her from his assessing gaze.

"So will we eat without speaking, then?" He took the plate when she pushed it in his direction.

"What do you want to talk about?" she asked, still keeping her gaze down as she filled her own plate.

She sensed more than saw him shrug. "Tell me about being the schoolmarm in these parts. Do you like teaching?"

"Most days. It's been a way to support myself and my sisters before they were married."

But now she was ready to start making a family of her own.

"You've been here for what…a coupla years?"

"Yes. Before that I was at the Normal School in Cheyenne."

Rude as it was, she would've been content to let the conversation die. Embarrassment still heated her cheeks.

"How're your sisters?" he asked after a short silence.

She glanced at him from the corner of her eye, trying to gauge whether he was asking after Sally. She couldn't tell.

"They're well. Both married." She wasn't jealous of her sisters or their happiness. She only wanted to find the same for herself. Her disappointment that today's event hadn't turned out differently was perhaps coloring her interaction with the horseman. He seemed sincere in his desire to have a pleasant conversation.

It wasn't the horseman's fault that no one else had bid on her basket. In fact, he'd tried to spare her humiliation by bidding. Shouldn't she offer him basic consideration while they ate? Could she?

As he enjoyed the picnic food, Oscar imagined his ma would've been proud of his manners. He'd apologized for offending the prickly schoolmarm—even if she hadn't accepted it with grace—and was holding his patience against her short, almost rude, answers. Maybe it was growing up with so many brothers, but part of him took pleasure in getting her riled up.

"Did Sally ever get down to Colorado? She talked about wanting to go to college there."

Sarah looked surprised. Surprised that he'd mentioned Sally or that he'd remembered something like that? "She did. That's where she met her husband—a gunsmith."

There was another pause, and he was considering giving up on them having a decent conversation, when she grudgingly asked. "And how is your family?"

He nodded, wiping his chin before he spoke. "Fine.

Jonas—my pa—has had a couple of good years with the crops, which helps because now he's got a couple new mouths to feed."

Oscar's adoptive parents had married five years ago, and having a woman like Penny around had changed the family—in a good way. She'd brought joy and laughter to Jonas, who could be too serious sometimes. She'd worked patiently—stubbornly—on the boys until their manners improved. Her main challenge now was taming Breanna, who wanted to do the same things as her brothers, and not be confined to the kitchen and barnyard.

And their natural children… Oscar missed the little tykes. Walt, at four, idolized the older boys and would follow Oscar around all day if allowed. Two-year-old Ida was precocious, but so adorable that a body couldn't even argue with her if she demanded the last of the dessert.

"And all your other brothers? And a sister, right?"

Six adopted brothers and a sister. It seemed a little crazy to think his pa had taken them all in when he'd been a single man. Each brother came from different circumstances, some orphaned by illness, others escaping a difficult family situation. And Jonas's compassionate heart big enough that he made a family out of them all, instead of turning anyone away.

"Maxwell has been away at college the last three years. He wants to be a doctor."

"That's a wonderful aspiration."

He admired his brother. Admired him, but missed him. Of all his adopted brothers, he and Maxwell were closest in age, and had often spoken of their hopes and dreams. He'd heard all about Maxwell's fears of not doing well at college—and told his brother he was being stupid. He'd known Maxwell would do well with his mind set to a goal, and Oscar had been right. Once Maxwell had gone through the first semester and received top grades, he'd been raring for more.

Maxwell would've been the only brother Oscar felt close enough to tell about the deep loneliness that had followed him around the past few months. But without Maxwell around, he hadn't told anyone.

He shook off those melancholy thoughts, unwilling to go down that path with Sarah Hansen looking on. He'd get this one last job done and go home to his new little cabin and his herd of horses.

"The rest of the boys are workin' the land with my dad. Once a couple of us hit eighteen, we were able to file for the nearby land and increase the spread. It's more work, but more land for the cattle to graze."

Her eyes had glazed over. Bored with life on a farm? She'd left tiny Bear Creek behind to go away to school, after all.

She lowered her face and the flowers on her hat shifted forward. His hand tensed with the desire to tweak the ridiculous ornament. He looked away, and thought he saw a shadow move between two wagons.

One of the saddle horses nearby whickered and Sarah's head came up, bringing his attention right back to her.

"If I remember correctly, your sister used to suffer from seizures. How is her health now?"

"Breanna's health is fine. She's gone a good long spell without an episode and Penny—my ma—hopes they're gone for good. My pa's been dealing with the seizures since Breanna was born and he's not so sure." He couldn't help smiling as his thoughts shifted to the last stunt Breanna had pulled before he'd left home this spring.

"What?" asked Sarah suspiciously, using a handkerchief to blot her lips.

"Just remembering. My sister wants to be a cowhand like the rest of us boys. It drives our ma crazy. This spring Breanna dressed in some of my brother Seb's clothes and tried to sneak along on a cattle drive. Ma was busy with the toddler and almost didn't notice."

Sarah's scandalized look was similar to what Penny's had been. "But that's so dangerous! Why, she could've been trampled by the beasts or bucked from her horse, or what if rustlers attacked?"

He shrugged. "Breanna's a good rider. Speaking of riding—"

He meant to ask her about her fear of horses, but another movement among the parked wagons caught his eye.

"Excuse me a second—" He rose and strode over to where he'd thought he'd seen…

There! Someone small darted between two wagons, and Oscar gave chase. They were close enough that the ground-tied saddle horses, like Oscar's, were getting restless. He didn't want the kid to end up hurt if they got too near the animals.

"Hey!" He clamped a hand on the kid's shoulder, surprising the young girl into a shriek.

"Leave her alone!" Another child flew at him, surprising him into banging his elbow on a wagon. It stung, but he didn't release his hold on the first child.

A nearby horse whinnied. "Calm down," Oscar ordered, voice as strong as he could make it. Just like he would've if he'd been at home.

The girl beneath his hand froze, looking up at him with wide, scared eyes. A second girl, half a head taller and alike enough to be a sister, came and locked arms with the first girl. This child carried a baby on her hip. All three had dark, silky hair cascading down their backs, not in pigtails like the other young girls he'd seen at the picnic.

"See those horses over there? You were scaring them with your playing and scampering around."

The girl with the baby lifted her chin. "We weren't playing."

"Oscar. Mr. White!" He looked over his shoulder to see a pink-cheeked Sarah picking her way through the wagons, glancing often at the horses, though they were too far away to bother her.

"I found these two—er, three sneaking around the wagons and upsetting the horses. I don't suppose you're acquainted with them?"

She looked over the girls, and he took the time to take a longer look, as well. Their dresses were threadbare, they had bare feet even though autumn had begun and dirt-smudged faces—much the way he and his brothers had looked before Penny had come into their lives.

"These are some of my students. Cecilia and Susie Caldwell. And…I'm sorry. I don't remember your little sister's name."

"Velma," the middle girl answered in a whisper. "Miss Hansen, we was just watching the picnic."

"We *were* just watching the picnic," Sarah corrected softly, absently.

The older girl, Cecilia, glanced back toward the blankets and people past the wagons. Her dark-eyed gaze had a wistful quality.

"Where is your father?" Sarah asked.

"Stepfather," Cecilia answered belligerently, jiggling the baby when it gurgled. "He's at home. But he said we could come and so we walked."

"All right. Well, Mr. White seems to think you shouldn't be playing here in the wagons, not if it's scaring the horses."

Now the younger girl glanced longingly at the picnicking people. Oscar had a sudden insight—they were hungry.

"We've got plenty of food from that basket Miss Hansen made. Why don't you girls join us and then you can go off and play with your friends?"

The two dirt-smudged faces lit up, but both glanced up questioningly at their teacher. The woman herself stared at Oscar with a drawn brow, again as if she didn't know who he was.

"Can we really eat with you, Miss Hansen?" the younger girl asked softly.

"Yes." Sarah seemed to shake herself from a daze, then led the girls back to their picnic blanket. Once, she glanced back questioningly at Oscar in the rear.

With the girls added to their party, Oscar was edged almost completely off the blanket. Sarah fixed the food so that the girls could use what had been serving platters for their meals, then accepted the baby from Cecilia, holding it on her knee.

As the girls ignored the utensils and ate hungrily with their fingers, smacking their lips and with crumbs flying, Oscar had a flashback to what Penny's first meal with his family must've been like. The thought was bittersweet. He missed his adoptive ma, too.

"Miss Hansen, *you* cooked this food?"

An intriguing blush bled into Sarah's cheeks, piquing his curiosity. She ducked her head and those infernal flowers fell into her face again. "I had help," she muttered.

"What do you mean?" He directed his question toward the older girl, who'd spoken in the first place. He guessed her to be about the same age as his sister Breanna. Ten or eleven.

"Um...just that everyone knows Miss Hansen doesn't—"

"She cain't cook," the younger girl, whom he guessed to be about eight, broke in around a mouthful of half-chewed food. "Some of the boys in our class say that's why she cain't get a man to marry her."

Oscar stifled the smile that wanted to escape. A glance at Sarah revealed her face was downturned almost into her lap, but he could still see the bright-red tip of her nose from under that hideous hat.

The baby reached up with one soggy hand and tried to grab the frilly fake flowers hanging from Sarah's bonnet, but she grasped the baby's hand and began to play pat-a-cake.

She was gentler with the infant than he expected. From what little he remembered of her back in Bear Creek, she hadn't been particularly patient with her younger sisters. And she certainly hadn't been a picture of kindness since he'd arrive in Lost Hollow. Not that he'd deserved it after he'd teased her. But watching her with the infant…something gentle, almost motherly had come out, and she was smiling a real smile.

Maybe she really did have a heart.

The babe reached for her hat again.

"Miss Hansen, did you wear that hat to match your basket?" Susie asked.

"Mmm-hmm," Sarah answered absently. "Your sister seems to like it. What about you?"

The young girl wrinkled her nose.

Oscar finally did what he'd wanted to do since he'd sat down across from her. He reached out and tweaked the flimsy flowers, sending them into a quiver. "It's been driving me crazy all afternoon. Those flowers are awful." He chuckled when the girls dissolved into peals of laughter.

Sarah reached up with one hand and deftly took out a pin. The ugly flowers tumbled to the blanket and Sarah glared up at him, making him chuckle even more. Her eyes flashed fire. If she had been one of his brothers, he would've expected retribution in the form of a prank, just when he wasn't expecting it.

"At least I've a bit of style. Your poor hat looks as if it's been stomped by a bull even more than you have."

He took off the item in question and examined it as if he'd never seen it before. The brown felt was dented in some places, faded and sweat-stained. It was his favorite hat, and he'd had it for years. He shrugged, and plopped it on Cecilia's head. The girl giggled.

"Here. I've finished. Let me hold the baby while you clean your plate." He didn't wait for Sarah to answer, just reached out and plucked the baby from her arms.

Maybe this lunch wasn't a total loss. With the girls surrounding him and Sarah and forming a buffer, he almost felt right at home.

Sarah couldn't decide whether to get up and leave—she'd have to hide in the nearby church until the Allen family was ready to leave, as she'd ridden with them in their wagon—or to stay and receive more of Oscar White's teasing. The man obviously had no solemnity in his personality.

But the Caldwell girls had certainly fallen for his charm, even the baby. She billed and cooed at him, waving her hands and squealing with delight when he made faces at her. Sarah knew the girls weren't fully accepted by the other children or families, due to their heritage. Their birth father, now deceased, had been an Indian, and there was some prejudice in town against them. But Mr. White seemed to neither notice their darker coloring, or to care.

It probably shouldn't be a surprise that he had a natural manner with children, not when he'd grown up as part of such a large family. And he'd charmed Sally, at least for a while. If he weren't so irresponsible, perhaps Sarah would find him charming, as well.

When she'd noticed the horses start to get restless, her stomach had clutched. And while he'd headed right for the trouble, she'd wanted to run in the other direction. It had only turned out to be her students, but still... what if it had been someone up to no good? What if the horses had bolted and Oscar had run right into the situation?

He was reckless at heart, not someone she should be attracted to.

But that didn't stop her pulse from reacting to his nearness.

She just needed to control her reaction to him. She corralled a classroom full of children each day. Surely she could find a way to ignore her feelings and continue working on a plan to find a husband who would be good for her.

Chapter Three

"Miss Sarah?"

On Wednesday morning, several days after the calamitous picnic, Sarah jerked her gaze up from where she'd been unconsciously staring at her desk. "Yes, Amelia?"

"I'm done with my assignment," the girl said shyly, chin tucked down into her chest. How long had she stood quietly beside Sarah's desk at the front of the classroom, waiting to be acknowledged?

"All right. I'll come to your desk and review it."

A glance across the twelve desks in the classroom revealed all heads bent over their work, save one. Miles, a frequent daydreamer, stared out the one dingy window. Sarah really needed to clean it.

She needed to get her muddled thoughts straightened out. Ever since the fiasco at the picnic, when no one save the horseman had bid on her basket, she'd been considering the need to expand her horizons, so to speak. If none of the men—at least the men she was interested in—in Lost Hollow wanted to court her, maybe she would have to look elsewhere.

But now wasn't the time to be thinking of herself and her plans. She had students to teach.

She was crossing the room, striding between the desks as she spoke, when she heard a peep from the Caldwell girls' cloth-covered lunch basket, tucked beneath their seats.

It wouldn't be the first time someone had brought a kitten or a bullfrog or a lizard to school, but it always caused a major distraction, and Sarah was surprised that these two sisters would do something like that. Susie and Cecilia were usually quiet and attentive, almost active in *not* seeking attention.

When she moved to the small space behind their desks, she noticed the large reed basket wasn't the normal pail in which they usually carried their lunch. She braced herself for what she might find and placed one hand on each girl's shoulder.

"Girls, do you have something other than your lunch in that basket?"

Susie looked up at her with terrified eyes, but Cecilia, the older, showed defiance with her tilted chin. "No, Miss Sarah."

A cry rang out. A baby's cry.

Beneath her hand, Sarah felt it as Susie sucked in a breath. Sarah quickly knelt and drew back the cloth covering the basket, and a startled little blue-eyed gaze met hers, much like she imagined Moses had looked when the Egyptian princess had found him among the rushes.

"Girls," she whispered. "I think you'd better come up to the front of the room and talk to me."

Cecilia scooped up the basket and followed her sister to the front of the room, Sarah trailing. Whispers from the other students crossed the room, and Sarah tried to combat them with a stern glance and a reminder to focus on their tasks.

Behind her desk, she sat in the chair while the two girls stood at the corner of her desk. Cecilia had taken the baby from the basket and settled her on her hip. Baby Velma clung to the shoulder of Cecilia's dress and stared at Sarah with a wide-eyed gaze the same as her older sisters.

"Susie. Cecilia. What is the meaning of this? You know we can't have a baby in the classroom."

"Miss Sarah…" Susie whispered, chin now bowed to her chest. "Are we…are we in trouble?"

Tears trembled on her bottom lashes, and Sarah's heart constricted for the girl. But as the teacher, she had no room to offer comfort, not until she got to the bottom of this situation.

"Can you tell me why you brought Velma with you this morning? Does your father know you have her here?"

Susie glanced at her sister. Cecilia stood with chin still jutted out, belligerent eyes on Sarah. The baby stuck her thumb in her mouth.

"Stepfather," Cecilia reminded her coldly. "He knows we got her."

When Susie's cheeks reddened, Sarah had to wonder if the older girl spoke the truth. She waited, letting the silence stretch, a technique that her own mother had used on Sarah and her two sisters successfully.

Finally, Susie relented, glancing tearfully at her sister. "F-Father can't keep Velma today."

Cecilia hissed at her sister, glaring balefully at Sarah for good measure.

"Girls, I just want to help," Sarah said. "Is your father—your stepfather at home?" She was disappointed that the girls had tried to keep having a baby in their basket a secret, instead of coming to her. Didn't she inspire trust from her students?

Susie nodded, again with a glance at her sister.

"But he can't watch your sister? Is he ill?"

"Not—not really."

Sarah touched the girl's arm, trying to get more from Susie, who seemed willing to talk. "What does that mean? Is he ill, or isn't he?"

"He's drunk, all right?" Cecilia's voice rang out loudly, the opposite of Susie's whispers. "Is that what you wanna know? He can't watch Velma because he might forget to feed her all day or let the fire die and it's plenty cold today."

Titters and whispers spread over the classroom again and Sarah had to silence them with a rap of her ruler on her desk. "Children, please."

This time, she laid a hand on both girls' shoulders again. "Velma can stay with you today. She seems like a very good baby."

Of course, if she got hungry or had an upset tummy, that could change in an instant, but what could Sarah do? It *was* cold outside today. The girls would be better off in the classroom than at home, if their stepfather was that bad. And Sarah couldn't leave a classroom of children to attend the girls at home.

"Is there no one else that can help you?" Sarah asked softly, compassion tightening her throat. She knew what it was like to have a father you couldn't count on. Knew the shame, the fear that perhaps the next meal wouldn't come. "What about relatives? Do you have any aunts or uncles? Or a grandmother, perhaps?"

Cecilia stared at her with glittering eyes—tears that refused to fall? Sarah couldn't tell, but the girl only kept her jaw clenched and shook her head.

"No, Miss Sarah," whispered Susie. "It's just us."

Sarah remembered how the girls had been on the outskirts of the basket auction, none of the other families inviting them to share the noon meal. She'd even seen some of the women in town shepherd their children the other direction on occasion. Did the entire town view them as outcasts due to the slightly darker color of their skin? It was a question for another time.

"Well, we'll figure out a solution later, girls. For now why don't you let Miss Velma sit with me and return to your lessons? Try to concentrate."

Sarah spent the rest of the day teaching with a baby on her hip. She had to admit that Velma had to be the most relaxed child she'd ever met, content to be held and watch the other children. The baby took a long nap in her basket after lunch, and Cecilia fed her mashed vegetables and some goats' milk late in the afternoon, unobtrusively as possible in the back corner of the classroom.

At the end of the day, Sarah got caught up with another student and the Caldwell girls managed to slip from the classroom before she could speak to them further. Disappointed, she knew she would have to talk to Mr. Allen. Hopefully the school board could find a way to help the girls.

But what if the town held the girls' heritage against them?

Later that evening, before supper, she still couldn't forget the girls' ashen faces and their humiliation as they'd spent the afternoon struggling with their lessons. It was a reminder of how her own home life had been after her father's accident. That one incident had changed the lives of her entire family, and not in a good way.

Sarah sat at the small desk wedged between the bed she shared with the Allens' daughter and the wall. Out the room's only window, she had a view of the corral. As the sun made its descent, Oscar worked with Mr. Allen's prized horse.

She'd seen him there almost every day since he'd come. Tonight he had one long line attached to the animal's bridle and what looked like a whip in his other hand. The horse was moving in slow circles around the fenced area.

She hadn't meant to watch him, but every evening her eyes strayed to the corral. He seemed overly patient with the horse. It surprised her. She'd expected something more dangerous, like him throwing a saddle on the animal the first day and riding it until the bucking and snorting stopped. But so far he hadn't seemed to lay a hand on the horse.

Now he released the horse and moved slowly into the barn. Sarah tried to shake off her distraction and focus on the letter she was writing to her sister, but she began thinking about the disastrous picnic again. She'd been putting off taking further action to finding a husband, but if she wanted to get married, she needed to move forward.

And she had an idea how. She sifted through the papers on her desk. She'd bought a newspaper in town before the basket auction…where was it?

She sank into her seat as realization dawned. She'd left it in the wagon. In the barn.

She waited as long as she could, hoping the horseman had gone. It was near to suppertime when she slipped out of the house and headed for the barn.

She peered into the dim interior of the barn, first looking for any animals that might be outside their stalls or without a rope. Then, she glanced around for Oscar White. He was nowhere to be seen, either.

Breathing a sigh of relief, she slipped into the barn, wrinkling her nose against the smell of animals.

She moved quickly to the unhitched wagon, hiking up her skirts to climb in the back. She searched through the box for the newspaper she must've left behind.

"Where is it, where is it?" she muttered, looking through the discarded flour sacks and a couple of empty crates.

"Looking for something?" a familiar drawl called out. She whirled, nearly losing her balance, and was forced to grasp the side of the wagon box to steady herself.

A lazy hand waved the folded newsprint above one of the stall walls. That was all of him in sight. The hand disappeared.

"I wondered why the page had been opened to the marriage ads."

Face flaming, Sarah hopped from the wagon bed, intent on getting her paper, even at the cost of her humiliation.

"Let's see what we think, girl."

Who was he talking to?

"'Bachelor seeks wife who can cook and clean house.' Hmm. Sounds like that one wants more of a housekeeper than a wife."

She peered around the edge of the stall; it was blocked by two boards, but not a full door. Inside, Oscar sat on a round barrel in one corner, the paper propped on one bent knee and slicing an apple. The horse that had almost run her down that first day stood against the opposite wall, its head not far from the opening. As she watched, Oscar sliced a piece of apple and offered it to the horse, which ignored him completely. He shrugged and crunched into the piece of fruit.

Sarah ducked behind the stall proper in case it decided it wanted out. Two flimsy boards weren't likely to hold a beast like that inside.

"May I please have my newspaper?"

"What about this one? 'Widower with six children seeks helpmate.' Hmm. Six children is a lot. I should know. Perhaps that one isn't 'the one,' either."

"Mr. White." She put all the authority she'd ever used in the classroom into her voice while extending a trembling hand into the open stall door.

"You really can't find anyone in Lost Hollow?"

Instead of the paper, something small and moist plopped into her palm. A slice of apple. Had his childhood teachers had as much trouble with the man as she did now?

"Mr. White." She kept her hand outstretched, hoping against hope that he would replace the apple with her paper and leave her be.

"There's no one you like around here? I've heard

some talk in the bunkhouse…there are a coupla cowpokes who'd come around if you'd give 'em a look."

Affronted, she whirled, temporarily forgetting her fear of the horse inside the stall. The animal bobbed its head but otherwise didn't move.

"My private life is no business of yours, *Mr. White,* but I'm not interested in a cowboy." She stretched her hand out, daring to reach into the stall, with the chunk of apple still in her palm. "May I have my paper, please?"

He considered her, eyes appraising. "Why not?"

She sucked in a breath of air, the last of her patience gone. She opened her mouth to order him to give her the paper, when the horse took one step forward and snuffled the apple right out of the palm of her hand, the tiny hairs on its nose tickling her palm.

Sarah froze, ready to bolt and leave the paper behind, but Oscar said, "Wait!" in a low, urgent voice.

He quickly sliced off another piece of apple and extended it to Sarah, moving slowly and steadily. "Will you try to feed her again?"

Sarah nearly choked on her fear. "I can't."

"Please," he breathed. "I've been sitting here for nearly an hour and she's ignored me the entire time. And she just ate out of your hand."

"What if—what if she charges at me? This panel won't hold her back."

"She won't. She's calm and as long as you don't shriek or do something to frighten her, she's going to stay that way."

Hand shaking, Sarah felt him press an apple piece into it. As he settled back onto his barrel in the corner, the horse again nibbled the fruit from her hand.

Fear still racking her entire body, she turned and fled.

"Sarah, wait!" She heard a plank slide back and his footsteps behind her. "Sarah—"

The barn door flew open in front of her, sending the last of the evening sunlight spilling onto the dirt floor. She couldn't catch her breath. Trembled all over.

"Sarah!" came an unwelcome bellow.

Oscar watched as his boss, Paul Allen, filled the barn doorway. He came alongside Sarah as she hesitated, probably gauging the man's anger by his flushed face.

Oscar could see her hands still shaking. He hadn't meant to frighten her so badly, but he'd been ecstatic when the mare had responded to her.

"What's this that Junior tells me about some girls bringing a baby in the classroom today?" Allen demanded.

Oscar knew the man was a hard boss from the tales the cowboys told, but he couldn't believe he'd approached and spoken to a woman that way. Oscar's hackles rose and he took a step nearer to Sarah, coming even with her elbow.

"Two girls had a situation at home and had no choice but to bring their young sister to school with them. I was planning to talk to you about it after supper tonight."

The older man shook his head. "There shouldn't have been anything to talk about. You should've sent those girls home instead of allowing something like that in the classroom."

"Mr. Allen, the infant didn't even cry. I doubt it was much of a distraction." After seeing her with those three girls at the picnic, Oscar wasn't surprised she was standing up for her students.

"Junior said it distracted him."

No doubt the boy had gone running straight to his papa to tattle. Oscar barely knew the boy, but could tell he was spoiled and entitled.

Sarah's lips tightened. "Your son would be better served paying attention to his own lessons, as I've expressed before."

The man's face reddened even more. Oscar sensed this was an argument they'd had before.

"Maybe you've been given too much freedom in your classroom. I'll remind you that the school board has the final responsibility for those children and their learning and I won't allow it to be jeopardized. If those girls bring the baby to class again, you *will* send them home."

The man slammed out of the barn, leaving them in near darkness.

She breathed in a small gasp. Was she crying?

"You okay?" he asked. If she'd been his younger sister, he would've reached out and touched her arm, but he didn't think Sarah would've welcomed his touch. They weren't exactly friends.

She started, as if she'd forgotten he was there. He wasn't even sure Mr. Allen had seen him; the older man hadn't acknowledged Oscar.

"I'm fine."

He couldn't see her face in the dim light, but her voice didn't sound fine. She sounded suspiciously teary.

"Here." He pressed the newspaper she'd been so worried about before into her hands.

She didn't answer, only moved out the door and into the evening air. He followed.

"Sarah, wait. Is there anything I can do?"

She shook her head and kept walking. For a moment, he wished he hadn't teased her so badly before.

"Please. Is it the same girls we ate lunch with before?"

He reached out and snagged her arm, pulling her to a halt and so that she faced him. "Sarah, I'll help."

She brushed a hand across her face and he saw lines of weariness etched in her features. "Yes. It was the Caldwell girls, but I don't know how you could help. They said…"

She swallowed audibly. "Their mother died several months ago, just after the baby was born. A fever, I think. They told me their stepfather was too drunk to care for the baby. That's why they brought her to school."

Oscar's memories took him back to Boston. His uncle had taken him in after Oscar's parents had died, but the man hadn't been any kind of parent. In the end, Oscar had run away from the man's cruelty and emotional abuse, and that's when he'd met Jonas. Without Jonas, where would he have ended up?

"They're awful young to be dealing with something like that." His mind worked, as he considered the girls and what he might do. "Can the local church do anything for them?"

"I don't know. Their father—stepfather—might not accept it. I've heard him rail against the church before. And there's—there's more besides. People may not want to help them." She clutched the newspaper to her midsection. "But I'll have to try. I can't just leave the girls on their own."

"Sarah! Come set the table!" the rancher's voice rang out from the house.

A glance at the house showed the rancher's wife in silhouette in the light streaming from the kitchen window. Did she approve of her husband shouting at Sarah like he did?

Sarah's face pinched. "Excuse me."

Oscar took his meals in the mess, with the rest of the cowboys on the spread. But he wouldn't let her dismiss him so easily, not when something had upset her so. And he couldn't forget those little girls and their dirt-smudged faces from the picnic.

And it galled him to see Sarah so upset. "Sarah, wait—"

"Leave me alone!"

She stomped off toward the house, leaving him stinging with her dismissal. He didn't *need* to get involved. What he needed was to finish his job with Allen's horse and return to his cabin, his spread, his life.

And so he would.

Chapter Four

Midmorning the next day, Oscar finished a training session with Paul Allen's colt and released it to the near paddock. With no saddle or bridle, it galloped free, tossing its mane and whinnying in happiness. He planned to rope it later that afternoon for another session on the long reins.

His rioting thoughts weren't so easily marshaled. He'd been unable to sleep last night, thinking about Sarah and her predicament. She was competent. Bossy. She'd be able to get some of the women in town to help those little girls. Surely, she would.

But that might take time. He knew she had a full day of teaching today. What if something needed to be done right now?

How well he knew what it was like to be abandoned by a relative, even if the abandonment was figurative. He couldn't stomach the thought of those girls suffering.

So he found himself saddling the gelding and asking one of the cowboys for directions to the Caldwell place.

Riding up, the spread was a sorry mess. Fields empty where winter wheat should already be sprouting. The cabin hadn't been painted in years. Planks were missing from the barn roof. It didn't look as if the place would weather the winter.

Oscar dismounted and ground-tied his horse in the yard. A haggard-looking man answered his knock. Oscar could smell the stench of day-old alcohol on the man. His eyes were bloodshot. It was impossible to tell if he was drunk now or just hungover.

A baby cried from inside the cabin.

"What d'ya want?" the man snarled.

"Mr. Caldwell? I'm Oscar White."

The man's eyes widened slightly. Perhaps he'd heard about some of Oscar's exploits. In this one instance, Oscar could be glad of the stories people told about him, even if some of them were exaggerated.

"I'm a friend of Sarah Hansen—the schoolteacher?"

Now the man's eyes narrowed. "Yeah?"

"She mentioned to me how you've been having a hard time since your wife died…"

The baby squalled louder and Oscar took a half step forward, toward the doorway. "You mind if I come in?"

The man moved aside—a little wobbly, but eyes still suspicious. Oscar followed him inside the small living area. A ratty sofa took up one side of the room and on the other was a rickety table and chairs half in the kitchen. An open doorway led to what must be the only bedroom.

"Sarah—Miss Hansen, well, she's worried about the girls," he said, voice rising to be heard above the baby crying from the other room.

"That nosy busybody can mind her own business—"

"You mind if I…?" Oscar motioned to the bedroom,

not waiting for an answer, but walking right in. The man stumbled after him.

Inside the room, one bed took up nearly all of the floor space. Rumpled, stained bedclothes half hid the sobbing babe. Oscar picked her up and immediately understood from the smell why she was upset—she'd messed her britches. He held her in the crook of one arm, hoping that she wasn't going to soak through to his shirt, and dug around in the scraps of clothing on the floor until he found a cloth diaper that seemed remotely clean.

Caldwell looked on from the doorway. "I don't need no interference from anybody—"

"Look," Oscar said, giving the man a sharp glare over his shoulder as he changed the baby. "I know what it's like to lose someone you love. Some days it's hard to want to get up and do anything."

He picked up the baby, who was silent and watching his face now that she was clean.

"But you've got three little girls looking to you to take care of them."

The man's face went impassive. "They aren't my girls. They were my wife's."

"But they're your responsibility now." Oscar waved a hand around the room. "Your place isn't ready for winter. If you don't get a good crop, are you even going to be able to feed yourself?"

The man shook his head, turning away and going into the kitchen area. Oscar followed, only to watch the man take a bottle out from beneath a cabinet and unscrew the top.

The kitchen was messy. Dirty dishes overflowed the

dry sink and the remains of breakfast covered the table. The floor hadn't been swept in a good long while.

Oscar jiggled the baby on his arm while he considered what to say to the obviously bitter man before him.

"I'd like to help, Mr. Caldwell."

The man shook his head as if to clear it, but Oscar doubted what ailed him would be easily shook off.

Caldwell hiccuped, then shrugged. "I guess if you want to work, I ain't gonna say no. I cain't pay you."

"All right. We'll see how today goes," Oscar said, smiling down at the baby, who returned a toothless grin.

He was perhaps playing on Paul Allen's generosity by taking the afternoon, but Oscar didn't see a choice. He needed to make sure the baby would be cared for until her sisters returned home from school.

Time seemed to drag for Sarah. Cecilia and Susie had arrived at school on time, but had been subdued and quiet all day. Junior Allen caused problems at lunch, preventing her from having a moment to talk to the girls. After classes were over, they'd remained long enough to give her several quiet nonanswers while standing before her desk. Sarah had been conscious of the other children gathering things and speaking in small groups, and obviously the girls had been aware of the other children, too. She couldn't blame them for their desire to keep their family problems private. When all the troubles with Sarah's father had been going on, she hadn't wanted anyone from town to know how bad things really were.

But now that Sarah knew there was a problem, she

couldn't just let the girls suffer. She would just have to go speak to their stepfather herself.

She gathered her things and set off for the Caldwells' small spread. It wasn't close to the Allen place, so that meant she'd spend a good portion of her afternoon walking, and maybe even miss supper. But she had no choice.

She was disappointed but not surprised with the state of the farm. The fields hadn't been properly plowed after the summer's crops had been taken in. Even from afar, she could see the dilapidated condition of the cabin. Outside, a broken clothesline hung down to the ground and debris littered the yard.

But someone was singing.

A rich baritone voice filled the afternoon, lifting in a familiar hymn. It slowly faded and as Sarah approached the cabin, rose again.

As she neared the place, she saw Cecilia and Susie sitting on the worn plank porch, legs swinging beneath their skirts. She moved to join them, and that's when she saw him.

Oscar White, with a bundle of some sort strapped around his broad chest, working a horse and plow. Singing.

He had a nice voice, soothing and even.

"What is going on?" she asked the girls as she stepped up onto the porch.

"The horseman is here," Susie said in an awed voice.

Cecilia glared over her shoulder at Sarah. "You sent him."

"I did no such thing." She wouldn't have even if she'd thought of it. After he'd witnessed her dressing down by

Mr. Allen, she'd only wanted to escape him. She didn't even *like* the man.

She never would have imagined he would come here on his own.

"Where's your fath—stepfather?"

Both girls shrugged, faces turned back to watch the horseman wield the plow.

Sarah took it upon herself to peer inside. The cabin was quiet. "Mr. Caldwell?"

She moved through the open room, sniffing what smelled like stew. A line had been strung from one side of the kitchen into the open living and it was strung with diapers, sweet-smelling and white.

Had *the horseman* really washed baby diapers?

A glance at the stove did indeed reveal a bubbling pot of stew. The kitchen was clean, though the floor needed to be swept.

The girls' stepfather wasn't indoors, and when Sarah slipped out the back door it was to see Oscar leading the now-unhitched horse to the barn.

"Is Mr. Caldwell there?" she called out to him.

He turned and saw her. Then he took off his hat and waved it at her. "I'll be there in a minute!"

The girls' feet pounded inside; Sarah joined them in the kitchen, where they looked with wide eyes at the linens hanging above their heads.

"I've got the horse settled for the evening," Oscar said as he banged in the back door, backing inside. "Your pa left on the donkey a while ago."

Cecilia and Susie looked at each other, acknowledging they knew where he'd gone. Sarah's heart pinched for them.

Oscar turned around and Sarah realized that the bundle strapped around his wide chest was the baby. She hadn't even thought about the tot, and he'd had the baby out with him while he'd plowed. Now he spoke softly to her while he unwrapped the makeshift sling—a bedsheet?

Cecilia reached out for Velma when he'd gotten her out of the sling and he relinquished her with a final slurping raspberry on her cheek, to which she laughed.

"Y'all don't have to stay," Cecilia said, moving toward the table. "Our pa will be home in a while. We can take care of supper for ourselves."

Sarah moved toward the girls, laying a hand on each of their shoulders. "Girls, is there anyone else who could possibly help you? Do you know if your mother's parents are still alive? Did she have any siblings?" She'd already asked about family connections once, but perhaps the girls had kept something back from her before. Cecilia certainly had not been forthcoming about anything that was going on.

Cecilia's face went perfectly blank, but Susie's features screwed up and she turned her face away.

"There's no one who wants us," Cecilia said quietly.

"What—" Sarah started to ask more, but Oscar caught her elbow and shook his head slightly.

"Girls, I sampled the stew earlier and it should be about right. Can you serve yourselves?"

They nodded. "Thanks, mister," Cecilia whispered, surprising Sarah with her gratitude toward the man. She'd been nothing but difficult toward Sarah since the baby had appeared in the classroom.

Oscar used his hold on Sarah's elbow to propel her

through the cabin and outside. She shrugged off his hand as they crossed the threshold.

"I wasn't done asking them about their family."

"No, but they were done talking to you. You push too hard."

Her back went up. "I was trying to help," she hissed.

"I know." He wasn't ruffled by her tone at all, only amused. The corner of his mouth turned up.

He motioned toward his horse, now saddled and waiting for him just off the porch. "If you don't mind riding double, I'll give you a lift back to the Allens' place."

"No, thank you." She had no intention of getting on his beast. How easily an animal like that could throw them and break their necks!

"Aw, he promises to behave. And I do, too."

If she was a weaker woman, the grin he gave her—a flash of white teeth against his tanned skin—would've made her knees knock. But she wasn't weak, and she started walking toward the road.

"No, thank you."

"C'mon, Miss Schoolteacher. I promise this guy's as gentle as a kitten. It's a long walk."

She just shook her head and kept going. Finally, he fell in step beside her, the animal trailing behind him as the man held the reins loosely. She couldn't keep from noticing the brawny shoulder beside hers.

"It isn't necessary for you to accompany me home," she said stiffly. "I'm sure you have things to do if you've been working here all day."

He nodded. "My ma would have my hide if I let a lady walk home alone, daylight or not."

"I can't believe you washed and hung those diapers,"

she murmured, because she couldn't forget the bobbing string of white linens.

He chuckled. "It's not the first time I've had to help out with the little ones. And there wasn't much choice— there weren't any more clean ones to be had."

She shook her head, glancing at him from the corner of her eye. Imagining such a big strapping man doing a menial woman's chore…she couldn't picture it.

"And the stew?" she asked.

He shrugged. "They needed something to eat for supper."

"And the baby? The singing?"

"I couldn't very well leave little Velma inside by herself all day, could I? The sling is a little trick I picked up from my pa when Breanna was an infant. The singing, well…"

His voice trailed off and she glanced at him. Beneath his hat, his cheeks looked red. Was he embarrassed?

"At first, neither the baby or the horse really wanted to work with me, but once I'd started singing, they both calmed right away."

"Are you planning on going back tomorrow?"

He frowned. "I don't know. I doubt that would make Mr. Allen very happy. I've got responsibility for that colt. I don't know if I can really get involved."

That was the response she'd expected. He wasn't a resident here in Lost Hollow. And the girls weren't his responsibility.

But they were her students. And she refused to let them fall through the cracks, like she and her sisters had after her father's accident.

"Can I ask why no one else in town seems to want to

help this family? Caldwell is no peach to be around, but I would think there might be some women who could provide the occasional meal to ease the burden on the girls a little…."

She hesitated, but finally said, "I'm not sure on all the details. I believe it has to do with the girls' real father being an Indian. He died before Velma was born, but I don't think he was fully accepted in the community."

"That's a shame. Those girls shouldn't be punished because of their parentage."

"Mr. Caldwell seems to make it worse with his behavior. He isn't exactly sociable, and can be…unkind—" it was a very softened description of how she'd seen him "—when he's under the influence of drink…" Her voice trailed off.

He was silent, thoughtful.

"Listen, there's something else I wanted to talk to you about," he said, half turning toward her as they walked. "About last night."

"What?" she asked. "More of your courting advice?"

He smiled and her traitorous heart tripped. "No. It's about the horse. I've been trying for almost a month to get that mare to warm up to me, and she ate that apple chunk right out of your hand."

Sarah raised one brow. The excitement in his voice and the sparkle in his eyes had had her interested. Right up until he'd said "horse."

"Would you consider helping me gentle her?"

Sarah was shaking her head before he'd finished speaking. "No. Absolutely not."

"But she's responded to you—"

"I have no interested in helping you with that—that beast." Sarah was shaking just thinking about it.

"I know you're scared—"

She glared at him and he went silent. "I think I have a right to be a bit nervous around that animal after it nearly ran me down."

"It's deeper than that," he said quietly.

She blocked out the memories from her childhood, when she'd been trapped and frightened. She refused to give him the satisfaction of seeing her in a pathetic state.

They walked the rest of the way in awkward silence. She wished he would just ride on without her, but the stubborn man insisted on remaining at her side the entire way. As they entered the Allens' yard, Sarah saw her boss standing on the porch, watching their every move.

If she thought he had any way of knowing she had visited the Caldwell place, she might've expected her boss to be angry. But he couldn't know where she'd gone after school, could he?

He was obviously waiting for her, so she simply nodded a silent goodbye to Oscar and went to meet Mr. Allen.

"Where have you been?" he demanded.

"My afternoons are my own," she replied softly, attempting to hold on to her patience as best she could. The man didn't own her, even if he was her boss.

He crossed his arms over his chest, eyeing her with narrowed gaze. "The school board wishes to remind you of the upcoming Christmas pageant. We'd like to see your plans and a list of the children you expect to have speaking parts for our approval. And we also want to discuss the possibility of a new script."

"The school board has left the pageant under my approval the past years," she reminded him, keeping her voice low so he wouldn't suspect how angry she was at his controlling maneuver. "And we've used the same lines for the past three years and never had complaints from parents or students."

"Yes, but as there has been some suspect behavior in your classroom as of late, we've decided that we need to approve what you have in mind for this year."

"Is this because of what happened with the Caldwell girls?" She gripped her fingers together until they pained her. She couldn't afford to lose her temper with this man.

He didn't answer directly, only stared at her until she knew she was right. The man had no compassion in his body. Couldn't he understand that those girls needed help?

"We want you to get started immediately. It's already coming up on Thanksgiving, so there's not much time left for preparation."

"I believe there's plenty of time."

"The school board is insistent."

She knew what he really meant was *he* was insistent. He was trying to control her movements and limit how she could help the Caldwell girls. She didn't know if he had a personal agenda against the family, or just wanted Sarah to bend to his will. Either way, it galled her.

"If you don't heed the school board's guidance for your classroom, we may have to think about getting a replacement for next year."

She couldn't believe he was serious. She'd done a good job for the Lost Hollow school. She'd had several parents comment on the improvement in their children's learning. But he would remove her simply because he didn't like her helping a family in need? Was it because of the girls' parentage? Or was there something else?

His face said he would brook no argument. What could she say? She had little savings after supporting her sisters all these years. She needed the job, even though it pained her to have to agree.

"Excuse me. I need to wash for supper." He barely moved aside to let her pass. Tears blurred her vision, but she refused to give him the satisfaction of seeing how he'd upset her.

She would just have to discover another way to help the Caldwell girls, if her time would be limited by the pageant.

Oscar waited until Sarah had gone inside before approaching the older man on the porch. If he'd known Allen's character before he'd agreed to train the man's colt, he wouldn't have taken the job. Probably.

He needed the money from this job for his stallion. He needed to remember his purpose here, not get distracted by a pretty face and those little girls. But their situation reminded him strongly of his own childhood, and the hurts his family had caused him.

He wouldn't go back on his word. He'd train the colt, but he didn't have to be happy about Allen treating Sarah the way he was.

"Got a minute, Mr. Allen? I'd like to talk to you about the colt."

It was hard to tell since dusk was falling, but the man's gaze seemed to be taking Oscar's measure.

"I noticed you didn't work with him this afternoon. Where were you?"

Oscar refused to be intimidated. He ignored the presumptive question. "He's making great progress. Been on the long reins and I'm guessing he'll be ready for a saddle in the next few days."

The man nodded, posture easing slightly.

"Listen, I went over to the Caldwell place today. That family needs help."

Allen's shoulders tensed and a deep frown took the bottom half of his face. "That's Caldwell's problem. I hired you to train my horse and that's what I expect you to do. Your responsibility is to me."

He was almost bellowing now, but Oscar didn't back down. "If I can help that family while I'm in town, I will."

"You'll be *here,* from breakfast to suppertime, working with my horse, or I'll fire you. And spread the word that you backed out on your commitment to me. I'm sure that story will spread just as fast as your adventures do."

The threat didn't even make Oscar blink. The man had given him an opening, though it wasn't much.

"That's all I needed to know," said Oscar steadily, then headed to the mess to find his supper.

Allen's callous attitude was enough to anger, but it wasn't the real reason Oscar felt the need to help out. He'd been forced to rely on the charity of his uncle for those few years of his childhood, and the man had never warmed to Oscar, never really cared about him. He refused to see three little girls suffer the same fate, not if he could help it.

Chapter Five

The next morning, Oscar went to the creek to wash up, like he usually did. He needed to speak to Sarah before she left for the schoolhouse. The answer he'd been looking for had come to him last night as he'd left Allen on the porch, but he needed her help to make it work.

And some part of him wanted her to know she wasn't alone.

He'd just splashed his face with the bracingly cold water when he saw her. She sat on a plank swing hanging from a tree not far away, blond hair loose down her back, head bent.

The sight of her, the very beauty of the picture she presented caught his breath in his chest. Heat flushed through him, making him acutely aware of the cool drop of water that slid down his throat and beneath the collar of his shirt.

His feet took him toward her before he realized it, and he knocked his hat against his thigh. Nervous as a schoolboy.

She looked up and their eyes met and locked. He nodded a greeting, scratched the back of his neck, uncomfortable as all get out with this new awareness of her. He knew she was pretty, but to see her like this... to know they were on the same side...

"I need to talk to you for a minute."

She shook her head, the long blond strands slipping over her shoulder. She pushed them back into place, and Oscar swallowed hard.

"I don't think we have anything further to say to each other," she said as she avoided his gaze and began tucking her hair into a long braid down her back. His every thought fled. It seemed like such an intimate thing, to watch her fix her hair, even though they were outdoors, where anyone could see them, with murmuring cowboys not far away at the corral.

"You know—" His voice emerged strangled, hoarse, and he had to clear it before he could go on. "I heard what Allen said to you last night."

Her cheeks pinked, but her fingers kept flying over the braid lengthening down her back.

"Are you sure his threat is valid? What about the other members of the school board?"

She shook her head slightly. "They follow Mr. Allen's lead. They won't disagree with him."

"What's his agenda against the Caldwells?"

"There's some prejudice in this town against them for being half white. I don't know if Mr. Allen's disapproval of them stems from that, or something else." Her voice was barely a sigh. Had she given up? She still wouldn't look at him, so it was hard to tell her mood.

"I want to help, Sarah. I've got an idea, but it's going to take some doing on both our parts."

Now her chin lifted, those blue eyes considering him.

"What do you get out of it?" she asked suspiciously.

He didn't want those little girls going through what he had as a child. It was that simple. But he doubted Sarah would understand. So he wouldn't try to explain it to her.

Sarah had a hard time believing Oscar was sincere in wanting to help the girls. With the top button of his woolen shirt unbuttoned and his hair curling and damp around his face, it was hard to marshal her thoughts.

Why didn't she think he really wanted to help?

He shifted his feet, bringing her attention to his powerful legs. She forced her gaze away, back to the Allens' house.

"I know there's no love lost between us," Oscar said. He was certainly more serious this morning than she'd ever seen him. "But I think we can set aside our differences to help those little girls. Friends?"

He extended his hand to her. She considered it, considered him. Could she trust him?

He'd surprised her by working all day at the Caldwell place yesterday. And the gentle way he trained Mr. Allen's horse hadn't been what she expected.

He still irritated her like no other.

But she couldn't help the Caldwell girls on her own, not with the demands Mr. Allen had put on her with the upcoming pageant.

With no other choice, she reluctantly slipped her fingers into Oscar's. His warm dry grip surrounded her hand. His white teeth flashed in a smile that threatened to curl her toes, and she quickly reclaimed her hand, grasping the rope swing.

"What time will you be back from the schoolhouse?" he asked.

"I've got a meeting with the school board right after classes end. Then I'll still need to clean up the classroom. I probably won't make it home in time for supper."

"Fine. I'll come for you at the schoolhouse and escort you home."

She started to protest, but he was already striding confidently toward the barn.

That man!

Oscar found Paul Allen in the yard, speaking to his foreman. When the men were done, Oscar quickly stepped forward to talk to the boss, nodding his hello.

"What's this about?" Allen asked, eyes narrowed.

"I've been thinking about what you said the other night. About me bein' here from breakfast to suppertime to work with the colt." How could Oscar phrase it best to try not to offend the man? Or play on the other man's sensibilities? "I figure if I stay elsewhere I'll save you a bunk and two meals a day—breakfast and supper. And be able to help out a friend in the meantime."

Allen's cheeks reddened beneath his hat. "And where might that be?"

"Caldwell's."

Allen crossed his arms. He did not look happy, but what could he say in the face of Oscar's proposal—it would save him grub and Oscar would still be holding to the deal they'd struck to train the colt.

"If I were you, I'd be careful choosing my friends. A man like Caldwell doesn't have many and there's a reason for that."

Oscar smiled, because he had the boss right where he wanted him. "I was talking about helping Sarah. She cares about her students and I'm glad to help her out."

Allen's eyes narrowed to slits. "She needs to be careful she's looking out for the *right* students."

The man's audacity riled Oscar, but he worked to keep a neutral expression fixed on his face.

"I think she is. Good day," said Oscar simply, and turned and walked toward the barn. He'd gotten what he wanted, and it made him more determined than ever to make this plan work.

That evening, Sarah furiously scrubbed the blackboard with a damp rag. It was silly to take out her frustration in this way, but the school board's unrelenting stance on the Caldwell family—led by Paul Allen's stubbornness—infuriated her. They refused to acknowledge that the family needed help, and they wouldn't budge on their request for a completely new script for the Christmas pageant.

"You gonna scrub right through that poor, defenseless blackboard?"

A familiar male voice, laced with laughter, came from the doorway and Sarah whirled toward the horseman, one hand at her heart.

"Sorry. Didn't mean to startle you. I told you I was coming to get you. You about ready to go?"

He leaned one brawny shoulder against the doorpost, hat tapping lazily against his thigh. His cavalier attitude was the last thing she needed right now when she was strung tight, with no idea how to help the Caldwell girls and her job under threat from a heartless school board.

Sarah turned back to the blackboard, this time careful to disguise her upset with smooth strokes. "I have things to finish up here. It won't be the first time I've walked home in the dark."

"I want to talk to you about the Caldwell girls and their father."

She wasn't sure she could talk about the situation without her anger prompting tears. "Perhaps we could speak tomorrow."

Without warning, he clasped her hand, stilling her scrubbing. When he tugged the damp rag from her grasp, Sarah released it to him, prepared to insist he leave her alone. Except he turned and began washing the blackboard, nudging her aside with his shoulder.

"What are you doing?"

"Helping you." He didn't stop erasing the chalk marks left behind from today's lessons.

"Why?"

Now he looked over his shoulder at her. And winked. "Because I'm hungry. The sooner you finish up, the sooner we can get going."

Stubborn man. But if he wasn't going to leave without her, she might as well attend to her other evening chores. She moved to the now-dead fire in the potbellied stove and used a stick to stir the cold ashes, then prepared the tinder for lighting first thing in the morning. The days were getting colder. It was one major reason she was concerned for the Caldwell girls. While Susie wore shoes—a scuffed pair, likely Cecilia's hand-me-downs—Cecilia still came to the classroom each day with bare feet. Did their stepfather know she needed shoes? Could he even afford them?

By rote, Sarah finished setting the fire and moved to the broom, intending to sweep out the aisle and vestibule, where the children tended to track in the most dirt, but Oscar moved to take the broom from her and began the task.

"I guess your meeting didn't go so well."

He didn't look at her, focusing on the broom in his hands.

She hummed an affirmative as she gathered the schoolbooks she wanted to take with her to review for tomorrow. Several of the children had seemed to have trouble with the arithmetic today, so she wanted to spend extra time on that lesson in the morning.

He mumbled something that sounded like, "that might be my fault," but she couldn't be sure. "Did they outright tell you not to help the Caldwells?" he asked.

"No." She stuffed the books into her satchel, keeping her head down so he wouldn't see the bitterness in her expression. "But they've made it nearly impossible. They're insisting on a new script for the Christmas pageant, and between that and making backdrops and props and rehearsing with the children, I likely won't have time to do much else."

"Well, I've got a partial solution for you."

She hefted her bag and watched him put the broom back into the small cupboard in the corner. They met near the front door, and he reached to take the satchel from her.

"I've got it." She kept her voice soft this time. How could she be sharp with him when he'd helped her clean up the classroom—when he hadn't had to?

"Blame my ma," he responded, taking the bag from

her, anyway. He shot her a surprised look and weighed the bag in his hand. "You carry this thing home every night?"

Though it was a question, he didn't seem to require an answer, only pushed the door open for her and followed her out, securing the door behind them.

Down the stairs, he used her elbow to turn her toward the back corner of the school. "Let's get a move on. I'm starved."

That's when she saw the horse standing placidly—for now—at the corner of the building. Sarah pulled back, removing her arm from Oscar's grasp. "I can't—I'm not riding that thing with you."

"Aw, c'mon," he groaned. "Can't you have pity on a man? Just this once? I promise the horse won't cause any trouble. I've had him for years and he's never bucked me off. He's a gentleman."

She didn't—couldn't believe him. Her feet seemed glued to the ground. "I told you I'd be fine walking. Really. I'll see you back at the Allens' place."

"Sarah." She waited for him to voice his exasperation, but instead he grinned at her, a white flash of teeth against his tanned face. He took her arm again and urged her forward, though she dragged her feet.

As they turned the corner of the schoolhouse and neared the animal, Sarah saw the buggy it was hitched to.

She glanced toward Oscar, who continued to smile at her in the dimming light. "You rented a buggy?"

"Borrowed it." He patted the horse's neck as they passed the animal. "This guy's a little perturbed at me, asking him to do such a menial job as pulling a buggy. You game to ride home with me?"

She allowed him to boost her into the conveyance. The buggy dipped and settled as he hefted himself in next to her. His bulk filled the seat, leaving them sitting almost shoulder-to-shoulder, closer than Sarah would've liked.

He stowed her bag beneath their feet and released the brake.

Sarah couldn't believe she was riding home next to the horseman. She might've expected him to cajole and push her into getting on a horse with him. But he hadn't. After the past few days, it was obvious she needed to revise her expectations of the man. He hadn't been anything like what she remembered from Bear Creek years ago.

"So tell me about this plan of yours." She tucked a strand of hair behind her ear.

"It came to me when I was speaking to Mr. Allen last night. He said he wanted me working with the colt all day. But he didn't say I had to board at his place."

He looked at her for a long moment, waiting for her to come to the same conclusion he had.

"You're going to stay at the Caldwell place?" she guessed.

"Yup. In the barn. I figure maybe Mr. Caldwell could use a listening ear, and some help with the work around the place. Maybe if he can work through some of his grief and doesn't feel so alone, he'll dry up. And I'll be there to watch over the girls most times, except during the day. When you'll be with them."

"How did you get Caldwell to agree to that?"

"Told him I'd take a share of the proceeds from the winter wheat crop when it comes in. A man's gotta have his pride."

"But you'll be gone by then, won't you?"

He nodded. "I doubt I'll be here past Christmas, with the way Allen's colt has been taking to the training."

"So then, you're doing this out of the goodness of your heart?"

He chuckled at her skeptical tone. "I *am* looking for a trade, but not with Caldwell. You seem to be the only other person in town who cares about those little girls. I want to make a deal between us."

Her cheeks warmed. What could he possibly want from her?

"Look, I'll lay this out and you can think about it. You're the only person my mare has responded to."

His words froze everything inside her.

"Now, don't get all tense, all right?" His warm, broad hand clasped both of hers in her lap and Sarah realized she had clenched them so tightly she could barely feel her fingers.

"I'm not asking you to ride the horse. All I'm asking is you to spend time with the horse—and me. Maybe walk her around on the lead rope if we get that far before I leave. If she trusts you, I can use that to get her to trust me. That's all I'm asking."

"It's too dangerous," Sarah whispered. She couldn't trust her voice for more.

"Just think about it, all right? I won't let you get hurt."

He reclaimed his hand and deftly turned the horse and buggy into the Allens' yard. The Allen children played in the yard, but began shouting and waving when they spotted the buggy. Sarah braced herself as best she could as they started running toward the buggy. If the horse bolted, the buggy could flip—

"Whoa, boy." Oscar neatly pulled back on the reins and the horse slowed, acting as if it didn't even notice the rowdy children.

Sarah let out a shaky breath. Oscar hopped to the ground and reached up for her waist, lifting her down as if she weighed next to nothing. When he pressed her satchel into her hands, their fingers tangled. She looked up at him, aware that he was too close, his eyes saw too much.

"I told you, I won't let anything happen to you."

But the reality was that she wasn't sure she could believe him.

Oscar watched several emotions cross Sarah's expressive face. He wouldn't have seen her struggle in the dim twilight, except for how close they were.

He continued to be struck by her beauty. This close, he could see the spray of freckles that dusted her pert nose. He had the insane urge to lean forward and steal a kiss, but could still hear his ma's voice reprimanding him for the kiss he'd stolen from Sarah's sister all those years ago. And he didn't particularly think Sarah wanted his kiss. Besides, the Allen kids were closing in on them, loud and raucous.

He released Sarah as the youngsters clambered toward them, then turned to unhitch Pharaoh from the buggy.

"Miss Sarah, Pa said not to save your supper if you was too late," the oldest boy, Junior, said. His voice carried across the yard, he was so loud. And he was almost gloating with his announcement.

"Ma tried to save you some, but Pa seemed kinda upset and wouldn't let her," Ham, the younger son, added quietly.

A glance at Sarah's face revealed her expression had tightened and lips clamped down.

Oscar kept unbuckling the harness, stuffing down the flare of anger at the boss's order. The man had called the school board meeting with Sarah in the first place, then penalized her for having to take the time to complete her day's tasks?

"I'll see if Cookie can make up two plates of grub. He always holds some for the hands who come in late." Oscar couldn't defend the prickly schoolteacher to Allen's face, not when he needed to keep his job. He still needed the money for his stallion. But he could make sure she got fed.

"I can't eat in the mess," she murmured. "It's not proper."

"Well, then…maybe tonight's a chance for you to get to know my mare a little better. We can eat in the barn."

Oscar turned in time to see Sarah wrinkle her nose, but Ham came closer and so did the teen girl, Barbara.

"Are you gonna help the horseman?" the girl asked breathlessly.

The older boy lost interest and wandered off toward the corral.

Sarah frowned at him, but Oscar shrugged at her and began to lead the horse off. "It's either that or go hungry, Miss Schoolteacher."

He gave the gelding a good rubdown and put the animal in its stall. Stopped to dunk his head in a barrel of rainwater to freshen up, then begged off two plates of grub from Cookie. The man raised a bushy brow, but didn't comment.

When Oscar returned to the barn, he found Sarah hesitating in the large double doorway with two children still tagging along.

Her raised chin challenged him to comment, but he only smiled at her and tilted his head to urge her inside.

She froze well before the mare's stall. The children didn't seem to notice, rushing ahead of Oscar.

"Here." Oscar handed the food to Sarah. "Stay outside," he called to the children, who obeyed but peered curiously over the planks that kept the horse inside its enclosure.

Oscar ducked into the stall and maneuvered the empty barrel he'd used before out into the barn proper, nudging aside the planks as he needed to.

"Don't let her out here!" Sarah cried.

Oscar looked over his shoulder. The horse hadn't moved a bit. He winked at Sarah as he pushed the barrel into place just outside the stall door. He put the planks back in place, then pushed a bale of hay across the floor next to it. Still well outside of the compartment.

Returning to Sarah, he took her elbows and gently drew her forward to perch on the bale of hay, facing the stall. The children settled next to her, one on each side. He rested on the barrel and took one of the plates from Sarah.

She didn't move, only stared down at the plate before her. He wanted to jar her out of her fear, but how?

"Mr. Horseman, where'd you get this horse, anyway?" the young boy asked. "She sure ain't very pretty, is she?"

Oscar nudged the tip of Sarah's practical shoe with his boot, finally getting her to look up at him. Her face was white. What could he say to break her concentration on the horse?

"You can't judge a horse just by how she looks. Maybe she is a little long in the tooth…"

Aha. That got her attention as she graced him with a scathing look. He grinned. She turned her face back toward her plate, but this time she took the fork and scooped up a bite of baked beans.

"But maybe she's got a beautiful gait. Or can rustle up a herd of cows faster than you can snap your fingers. A horse is much more than what color her coat is."

Sarah's eyes flickered to his, held for a moment, then darted down, hiding behind a veil of golden lashes.

"What do you plan to do with this horse?" Barbara asked. "She doesn't look like she's built for racing."

"The man I bought her from wanted to use her for farming and such, but he hadn't trained her well and wasn't very kind to her. That's why she's so skittish now."

Oscar looked over his shoulder at the mare. Sometime while they'd been talking, she'd moved one step closer to the planks and the edge of the stall. She seemed cautious, but curious about the voices coming from outside her stall.

"But I think she'll made a good saddle horse, for the right rider," Oscar finished, returning his gaze to Sarah, who met his eyes squarely this time.

She nodded once, and he knew she was agreeing

to his plan, agreeing to help him with the horse. Suddenly, the barn door slammed open, banging against the outer wall.

"Sarah!" Allen's voice bellowed.

The horse backed up in its stall, bobbing its head and neighing its agitation at the loud interruption.

Sarah jumped, and Oscar quickly moved between her and the horse, standing steady and tall in case the mare decided to kick out.

Allen rushed into the barn, gaze scanning and breathing rapidly.

"Is there a problem, Mr. Allen?" Oscar asked, bringing the man's attention to their little grouping.

Allen's face showed his surprise. But at what? Finding Oscar and Sarah together or finding his children present? "Where have you been?" the older man demanded.

"After our meeting, I had to clean up the schoolroom." Sarah glanced over her shoulder, but by some miracle, the mare was standing still in her stall—not exactly calm, but at least not rearing.

Oscar touched beneath Sarah's elbow. Letting her know he was here.

"And then Mr. White was kind enough to escort me home, since it was nearly dark."

"Where have you been since then? The Lost Hollow schoolteacher must be above reproach, and if you've been dallying with—"

Oscar interrupted before the man could go on and disparage Sarah or her reputation. "I hope you're not suggesting Sarah did anything wrong. Your kids were kind enough to tell her supper hadn't been held, and

I got Cookie to share some of the grub. Can't let our schoolteacher go hungry, now can we? And your kids were keeping us company while we ate." Oscar purposely kept his voice cool, though his temper was flaring. He was tired of the way Allen treated Sarah. But if Oscar lost his temper, he wouldn't do anyone any good.

The older man's eyes flashed. But with his young son at his side, gripping his hand, and his daughter looking on, he couldn't exactly accuse Sarah of impropriety, not when they'd witnessed the entire exchange over supper.

"One step out of line…" the man threatened with a last glare at Sarah, then spun and stormed out of the barn, his children following, though the girl threw a sad look over her shoulder.

"I'd better go," Sarah said, voice subdued and face downturned.

Oscar squeezed her elbow gently. "I'll get your satchel."

He carried the bag for her across the yard, not relinquishing it until they reached the porch, where they could stand in full view of the lit windows or anyone in the yard or corral could see them. He hated that the upbeat moments between them had been destroyed.

"What's he got against you?" he asked her quietly.

"He doesn't like anyone to contradict him," came her near-silent answer. "He's got it in his head he doesn't want me helping the Caldwell girls."

"What about his wife? How can she let him treat you like he does?"

Sarah just shrugged, still not looking at him.

"I'm helping that family just as much as you are."

"Yes, but he needs you. He talked you up so much

around town before you got here that if he fires you everyone will want to know why. He won't come outright and say what he's got against the Caldwells and he doesn't want to ruin his own reputation."

Oscar shook his head. "It's not right."

She looked over his shoulder, not really looking him in the face. "At least you're doing something for them, when I can't."

"You might feel out some of the ladies around town or from the church. Yesterday I noticed there was hardly a stitch of clothing in that cabin, and winter's coming on. The girls need some new dresses, coats. If you can get the women behind you, maybe you *can* do something more."

Her shoulders lifted briefly and then dropped. "They might not be willing to cross their husbands. But I'll try."

She slipped inside before he could say a proper goodbye.

He didn't like the fact that he had to finish working with Allen's colt, but Oscar needed the money. And now he felt as if he couldn't leave without seeing this situation through. He couldn't walk away from Sarah, who was only trying to do a good thing for those girls, when she was at that tyrant's mercy.

But what happened when his time with Allen's colt was up?

Chapter Six

Three days later, Oscar cleared the breakfast dishes from the table as Susie and Cecilia rushed out the door to head for school. Velma toddled after them with a toothy grin, then banged on the closed door once they'd skedaddled.

Caldwell scooted his chair back from the table with a scrape of wooden legs against the plank floor. "Good breakfast. Didn't know a cowboy could cook."

Oscar dropped the dishes into the soapy tub of hot water, and began rolling up his sleeves as the other man didn't appear concerned about cleanliness. Caldwell seemed a bit more settled since Oscar had moved into the barn. The other man hadn't visited the saloon that Oscar knew of and had attempted to work on the outside chores. But it bothered Oscar that he didn't seem to care much for the girls.

"I'm glad you liked it," Oscar said. "Listen, there's something I wanted to talk to you about. Have you noticed that the girls' dresses are getting real short? And I couldn't find any shoes for Cecilia, or coats, either."

Caldwell's shoulders tensed and his mouth turned down, but Oscar went on.

"If you've got a few dollars, I can run into town and get what the girls need."

The man shook his head, stuffing his hat onto his head and heading toward the door. "Ain't got no money."

"Well, what about credit? Will the general store grant you enough to get some necessities? They can't go all winter—"

Caldwell didn't seem to be listening as he snapped his suspenders and turned for the door. He shook his head. "That old man won't grant me a nickel."

Oscar wasn't terribly surprised. If Caldwell spent any measure of time at the local saloon, likely his funds wouldn't cover all his bills and other proprietors tended to know things like that. But the girls *did* need winter clothes.

"But—" Oscar's protest was cut off as the man slammed out of the cabin.

Although Caldwell hadn't touched a bottle since Oscar had arrived a couple of evenings ago, he had to have gotten the money for that previous binge somewhere....

Oscar finished the dishes while Velma played on the floor and then delivered the little gal to her stepfather, who was lazily digging the last of the potatoes from the small garden plot—something that should've been done weeks ago. Oscar couldn't imagine that the tubers would be very tasty, but at least the man was working.

Cecilia and Susie and Velma needed more than their stepfather could give. How could Oscar make the man see the light? He didn't know, but he was determined that they wouldn't be without the things they needed for the winter.

After the school day had ended, Sarah was sweeping out the classroom when the children playing outside went silent.

"Knock knock," called a familiar voice. The horseman.

Sarah went still as his bootsteps climbed the rickety steps. She hadn't seen him since the other night when Mr. Allen had threatened her job and questioned her character. She'd been embarrassed for him to make those accusations in front of the horseman.

But she'd also been conscious that if his children hadn't been present, his accusations would have been spot on. She was attracted to the horseman, and although he only seemed concerned about the Caldwell girls, if they were together alone the town could spread gossip about them.

"You doin' okay today, Miss Schoolteacher?"

She found a smile as he filled the doorway, then moved to put the broom away and went behind her desk. Without waiting to be invited, he came inside and leaned casually against one of the far student desks.

Behind him, she saw moving shadows in the open doorway. Probably some of her students wanted a tidbit of gossip about the schoolteacher and the horseman.

"I'm fine. What are you doing here?"

The side of his mouth pulled in a half smile at her greeting. It didn't seem to bother him that she wasn't as welcoming as she might've been.

"I thought I'd escort the girls home and it gave me an excuse to come in and see you."

Aware of the flush rising in her face, she shuffled a pile of papers on the corner of her desk into better order, then focused on lining up several small pieces of chalk in order of size. Anything was better than facing the man, who seemed to bring out the schoolgirl in her. Which was ridiculous, because she was nearly a spinster.

"I don't suppose you've had a chance to make it into town to see about rustling up some clothes—" He looked over his shoulder as something banged in the vestibule. When he looked back at her, his brows were raised. "To talk to some of the ladies about the project we'd talked about?"

Sarah's heart swelled with his intuitiveness and compassion. He'd figured out that there were children listening at the door. Children who could be cruel if they found something—like a lack of appropriate clothing—to pick on in another child. And he'd found a way to communicate with her that the children wouldn't understand.

Sarah swallowed against the sudden thickness in her throat. "I've been buried under writing this new script for the play. I haven't had time."

"Good."

She raised her brows at his satisfied answer.

"I'll escort you into town on Saturday. You can call on some of the ladies and we'll have a chance to talk."

She crossed her arms over her chest and raised one brow. Did he realize how high-handed he sounded?

"Plus, you agreed to help me with my mare."

"I did not." Although she had intended to before Mr. Allen had burst in and ruined their camaraderie. "But I might consider accompanying you on Saturday if you should *ask*."

His teeth flashed in a grin. "I'll pick you up mid-morning and you can instruct me on my deficiencies the whole way into town."

She narrowed her eyes, but couldn't find it in her to be perturbed at his teasing. She'd known before now that he couldn't be serious. "Fine." She began gathering her books and notes strewn across the desk. "How are things going for you and Mr. Caldwell?"

He glanced over his shoulder briefly and back at her meaningfully. "Things seem to be all right for now. We can talk more on Saturday."

Sarah stuffed things into her satchel and moved toward the door, allowing Oscar to escort her through and close the door behind. The children, mostly girls, scattered at their exit, murmuring and giggling. No doubt they would be sure to tell their parents this evening. Tongues would be wagging in every home in Lost Hollow.

But would any of the gossips spare a thought for three little girls who needed help?

Saturday dawned bright and unseasonably warm. Although it had taken her several late nights of working by candlelight into the wee hours, Sarah had finished a new script for the pageant. She'd also been compiling a mental list of the children she would assign to each part and the mothers she could call on today.

But those calls weren't the reason she had taken extra

care on her hair or chosen the one dress she had that most flattered her figure.

No, the horseman was behind her increased pulse and the slight flush in her cheeks.

And it was incredibly silly. He wasn't courting her. He was helping her with a project. And she wouldn't welcome him if he were courting her. She didn't want a cowboy interested in her. Didn't want someone reckless and careless.

So why then was her heart pounding, knowing he was coming for her? He was probably on his way right now.

She needed to get ahold of herself. Needed to be realistic. Sarah thumped the hairbrush she'd been holding onto the end of her mattress and forced herself to sit at the desk wedged into the corner of the room.

With Barbara already out doing chores, Sarah was alone. Thank goodness for small favors. She didn't want the curious girl telling her father what Sarah was up to.

She opened the newspaper she'd tussled with Oscar over and skimmed to the two ads she'd circled in pencil. One man from Montana and one from Colorado. Her heart thundered for another reason as she contemplated writing an answering letter to one or both of these gentlemen. Did she dare?

Did she have a choice? She wanted to be married, wanted to start a family of her own. None of the respectable, available businessmen in Lost Hollow seemed interested. With Sarah's involvement with the Caldwell girls, it seemed less likely than ever that one of the men in town would want to court her.

Being a mail-order bride was the only option for her

if she wanted to marry, unless she relocated. And with her limited funds, relocation was a risk. She'd prayed and prayed about it and the answer still didn't seem clear. She just knew she wanted to get married. Answering a marriage advertisement might be her only chance.

Before she could change her mind, Sarah took out a blank sheet of stationary and penned a short note expressing her interest in obtaining more information about one of the prospective grooms. She found an envelope and addressed it, intending to post it between one of her calls in town.

As she stood and slipped the letter in her dress pocket, movement outside the window drew her gaze. Sitting tall in the buggy seat, with that beat-up brown Stetson perched on his head, there was no mistaking the identity of her caller.

Sarah hurried out of the house, only to find her boss and his wife standing on the porch.

Oscar approached, tipping his hat off his head. His hair was matted with sweat, as if he'd already put in hours of work, though it was only midmorning. His chambray shirt heightened the breadth of his wide shoulders and Sarah's pulse began to dance, even after the talk she'd given herself inside.

"Morning, Mr. Allen. Mrs. Allen." He paused, too-sharp gaze taking in Sarah's dress and her cheeks that were now flushing with heat at his appraisal. "Sarah."

Mr. Allen crossed his arms over his chest. "Going for a drive? Miss Hansen, do I need to remind you that your character must remain at the highest standard?"

Oscar opened his mouth, but before he could say

anything—in defense of her or denial—Mrs. Allen broke in.

"Oh, Paul. Let Sarah enjoy an outing with a charming young man. She's never done anything to make you question her before."

Sending a grateful look at the woman who rarely dared speak out to her husband, Sarah hurried down the steps before Mr. Allen could protest any further. Oscar matched her stride across the yard to the buggy, where she hesitated when she saw the mare tied behind the cart.

Oscar raised his brow at her, as if daring her to return to the house. She accompanied him the last few steps.

"You're sure she won't be a danger—bolt or rear or turn the buggy?" Sarah murmured as he boosted her up into the seat.

"Not really," he answered as they came face-to-face. Then he settled her on the seat, giving her another of those half smiles and rounding the front of the buggy before she could protest.

"You look nice today." He turned the buggy easily out of the Allens' yard and into the two-rutted lane toward town.

"Thank you." She fidgeted with her hands in her lap. She glanced over her shoulder to see the mare following the buggy placidly. "How is the Caldwell place shaping up?"

"All right. I don't think Caldwell has been at the bottle again since I've been there. He hasn't really talked to me, but the toddler has been happy and the girls have seemed more settled. I did ask him about money for getting the girls clothes but he claimed he didn't have an extra dollar."

She wrinkled her nose. "Well, Cecilia can't continue much longer without shoes, even if we've been having a particularly mild autumn. And they both need winter coats. Pray that today will be successful and someone will offer to help."

"How've the children been in class? And your plans for the pageant?"

"Would you believe my worst pupil is Junior Allen?"

Oscar's huff seemed to indicate his agreement.

"He's restless and spoiled—his father refuses to believe he could do better in school if he would apply himself. And he tries to show off for the other boys, his friends, and causes trouble in the classroom."

Oscar nodded. "I knew a boy like that in my school days."

She gave him a sidelong glance. "I had you figured for that boy."

He grinned at her but shook his head. "Maybe before Jonas got ahold of me, but he would've skinned me alive if I had caused trouble. My brothers Mattie and Ricky, though…"

"You sound as if you miss your brothers. Will you be traveling home for the Thanksgiving holiday this weekend?"

She, for one, was looking forward to an extra day without the schoolchildren. Although she'd gotten the script worked out for the pageant, there was much still to be done and without the children underfoot, she could try to catch up.

He shook his head, face gone serious. "I've got too

much to do with Allen's colt. Making good progress, but I'm hoping to be back to my place before Christmas. I've got this little cabin built and my horses are just waiting for me...."

"It sounds nice."

"It is. Just a two-room cabin, but it's on the lee side of a hill, surrounded by pine forest and real quiet. Got a barn and a little corral, and it's all mine and mine alone."

The arrangement sounded lovely, but what about his family? Why was he so thrilled about being alone?

"What about you? Picked out a husband yet?"

She flushed, a wave of heat sliding up her neck and into her face.

"What's that blush for?" He nudged her elbow in the close confines of the buggy seat. "You sent a letter?"

She didn't answer.

"Sending one today? Ah. Was it the man with six children?"

The meddlesome man! Couldn't he leave it alone? Even if he was joking, it wasn't any of his business.

"All right, you won't tell me. I thought I'd drop you in town for your visits and we could meet for lunch at say...noon?"

"Fine," she said. "At the hotel dining room?"

"No, I've got something else in mind."

He didn't give her a chance to answer as they turned onto Lost Hollow's main thoroughfare and he pulled the buggy up against the boardwalk beside the bank.

"I'll pick you up right here." He took her waist in his broad hands and lifted her down. "I hope your calls go well."

It was the most serious she'd ever seen him, as he

gazed down into her eyes and squeezed her hands between his. If the man was ever to turn that intensity on a gal, one would certainly be hard-pressed to ignore the flutter of butterflies his coffee-colored eyes engendered.

Which was why it was a relief when he grinned and sent her off with a gentle push.

Mostly a relief.

Her first call seemed promising when Mrs. Anderson, the mother of one of her students, welcomed Sarah and ushered her into the kitchen with a smile. They sat down and Sarah accepted a cup of tea, wondering how best to broach the subject of the Caldwell girls.

"Minnie tells me you and the horseman are courting."

Sarah choked on her first sip of tea. Eyes watering and throat burning, she dabbed her mouth with a handkerchief. "Excuse me. I'm so sorry."

The other woman winked conspiratorially. "Should we be worried about finding a new schoolteacher next year?"

It would be necessary if Sarah were to marry. Most schools didn't accept married schoolteachers, unless they were male.

Heat rose in her face, but Sarah knew she had to find some way to be polite. She tried to think of the girls she wanted to help instead of the fact that people in town were clearly gossiping about her. "I'm sorry—I don't know where your daughter got the idea that we were courting, but it isn't true."

Now Mrs. Anderson's brows lowered. "Minnie isn't one to tell tales," she said. "She said he'd called for you at the schoolhouse and some of the children heard you making plans to see each other."

Then the other woman's face smoothed. She reached across the table and patted the back of Sarah's hand. "I'm sure it's all new and you don't want the man getting a little nervous if he overhears something in town. Well, don't worry, dear. Men don't pay attention to the sort of gossip that we women love to partake in."

"I'm not worried," Sarah said sharply. Working to soften her tone, she went on, "There's nothing between the horseman and myself." Even if her stomach was full of butterflies, it didn't mean Oscar White held any attraction for her. "I actually came calling today to talk to you about another matter. There are a couple of girls in my classroom who are in need. I was hoping that… perhaps you and some of the other women in town— other mothers who understand the importance of a child being properly clothed during the kind of winters we have up here—might show some charity toward them."

Mrs. Anderson went stiff in her hard-backed chair, teacup clacking against the saucer as she set it down. "I know who you are speaking of and I'm afraid it's impossible."

Heat worse than what Sarah had felt when the woman had brought up Oscar scalded her cheeks. "I'm disappointed to hear that. I thought that such a fine, upstanding woman of the community such as yourself would want to help with this situation." Sarah knew she should temper her words, try to cajole the woman into helping in some way, but she couldn't. Not after being disarmed by gossip about herself and the horseman and the woman's quick dismissal of Cecilia's and Susie's needs.

Now the other woman's cheeks blazed pink. "Perhaps you would be better served worrying about yourself and your marriage prospects instead of prying into matters better left alone. And insulting me—"

Sarah stood and excused herself with a nod, afraid that if she opened her mouth, the words that would erupt would only deteriorate the situation further. She swept out of the house.

The rest of her calls fared no better. Each woman seemed happy to see her, eager to gossip about the horseman. But when Sarah expressed her reason for the calls she was shut out in every case.

Did the people of Lost Hollow have no compassion?

And without their help, how could Sarah and her meager salary provide what the girls needed?

Chapter Seven

Oscar could guess Sarah's meetings hadn't gone well by the tense set of her shoulders and the white lines around her mouth when he next saw her.

What were they going to do for the girls if no one was willing to help? He supposed he could dip into his savings, but if he spent the funds he'd been saving for the stallion he wanted, he'd have to take another job before he could return home, before his dreams could be fulfilled.

But what of the girls and their needs?

His grumbling stomach made it hard to concentrate on anything else, but he gave it an attempt, tucking Sarah's arm through the crook of his elbow and leading her toward the edge of town.

It was a measure of how upset she was that she didn't seem to notice the two horses he led by their reins, walking behind.

"Let's get something to eat and you can tell me all about it."

"I don't want to talk about it. I'm so angry I could just scream."

At the edge of town, they reached the same picnic area where the basket auction had been held weeks ago, and this seemed to finally break through to Sarah's consciousness. She looked around, noticed the horses and her arm tensed in his.

"I suppose you're really not taking me to the hotel dining room, then?" she asked. But she didn't sound terribly disappointed. Almost sounded relieved, and he wondered if he should be insulted she didn't want to be seen with him in public. Or perhaps it was something else entirely.

Oscar released her arm and moved to untie the blanket he'd stowed behind Pharaoh's saddle. He passed it to Sarah, who watched with narrowed eyes.

"I'm going to ground tie the horses. They won't be too close to us," he reassured her. "Spread the blanket, Miss Schoolteacher."

She did, not commenting when he tied the horses probably closer than she would've liked. The animals seemed happy enough to graze in the crisp fall grasses. Oscar returned to Pharaoh's saddle and unhooked the picnic basket he'd packed that morning, joining Sarah on the blanket.

She stared off to the horizon, and startled when he bumped her knee as he settled.

"You okay?" he asked.

"Yes. No! I can't believe there's not one woman in town whose heart is compassionate enough to see that those girls need help. The lot of them are worse than gossiping schoolgirls...." Her voice trailed off and she shot him an embarrassed look at him before going quiet.

Oscar set out two plates, smiling to himself when she

dove into the basket and came up with the silverware. He flinched when she gestured wildly and the knife came his direction.

"Do you know, one of the wives actually said she wanted to help, but she couldn't go against her husband? We were alone in the house, but she whispered it as if he could hear her."

Because he couldn't hide his smile at her fervor, he was careful to keep his face averted as he took out the roasted chicken he'd made for the girls' lunch today and saved a portion of.

"I thought you didn't want to talk about it," he said, keeping his voice as level as he could.

She met his eyes and he couldn't help the smile that quirked his lips.

"This isn't funny."

"You're completely right," he said. "It's just you're delightful when you're angry—as long as it's not with me."

Now it was her turn to keep her face averted. Was she blushing? Yes, the tip of her nose was bright-pink.

He handed her a plate piled with chicken and the potatoes he'd roasted with it and a buttered slice of bread from a batch earlier in the week. "Maybe we've just got to think of something different. Don't know why I didn't think of this before, but I'll send a telegraph to my ma and pa. I'm sure they've got some things from the tots that would fit Velma. And they might be able to send some money for Cecilia and Susie. Oh, and what if we wrote to the church in Bear Creek? Even if they took up a small collection, it would help the girls and maybe even help Caldwell figure out a way to get through the winter."

"Would they really be willing to help?" The seed of hope in her voice warmed him.

"I don't see why we couldn't ask."

His idea seemed to calm her a bit. She tucked into her food as if the morning's business had fueled her appetite.

They ate for a while in silence, until he asked, "You mail your letter?"

Her face turned charmingly pink again, and he grinned, stretching out to lean on one elbow while he finished his food.

"So how come you haven't married yet?" he asked. "If you want to get married so bad."

"I haven't had time for courting." She didn't quite meet his eyes when she said it.

"Seems like you'd make time for that, if you really wanted to get married. Maybe your standards are too high. What's wrong with cowboys, anyway?" He was teasing her, but one little part of him was curious. What was so wrong with the profession? He'd done well for himself both working cattle and participating in cowboy exhibitions—well enough to get a start on the life he wanted.

She looked up at him sharply. "For one thing, they're arrogant and nosy."

Oscar just grinned. He loved to rile her up.

"And also, their jobs are particularly risky. How can a cowboy support a family if he gets hurt trying to do his job?"

"Some are risk-takers—it's the nature of the cowboy's personality. But not all," he argued. He considered himself a cautious sort. Of course, there were no guarantees one wouldn't get hurt on the job, but he made an effort to be aware of the animals he worked with and not take any unnecessary risks.

She gave him a look that said she begged to disagree. But when she spoke, her question surprised him. "Why aren't you married?"

He considered the question momentarily. Had considered it before, especially when loneliness and being away from home started eating at him. The truth was, everyone he'd loved had up and abandoned him. Why trust his heart to a woman when she'd likely do the same? He was better off making his own plans, taking care of himself.

He shrugged. "Just haven't. Anyway, we were talking about you and your marriage prospects. There hasn't been anyone you'd consider courting?"

She shrugged. "There was someone back when I was at the Normal School, but there were other circumstances and he...he didn't want to wait."

"What circumstances?"

Her eyes flashed at him again. "Do you always have to ask so many questions? If you must know, someone had to provide for my sisters!"

At her exclamation, the horses shifted, and Sarah looked frantically in their direction, clapping one hand over her mouth.

Oscar chuckled. "They're just moving around a little. Nothing to worry about."

"How—how can you tell?"

"You might think a trainer just slaps a saddle on and bucks the spirit out of a horse."

Her cheeks turned another interesting shade of pink. Had she really thought that was what his job was about?

"But each horse is a little different," he continued. "And if you can learn to read them, you'll realize what mood they're in. And know when you should move outta their way or when they welcome you."

He sat up and edged closer to her on the blanket, bringing them shoulder-to-shoulder. "Look at Pharaoh, here. That's the gelding."

He pointed to the nearer horse, grazing placidly not far from their blanket. "He's pretty much ignoring us. See how his tail is flicking and his ears are forward? Even his posture is pretty relaxed—he's just enjoying his snack."

"And the other one?" Their heads were so close that her softly spoken words were barely more than a puff of warm, moist air across his cheek.

Close enough that if he turned his head, he could capture her lips with his. But she'd just told him she wasn't interested in cowboys—him included.

"She's a little more skittish, as you know. Look at her ears...." He gestured toward the mare, whose ears were flicking forward and back, a sign she was paying more attention to Oscar and Sarah than the other horse.

"And she hasn't turned her back to us. As a prey animal, that would make her too vulnerable. But she's not scared—just aware."

Sarah remained still at his side.

"What's her name?" she whispered.

"She doesn't have one yet."

"You've had her for weeks and you haven't named her?" Now she turned slightly toward him, bringing their faces into close proximity. Her eyes widened slightly as she seemed to realize just how near they were.

For his part, Oscar couldn't look away. Her golden lashes surrounded those deep blue eyes. And mesmerized him.

"I like to get to know the horse—really know her— before I name her," Oscar murmured, his voice caught somewhere between his breastbone and his mouth.

She blinked, and abruptly turned her head and shoulders away, even scooted away from him on the blanket.

"So why'd you have to support your sisters?" he asked quickly to cover the awkwardness of the moment. The closeness had been shattered. Obviously, she still felt he was not to be completely trusted. "What about your parents?"

She nervously plucked at the gathers on her skirt. "My mother died when I was thirteen. After that, my father got a wild idea to join a couple of men in a gold mine venture. The mine collapsed on them. One man died and my father was injured badly enough that he could no longer work. He had had a little money saved up, but that ran out quickly without him being able to hold a job."

Oscar could guess the rest. "And you left school early and went on to be a teacher to take care of your sisters."

Her nod was all the response he got but less than he needed. He'd had no idea what her family situation had really been like. It made sense for the fact that he hadn't been close to Sarah back in Bear Creek, but even Sally had never made any mention of their circumstances.

No wonder she was so concerned with a trio of little girls who didn't have anyone else to take care of them— she could identify with their plight. Had she and her sisters had to scrounge for food? Clothing?

His admiration for her grew. She'd been thrust into a bad situation—much like he had. But she hadn't had the choice to run away when she'd been abandoned. She'd had to take care of her two younger sisters. And she'd found a way to do it successfully, putting their needs above hers, and above the family she wanted for herself.

She was so much more than the bossy girl he remembered from Bear Creek.

Sarah glanced at the man beside her from the corner of her eye. She was uncomfortable with the turn the conversation had taken—and uncomfortable with the way he'd been looking at her.

Like he wanted to kiss her.

For a moment, she'd thought he would. For a moment, she'd wanted his kiss.

How foolish was that? If someone drove by on the road and saw them, and reported back to Paul Allen, her job could be in jeopardy.

Worse, what if she started developing feelings for the horseman? She absolutely couldn't act on the attraction she felt for him. No matter what. Her heart could not become involved.

And the compassionate look in his eyes was only confusing her. Almost as if he understood what she'd been through.

She spared a thought for what her sister Sally might think. Likely she would cheer Sarah on, encourage a pursuit of the horseman. Sally knew how deeply Sarah longed for a family of her own. And even after their childhood romance had changed to strictly a friendship, Sally was fond of Oscar.

Those thoughts weren't helping.

She reached for the picnic basket on the corner of the blanket and dug inside, grabbing the apple she'd seen earlier and a knife that had slid to the bottom.

Right now, the man was more dangerous than the horse, and she would rather face the hazard she could see.

"Will she… Can I share this with her?" she asked, not quite able to meet Oscar's eyes.

"Sure, we can try. Here—" He knelt on the blanket and assisted her until she was standing.

"We won't approach her." He halted Sarah with a hand at her elbow, just past the edge of the blanket. "Let's wait and see if she'll come to us."

He took the apple and knife, and started slicing it into small pieces.

"What should I do?" Sarah's heart pounded frantically now that she'd committed to this course of action. What if the horse spooked and charged her, the way it had that first day of Oscar's arrival? Where could she go to escape? The field was wide-open.

"Relax. Didn't I promise I wouldn't let you get hurt?"

He plopped a moist piece of apple into Sarah's hand. "They can tell when you're frightened, and then they wonder what's making you so nervous."

"But I *am* nervous."

He considered her, leaning his head to one side. "Do you remember your first day teaching? The very first time you stepped in front of that classroom?"

"Yes." She'd been shaking and nearly sick to her stomach.

"What did you do? Tell the kids you were scared and ask them to take it easy on you?"

"Of course not. They would've seen that as weakness and I never would have been able to control the classroom." Ah. She saw his point. Sort of. "But this is different. I'm not teaching the horse anything."

"Sure you are. You're teaching them that you can be trusted. That you aren't going to do anything to hurt them."

His words sounded logical. But that didn't stop her from jumping when the nearest horse, the male, moved. Oscar closed one hand over her wrist, the warmth both surprising and calming her.

"Easy. He smells the treat you've got."

The horse stepped toward her, and swung that enormous head in her direction. She barely restrained her flinch, but managed to keep her feet rooted to the ground and not run away.

"Should I give it to him?" She could barely force the words out, couldn't find breath at all.

"Yes." Oscar chuckled and reached behind her to press down gently on her shoulders, one at a time. Manually relaxing her posture.

Her hand shook badly, but the horse didn't seem to care as it slurped the apple piece out of her hand with a soft "whuff" of air against her palm.

"She's watching him. Even if she isn't looking, she

knows that he got a treat from your hand and nothing bad happened. We can use Pharaoh to teach the mare that you're safe."

The horse nosed around her midsection and Oscar plopped another piece of apple into Sarah's palm, which the horse quickly took.

The horse neighed softly and bobbed its head, scaring Sarah into taking a step back.

"It's all right." Oscar reached forward and ruffled the horse's neck. "This guy is a hog for goodies. He's telling you he likes it. He likes everything. Apples, carrots, grain…"

Sarah found a store of courage to step up to Oscar's elbow.

"Watch his ears." Oscar didn't stop petting the horse, even though the animal was nudging his opposite hand, attempting to get at the rest of the apple. "Forward means he's at ease. Pointed back behind his head means he's upset or fearful."

"Has he ever bucked you off before?"

"This guy? No. He's even-tempered and we've been in accord pretty much since we've been working together."

She still stood half-behind Oscar's shoulder, and he looked back to grin at her. "I've had my share of spills, though."

Sarah couldn't find any humor in that. "Have you ever been hurt?"

"Naw. A bruised rib or sore ankle, maybe. When you grow up with a lot of brothers, you learn how to duck and roll."

She could only imagine. Two years ago, she'd had

a passel of boys from one family in her classroom and they'd spent all day tussling and wrestling each other. They'd moved midyear, but she'd never forgotten the rowdy family.

The horse certainly seemed calm. It almost acted as if it was enjoying Oscar's scratching of its neck and shoulder.

Sarah didn't know if she dared, but she had to try. "Can I…?"

He glanced at her again and his eyes lit from within. He reached down and took her hand, his warm fingers enclosing hers and causing a tingle all the way up her arm. He pressed her palm against the horse's neck, his hand covering hers completely.

It took a while, but eventually Sarah stopped shaking. The horse stood patiently and Oscar didn't move, either, providing his shoulder and hand for support. Finally, the sound of the horse crunching into the apple in Oscar's other hand broke Sarah's concentration.

Oscar let the horse take the whole apple between his teeth and with a final pat, urged the horse away.

"But what about her?" Sarah asked, nodding toward the mare. "She didn't step over to us. Isn't that what you wanted?"

Oscar squatted and began putting the plates and utensils back in the picnic basket. "It's not a failure. All on her own, she got closer to me—to us—than she ever has before. Maybe it's next time that she comes and eats out of your hand. And she stayed close the whole time."

They moved to fold the blanket, Oscar taking one side and Sarah the other. When they met in the middle, his fingers closed over hers as he took the half-folded blanket from her. Their eyes locked and her breath froze in her chest.

"When you're gentling a horse, even a small step forward is a win."

Sarah moved away, bending down to scoop up the picnic basket. His words, his manner.... If she were younger, or more attractive, less bossy...she might think his words had a double meaning. That he'd wanted to get closer to *her,* Sarah.

But he couldn't have meant that, could he?

Before she'd quieted her swirling thoughts, he had come beside her, falling into step on the path toward Main Street. "Want to hold the reins while we walk back to the buggy?"

"No!"

He laughed, the sound rich and full, and a funny little tickle deep in her belly responded to him.

Surely he hadn't intended anything deeper by his words...surely.

Chapter Eight

The mild autumn weather lasted several days past Thanksgiving, but as it got colder, Sarah worried about Cecilia's exposure to the cold with no shoes.

With none of the mothers or women from town willing to help, she had no choice but to come up with a solution on her own.

She really couldn't afford to purchase a new pair of shoes for the girl out of her meager savings. And she couldn't imagine what the school board would say if she showed such favoritism.

So she'd stuffed an extra pair of thick socks into the bottom of her second, more worn pair of shoes and hid them under her desk when she'd arrived at the schoolhouse this morning. She would try to find a time when the other children weren't paying attention to give them to Cecilia.

When the temperature dropped noticeably before lunchtime, Sarah called Cecilia up to her desk as the other children filed out for the midmorning recess.

"I've noticed that you don't have shoes." Sarah purposely kept her voice low as the last child exited the schoolroom.

Cecilia bristled, her arms immediately crossing over her middle and lips tightening into a frown. Even her toes curled beneath the slightly too-high tattered edge of her skirt. "So what?"

"It's getting on to winter," Sarah responded gently. She knew that she needed to approach the girl with care or risk offending her. "I would hate for you to get frostbite because you don't have appropriate footwear."

The girl looked away, shrugging her thin shoulders.

Sarah reached below the desk and grasped the shoes with one hand, setting them on top of the desk in Cecilia's view. "These are for you. I'm sure they are too large, but a trick I learned with my younger sisters was to stuff an extra pair of socks in the toes of the shoes."

Poor Sally had been stuck with Sarah's hand-me-downs for years, and they'd often had to make do with what they had.

Cecilia looked at the shoes for a long silent moment, but remained perfectly still. "My pa won't take kindly to charity," she mumbled. "I can't take them."

"Yes, you can." Sarah pushed the shoes across the desk. "I want you to have them. And if your father argues with you, tell him that you can't perform your chores if you have frostbitten feet." She held her tongue on what else she wanted to say—that he should already be providing for his stepdaughters' clothing needs.

"Besides, how can you take care of your sisters if your feet are injured?" Sarah said the words casually, looking down at her desk as if she wasn't invested in whether the girl decided to accept the shoes or not. Perhaps it was a *bit* manipulative to play on Cecilia's sense of responsibility for her sisters, but Sarah did have the girl's best interests at heart.

Hesitantly, Cecilia reached out one finger and touched the toe of one of the shoes. "They're nice," she whispered.

"They're yours." Sarah turned to the blackboard, as if the matter had been decided. She heard a twin pair of clunks as the shoes hit the floor and rustling as Cecilia slid them on. Sarah regretted that she couldn't give the girl a pair of shoes that fit better, but this was better than nothing.

A bustle at the door preceded a loud giggle. "What are you doing?" asked Barbara. "Aren't those your shoes, Miss Sarah?"

Sarah turned to see a gaggle of girls tumble into the classroom, puffing hard from their outdoor exertions.

"Why're you wearing the teacher's shoes, Cecilia?" "She's too poor to have some of her own!" chorused two more voices.

Barbara looked chagrined, standing just inside the door. Sarah knew the girl most likely hadn't meant to draw attention to her classmate; Barbara wasn't cruel, she was just innately curious and always wanted to know why things were the way they were.

Susie pushed her way through the small knot of girls and ran to her sister's side. Cecilia's face had gone red, but her chin was in the air.

"Poor, poor Cecilia and Susie!" rang out a voice and rude laughter followed.

"Quiet!" Sarah called out.

From the back of the classroom, Junior Allen sent

Sarah a squint-eyed look and muttered something she couldn't hear, but it set off the children again.

"Children, quiet!" Sarah rapped a ruler on the edge of her desk, temper flaring at the children's cruelty and refusal to obey. Finally, she stuck two fingers in her mouth and let out a shrill whistle.

The room went silent. From just in front of her desk, Susie looked up at Sarah with tear-filled eyes. Next to her sister, Cecilia stood with a belligerent stance, arms crossed as if daring the other children to hurt her with their words. Sarah well knew how that stance tried to hide the tender feelings beneath the bravado.

"I am ashamed of you children," Sarah said. "There's more to your education than reading and arithmetic. I thought I had trained you better in the ways of kindness and respecting your fellow students. Cecilia and Susie are very special girls who are going through a hard time right now. Instead of belittling them, you should be asking your parents how you could help them."

There was a pause. Junior snorted, and several children laughed in response.

"You shoulda left things alone," Cecilia hissed at Sarah. The girl grabbed her sister's hand and ran for the door, pushing aside other children to escape the room. The outer door slammed amid tittering from the children.

But at least she had the shoes on.

Temper hot, Sarah felt the ruler she now clutched in her hands snap. She hadn't meant to do that. But it served to capture the children's attention. They went ominously quiet.

"Please sit down," she said firmly.

They were silent as they shuffled into their seats. Several of the girls wore guilty expressions and Barbara looked near tears. Junior looked particularly smug, and his attitude, so like his father's, infuriated Sarah.

"You will all copy this verse ten times on your slates."

Hand trembling with the force of her emotions, Sarah wrote out the Golden Rule, straight from Matthew chapter seven, on the blackboard.

There was rattling from behind her as the children got out their slates and chalk.

Sarah dusted her hands as she turned back to the room, hoping she appeared more composed now. "When you are finished, you will be dismissed for the day. I hope that you will all go home and think very seriously about the words you are writing at this moment."

That afternoon, Sarah worked at the schoolhouse, unwilling to go home and face Mr. Allen. No doubt he had heard all about the events of the day from his children. She still struggled with what had happened earlier.

Perhaps she'd overreacted, but after days of continued coldness from her boss, and the utter lack of compassion from the people of Lost Hollow, she hadn't been able to help her reaction.

She refused to give any credence for her turbulent emotions to the fact that she'd only seen Oscar in passing as he worked Mr. Allen's colt. They were barely friends, but after the picnic they'd shared, she'd thought…she didn't know what she'd thought, but his silence was unexpected.

Afternoon sunshine streamed around her, but the air had a particular bite and a stiff breeze blew her hair into her eyes. The schoolyard was blessedly quiet as she fought to cover a broken windowpane with thick paper. This side of the schoolhouse was wind-worn and really needed a new coat of paint.

She still needed to look over and mark lessons from earlier in the week, and was woefully behind on getting the pageant backdrops put together, but with winter so close, the one-room building needed to be secure to keep out the cold air. If she could just—

The wooden bottom of the sill broke off beneath her hand, and Sarah tumbled backward, hitting the ground unceremoniously with an "oomph!"

The thick brown paper fluttered to the ground at her feet, leaving a gaping hole in the windowpane.

Tears of frustration filled her eyes, but she quickly blinked them away. At least none of the students had been here to see—

"Miss Schoolteacher, you all right?"

Fast hoofbeats halted and then footsteps approached. Sarah didn't have to look up to know who it was. The prickling awareness heating the back of her neck was enough of a recognition.

"What are you doing here?" Embarrassment and a sharp pain shooting down her leg made her words sting as she struggled to get up. Her hair flopped down into her eyes, and she pushed it out of her face. She must've lost some pins when she'd fallen.

He was already there beside her, helping her up with a warm hand at her waist and the other beneath her elbow.

"I was going to see about escorting the girls home from school today, but it's awful quiet around here so

I guess they're already gone. I saw you fall—you sure you're okay?"

She stepped away and brushed at her skirt. "Yes, I'm fine. I was trying to…" She motioned to the window with its missing pane and his eyebrows went down, making him look almost dangerous.

"Can't you get someone to fix that for you?"

"Keeping the classroom maintained is part of the job," she explained, moving to pick up the stiff paper and the piece of window frame that had broken off and caused her fall.

"But this is the building, not the classroom."

She moved toward the window again. "There's no one else." If she complained to Mr. Allen, he would only think she couldn't do her job. She didn't dare.

Oscar easily overtook her and took the paper and wood piece from her hands. "I don't suppose you have a hammer? No? All right. I'll come early tomorrow morning and fix the window and stoke the fire."

He examined the chunk of wood from the window frame before tossing it on the ground beneath the window. "Did you have a visitor before me? Is that why the children are already gone?"

"No. I sent them home early." She wouldn't admit that she'd been afraid she wouldn't be able to hold her temper.

"Hmm. I thought I saw someone riding away.…" Distracted from the broken window, he followed her around to the front of the schoolhouse, where she stopped cold.

A bulky burlap sack rested at the bottom of the steps.

"That wasn't here when I came outdoors," she said. "Did you get a look at the person riding away?"

"Not a good one. They were slight…might've been a woman." He approached with Sarah following reluctantly a few steps behind him.

"Be careful," she cautioned. "Is it moving?"

"What exactly do you expect to be in that bag?" he asked over his shoulder.

"In the past I've received snakes, feral cats, frogs… I'm sure you can imagine from your own school days. And with some of the townspeople being unhappy with me wanting to help the Caldwells, you never know…"

He squatted and reached for the bag. She held her breath.

"Or perhaps we've both underestimated someone's compassion," he murmured.

He held up the bag, with its mouth wide open so she could see the contents. Looked like something woolen.

"Dresses?" she asked, breath caught in her chest. She crossed to join him.

"Not quite." He pulled out the fold of material. "But enough yardage to make some."

Oscar watched Sarah's shoulders slump. Other than the day he'd arrived, when she'd nearly been run down by his mare, he'd never seen Sarah so disheveled and harried as she appeared now. He could only guess what mischief her schoolchildren had gotten into today if she'd sent them home early. That on top of all her other duties and the upcoming pageant…he could see she was overwhelmed.

And he wanted to help in some way.

"This is a good thing," he said.

The afternoon breeze was nippy and he motioned

her into the schoolhouse. Going up the steps behind her, he realized just how worn and creaky they were. He'd noticed it before, but now understood there might not be anyone to fix it—unless he counted Sarah. And he didn't.

"It's a nice gesture, but who is going to sew new dresses out of that?"

"You can't sew?" he teased.

Her face flushed pink as she moved toward a stack of wood and other detritus in the back corner of the schoolroom. "Probably only well enough to make a doll's dress."

He couldn't resist joshing her. It was too fun. "So you can't cook and you can't sew but you want to catch a husband? Are you really prepared for that?"

She bent down, and he lost sight of her face. "Perhaps I'm looking for a man with some house and home skills. It isn't an impossible request."

"Hmm...like a cowboy? A lot of us can cook and you've got to know how to darn your shirts if you get a rip out on the range. There aren't usually women around to do it for you."

She shot him a look. He grinned.

"What's all that?" he asked, leaving the burlap bag on one of the desks and joining her.

"It's supposed to be props—and a backdrop—for the pageant. One of the fathers brought it yesterday. He was supposed to have them fully installed, but instead he brought this pile of boards and some canvas. As if I don't have enough to do!"

She sounded close to tears. And if there was one piece of advice about women that his pa had passed down to him, it was to stay as far away as possible from a woman's tears.

"Look, I'll help you build whatever you need. But I'm not artsy, so any painting you're going to have to do yourself. And we'll figure out something about making the girls' dresses. Maybe I'll sew them."

He'd meant the last to be a jest, to pull a smile from her, but she stood and faced him, eyes glistening.

His gut clenched and he desperately wanted to erase that look from her face.

"I don't—I don't have anything to trade this time. You've already convinced me to help with your skittish horse...."

She looked so worried, in addition to her hair falling around her shoulders and the tremble in her lips, that he couldn't find anything to smile about this time, only a deep desire to make things better for her.

"I'm not looking for a trade," he said. "I'll do it for you."

She turned away quickly, reaching for her satchel, but not before he saw one silver tear spill down her cheek.

But he didn't know if her emotion was a good thing or a bad thing.

The next morning, Sarah woke before the rooster. Or maybe she hadn't ever really fallen asleep. She'd spent all night recalling Oscar's words and serious expression just before he'd left the schoolhouse yesterday.

He'd seemed completely sincere. And she'd been glad when he'd left because his intensity had frightened her.

She could see herself falling for him, given the chance.

She lay in bed, unsure what the future held and what she should do—if she spent any more time with the horseman, would she continue wanting something she shouldn't? A man that she knew couldn't be good for her? One with a dangerous vocation?

A distant whistle made her sit up, clutching the bedclothes to her. The chill in the room made her hesitate before putting her feet on the cold floor, but she couldn't resist a peek out the window to see if it was him.

She gasped at the feel of the cool planks against her feet, and quickly glanced to Barbara to make sure she hadn't woken the girl. With only a tousle of blond hair above the quilt, the girl didn't even stir.

The window fogged when Sarah pressed her nose against it.

She'd been right. It was the horseman, working the colt in the near corral. What was he doing out so early? Had he really finished repairing the schoolroom window?

Sarah laid her palm against the freezing windowpane as she watched him exercise the animal in circles around the pen.

With both arms extended, one with the line and the other with a long-handled whip, even from this distance she could see the muscles in his shoulders beneath the coat he wore.

He released the horse from its exercise and stretched.

Why would someone like him, someone virile and handsome, be interested in her?

Movement outside the corral caught her gaze. Two men rode up—young men—and dismounted in a hurry, hopping off their horses before the animals had even come to a complete stop.

Oscar slid between the panels of the corral fence and embraced one of the young men. Who were they? Some relations?

As if he sensed her perusal, Oscar turned toward the ranch house. She ducked to the side of the window, half hiding behind the curtain. She hadn't even donned a wrapper, only wore her long-sleeved flannel nightgown—but surely he couldn't see her, not inside and from this distance.

She needed to gain control of her emotions. Needed some distance from the man. But wasn't likely to get it, now that he'd agreed to help her with the pageant backdrops.

And she needed to do something about the materials to make the girls' dresses. Oscar had said he could manage with a needle and thread, but after what had happened in the schoolhouse the day before, Sarah didn't want to give the children any reason to pick on Cecilia or Susie. Perhaps she would have to raid her savings to have some dresses made. She would talk to the horseman about it and see what he thought.

Surely Sarah could guard her heart from one cowboy?

"What are you doing here?" Oscar embraced his younger brother, Davy, slapping him on the back through the younger man's duster.

The eighteen-year-old no longer had the build of a lanky teen—his shoulders and chest had broadened even in the couple of months since Oscar had made it home to see the family.

"Ma got your telegraph and sent me and Seb. She sent some things the kids had outgrown—shoes and such."

Relief and family pride soared through Oscar. He'd hoped his ma and pa would come through for the Caldwell girls, and they had. Now the material that had been donated by a mysterious benefactor could be used for a fancier dress for the girls for the pageant. Sarah should be happy about that.

Davy stepped back and Seb rushed in for an exuberant thirteen-year-old's hug. "And Ma wanted us to nag you for not making it home for Thanksgiving. She figures you got a gal or something or you woulda been back."

Oscar's thoughts immediately went to Sarah, and his checks heated even as a sense of guilt ate at his stomach. He turned back and gripped the corral's top railing with one hand while pointing to Allen's colt. "This is the reason why I didn't make it home—this guy is learning fast but needs a firm hand. My last job."

He hadn't made the effort to go home for Thanksgiving—because he hadn't really thought he'd be missed. Jonas and Penny were busy caring for the young tots, Maxwell was gone, and the other boys were getting older. It was only natural that Oscar move on.

It just hurt more than he thought it would. Made him think back to his childhood when his uncle had all but abandoned him. And he would rather keep busy working toward his dream than thinking about the past and things he couldn't change.

"Yeah, I think he's keeping something back from us, Davy," Seb teased. "Look at that blush on his face."

"Whoohee! Who is it? A local shopkeepers' daughter? Rancher's daughter? Who?" Davy asked with a laugh.

"It's no one." Sarah had made it immensely clear that she wasn't interested in him. Even if he did find her attractive, she was still bossy and determined. Set in her ways. But lovely. "There's nothing for you to tell Ma."

"Uh-huh." From Davy's tone, it was clear he didn't believe his older brother.

Oscar's throat closed off unexpectedly. He'd missed their teasing, the sense of camaraderie that he'd always felt with his brothers.

When he went back home, he'd be just across the valley from his pa's place. He could go to Sunday supper and poke fun at his brothers and sister.

But the sense of loneliness didn't lift. Maybe more time with his brothers would help. He could sure use their help getting the Caldwell spread in shape.

"I'm glad you boys are here." Oscar slung one arm over each brother's shoulder. "I've got a project I can use your help to tackle."

Chapter Nine

"**A**nd then Johnny put the frog in Lizzie's lunch pail—"

"No, it was Jeremy," Cecilia interrupted her sister's tale.

Sarah kept painting the large canvas backdrop Oscar and his two younger brothers had constructed for her. Even though the Saturday morning was chilly, it was blessedly dry and there was no wind on this side of the barn where the three brothers had set up the small carpentry area. They worked on building the other set pieces per the specifications Sarah had described to Oscar on the buggy ride over that morning.

"And it jumped out—" Susie continued as if her sister hadn't spoken. "And scared her so bad she threw her lunch all over the floor. And then he had to give her his lunch since he'd ruined hers."

"You know, one time before she was my ma, Penny put a dead snake in my bed, right under my pillow," the older of Oscar's two brothers, Davy, said.

"Ew!" both girls chorused.

"That was so funny! At first, you thought Ricky

and Matty did it, and got so mad at them—" Seb, the younger brother, chimed in. He wasn't much older than Cecilia, but seemed more comfortable in his own skin than the girl. Were all of Oscar's brothers so confident in themselves?

Sarah stepped back, propping one hand on her hip, to examine the paint she'd already spread across the canvas. She listened to the noise going on all around her, somewhat aware of Oscar's two horses, sequestered in the corral not far behind the barn. If they jumped the fence...but it was tall, and Oscar was nearby, hammering a frame for one of the pieces.

The chatter from girls and young men flowed all around her, but did not include her. She tried not to let it pinch her feelings. She sensed that the girls were still sore at her for embarrassing them earlier in the week.

She couldn't really blame them. She was sorry she hadn't paid better attention to the presence of the other children and sorry that Susie and Cecilia had been humiliated. They looked pretty in the new-to-them dresses that Oscar had told her his adoptive mother, Penny, had sent. And shoes! Slightly worn but perfectly serviceable shoes that fit for all three. Somehow he'd gotten the girls to accept the dresses and shoes, and some small-size shawls as a gift without hurting their feelings—something Sarah had failed at doing.

And she couldn't begin to guess what Oscar had told his brothers about her, but both had greeted her with a perfunctory hat-tip and had barely spoken to her since, although they interacted with the girls as if they had been born siblings.

Oscar had kept busy building the other props she'd

asked for. He hadn't made any effort to engage her since they'd arrived in the buggy.

She was surprised to find she could still feel left out. The same way she had seven years ago in Bear Creek, when she and her sisters had been different from the other children in that they had had to take care of themselves.

She was a grown woman now. Hurt feelings didn't have any place in her life, not when she had things to do, students to care for. But it didn't make it any easier to be the one on the fringes of the others' merriment.

"Miles picked on us yesterday. He called us 'charity cases,'" Susie confided to Davy in a low voice. They stood close enough for Sarah to overhear.

Velma toddled to Sarah and stretched her hands upward to be picked up.

"Hello, sweetie." She put down her paintbrush and scooped up the toddler. Well, at least one person here seemed to be happy for Sarah's presence.

Velma cooed and giggled.

Davy glanced up at Sarah from where he knelt on the ground, fiddling with the back of a piece of wood he'd hammered to another one. "Seems like I remember some big hullabaloo when our big brother called your schoolteacher here a shrew in front of our whole class."

Sarah's face heated. Susie's eyes went wide and Cecilia went silent, too, watching from her perch on an overturned crate between Seb and Oscar, who didn't look up.

"I don't remember that," said Seb, only half paying attention as he measured and marked on another piece of wood.

"You were little," came Oscar's voice, though he

kept his head down. "And I was a stupid kid." Now he glanced up briefly, apologizing silently with his eyes.

Sarah realized she didn't know that boy anymore. She only knew the man he'd become—and she couldn't imagine him doing something like that now. Not when they were working toward a common goal.

"Miss Sarah, the horseman really picked on you when you were in school?" Cecilia asked, breaking the tenuous, invisible connection between the two.

"Well, he wasn't the horseman back then. We were just kids, like you are now. And sometimes kids say things that aren't very nice."

"Sometimes grown-ups do, too," said Susie matter-of-factly, bending over Seb at work. "I heard the shopkeeper say we should just leave town 'cause no one wants us here."

Sarah felt a flash of annoyance. From this distance, she saw Oscar's jaw tighten and their eyes met in shared frustration.

"Susie!" Cecilia hissed. She looked around at the teen boys and grudgingly at Sarah. "We don't need no pity. Our stepfather says Oscar's trading us some labor for some of the spring wheat, but we don't need no one to feel sorry for us."

Sarah knew the words had to be directed at her. She wanted to explain, but Oscar's brothers were still chuckling over the past.

"So what'd you do when my brother called you names, Miss Schoolteacher?" Seb asked, eyes dancing. "Didja wallop him?"

She turned her best schoolteacher look on the

teen. "Violence is not an appropriate response in the classroom—or anywhere else," she said firmly.

Instead of looking abashed, the young man grinned at her.

Davy chuckled. And Oscar ducked his head. Was he laughing at her, as well?

Heat flushed into her cheeks and Sarah set the toddler down. "Go get your sissy," she prompted the tot, and the chubby legs took off toward Susie. Sarah picked up her paintbrush from where she'd left it on an upended crate.

"She reminds me of Ma," the younger man murmured, loud enough that Sarah heard it.

Now Oscar made a choking noise. The heat in Sarah's cheeks boiled even hotter. She'd *thought* he was past all immature acts, but now with his brothers here, the man was cutting up with them.

She hated being laughed at. And she had no idea why the young men thought her comment was so funny.

"It's no wonder..." Davy added, still chuckling.

A hasty glance up from the canvas revealed the girls looking wide-eyed between the brothers, a mite confused, just as Sarah felt.

"'It's no wonder,' what?" she demanded, moving to one side of the canvas and propping her hand on her hip.

The three brothers dissolved into laughter, although Oscar's was a tad reluctant.

"Why don't you share the joke with the rest of us?" she demanded, shaking the paintbrush in their direction so hard that paint droplets scattered on the grass at her feet.

The two younger brothers hooted, but Oscar stood tall, attempting to pull a straight face, even as his neck reddened. He fanned his face and neck with his Stetson as if he couldn't cool off.

"He—he—he *can't!*" Davy cried, tears now falling from his face as he was nearly doubled over with laughter.

Sarah threw down her paintbrush and stalked off several paces, then turned back with arms crossed over her chest. "Your poor mother must have the patience of a saint. I can't imagine having the lot of you causing trouble in my school. And I expected better of you," she finished, pointing at Oscar, whose lower lip trembled and then broke into that familiar grin she'd begun to appreciate. Until now.

Then the expression of his face changed and he started toward her with one hand outstretched. "Sarah—"

Without warning, a blast of hot, grassy air hit her in the side of the face, as a horse blew loudly in Sarah's ear.

Sarah shrieked and backed away, feet tangling in her skirt in her hurry and she went tumbling down onto her backside.

The horse—the mare—took a step away from the corral fence where she'd had her neck outstretched. Its head bobbed and it whinnied once.

"She's laughing, too!" "The horse was teasing Miss Sarah, too!" Susie and Cecilia's voices rang out as if from a far distance. Laughter still resounded from the brothers, but Sarah could barely catch her breath. The horse had been close enough to nip her, or even knock her down with a jerk of its head….

But it hadn't.

The girls were right. The mare had…almost played a joke on her.

"Sarah! Are you all right?" A breathless Oscar knelt at her side, one warm palm pressing against her shoulder blades and the other curled around her near hand.

She took stock of herself. Her backside felt a little bruised, as was her pride, and she had a glop of blue paint on her open palm that she hadn't noticed until now. Probably got it on herself when she'd been railing at the boys.

She was fine, if a little rumpled. And she wanted to make sure Oscar got what he deserved for letting his brothers laugh at her.

"I'm...I'm..."

She pretended that she couldn't catch her breath, and he leaned closer. Just where she wanted him.

"Sarah—"

She smoothed her palm across his shaven cheek, spreading the blob of blue paint across his strong jaw.

"I'm fine," she said.

He looked stunned. So she reached out and knocked his hat off. It fell to the ground behind him.

The rest of the group went completely silent.

Sarah pushed herself up off the ground and offered a hand to the man, who stared at her with one of those half grins. Instead of taking her extended hand, he shoved off the ground with a roar and chased after her.

Sarah dodged, knowing she wouldn't get far with only a one-step head start on him.

The girls shrieked and she spared a glance to see that Davy and Seb had gone running after Susie and Cecilia, as well.

"Don't get paint—" she called out.

"—on their dresses!" Oscar yelled to his brothers,

finishing her thought, just before he grabbed her around the waist and tumbled her into a soft patch of long grass.

The two teens chased the girls into the field and Velma toddled after, shrieking in glee.

"Are you really all right?" Oscar raised himself on one elbow, his head throwing a shadow and blocking the morning sunlight from her eyes. Behind him the sky spread out like a vista of possibilities.

"Yes. I can't believe your horse did that."

His eyes crinkled. "I'm thinking maybe she wasn't meant to be my horse. She thinks she belongs to you, Miss Schoolteacher."

"No—"

Before she could form the full protest, the girls and teen boys dropped beside them in a pile in the scratchy fall grasses, laughing.

Later that afternoon, Oscar and his brothers loaded up the finished and mostly dried props and backdrop in the Caldwells' old wagon. Sarah said goodbye to the girls, who had seemed to warm to her with their play, but still seemed unsure about the schoolteacher.

"It was lovely to meet you," he heard her say as she extended her hand for Davy and Seb to shake.

"Manners like Ma's," whispered Davy, with a poke in Oscar's back as Seb helped Sarah into the wagon seat.

Oscar gave his brother a friendly shove and Davy chuckled as Oscar hopped into the wagon and settled next to Sarah. Oscar knew he'd be hearing more about the surprising schoolteacher later. He still couldn't believe she'd painted the side of his face earlier, or that she hadn't been more scared about the horse's trick on her. She would fit right in with his family.

He shook off thoughts of what his pa would say about Sarah and snapped the reins to set the horses off. He was getting distracted from his true purpose here and he couldn't afford to.

He needed to finish the job with Paul Allen's colt and get back to his snug little cabin. Start building his herd, the life he'd been dreaming of. Alone, but close enough to see his family.

"This afternoon was fun." Sarah folded her hands in her lap.

"Mmm-hmm," he agreed.

When the wagon jostled over a bump and Sarah's shoulder brushed his, his concentration slipped.

He couldn't forget the sparkle in her eyes when she'd painted the side of his face. If his brothers and those little girls hadn't been watching, he might've followed his instincts and stolen a kiss.

"What was the meaning of that?"

Sarah's question jarred him out of his distracting thoughts. "What?"

"The joke between you and your brothers. What did it mean?"

He cleared his throat. There was no way he was going to admit what his brothers had been teasing him about. Even if they had been right—as the day had progressed, several of Sarah's admonitions and mannerisms had re-minded Oscar of Penny.

"It's a private matter."

"Hmm."

He slanted a look at her and changed the subject.

"When I saw the mare stretching her neck over that fence, I didn't know what she was going to do, but I thought you'd be frightened."

"I was." She fidgeted with her skirt. "For a few moments, I wasn't sure what happened and I was scared. Then I heard the girls talking and I realized they were right—the horse hadn't tried to hurt me. It was…playing with me. Is that silly? I don't suppose horses really play, do they?"

"It's not silly at all. Horses have personalities, the same as people do. I've met some crotchety old fellas and some playful ones. But this was the first time that mare has shown any personality at all." He paused. "I was proud of you."

She brushed a hank of hair out of her eyes, her elbow bumping his. Her cheeks pinked. "Maybe next time I'll get up the courage to touch her. She needs a name."

He smiled to himself.

"What about the girls' dresses?" she reminded him. "If we both pitch in a bit of money, I can have the dressmaker in town sew them. Perhaps the girls would accept the gift better if it came from you. They didn't seem to have any trouble accepting the other dresses and shoes from your mother."

She still sounded a little miffed at the girls' easy acceptance of him and his brothers. He wanted to put her mind at ease. "I told Susie and Cecilia about my brothers and how we were all adopted. They seemed to feel a sense of solidarity because we share a lost parent. Maybe if you shared a little bit about your past, they'd open up to you more. They might understand why you care, instead of just thinking you're interfering in their business."

Her shoulders tightened up and it was a shame, because she'd been so open just a moment ago. She tucked that strand of hair behind her ear again. "Yes, but I have to be careful about becoming too friendly with my students. If they become too familiar, how will I maintain order in the classroom?"

"Susie and Cecilia don't seem the sort to cause trouble." Oscar turned the wagon into the schoolyard, where they would unload the props and things and then he would run Sarah home, hopefully before it got dark. He didn't want old Mr. Allen causing a stink for her.

She didn't seem to have taken his words too well, not speaking again except for directions on where to put things as they unloaded together. Even when on their way back to the Allens' place, she remained silent.

He couldn't leave things between them awkward, not when they'd spent such a pleasant afternoon together. "I'm sorry if my suggestion offended you," he said as he pulled the wagon into the Allens' yard.

"You didn't," she said, accepting his hand down. "It's just not easy for me to talk about my past and what happened with my father."

"You told me." He was perplexed, because he hadn't particularly had to press for her to reveal the truth about her parents.

"Yes. Yes, I did." Her blue eyes were luminous in the darkening twilight as she searched his face for he knew not what. She ducked her head and turned for the house. "Good night, Horseman."

"Good night, Miss Schoolteacher," he called out after her. She disappeared into the house.

It would be better for him to forget about the school-teacher, forget about the three little girls who needed so much. He could return home as soon as he got this colt trained and get on with the life he had planned.

But he couldn't seem to get his heart to agree.

Chapter Ten

The morning of the pageant dawned cold and clear. With only two days until Christmas, the weather had turned colder and even hinted of coming snow.

Still in her nightgown, Sarah huddled in bed beneath the covers, as the light brightened through the window. She fingered the letter that had come for her from Montana. Clara Allen had picked it up for her on a visit to town and delivered it to Sarah last night. The older woman had been curious about the letter, but Sarah hadn't known what to tell her, so she hadn't said anything.

She still hadn't had the courage to read it yet.

What if it was an outright rejection? What if the man who'd posted the mail-order bride ad had found someone else? Or he didn't like Sarah's letter?

What if it was an acceptance? What if he wanted to continue the correspondence? Or...offered a proposal?

Thoughts of Oscar White and their afternoon together weeks ago whirled into her mind. She'd seen another side of him when he'd been with the girls and his brothers. Since then, he'd stopped by the schoolhouse often on his way back to the Caldwells' after working all day at the Allen place. He'd filled the windowpane with a new glass pane. He'd even fixed the rickety front steps and the sticky handle on the potbellied stove, and the droopy shelf.

All that was left was painting the outside of the schoolhouse.

And with every smile, his little stories about Susie, Cecilia and Velma, and their escapades, and even telling her about his success with Paul Allen's colt, and his teasing about her naming the mare, he'd made himself a place in her heart.

And he was planning to leave after Christmas. His job here would be done. He'd helped Mr. Caldwell get the place in some semblance of shape, helped the girls get winter clothing.

With everything settled, he would leave.

Everything would be settled, except Sarah's heart.

It was that thought that had her slitting open the envelope and unfolding the letter inside.

Out in the corral, Oscar slid his foot into the colt's stirrup and boosted himself into the saddle. He'd waited for the horse to accept him as a rider. They'd been practicing this for a while now, and Oscar knew it was time to take the animal out on the open range.

But first, the warm-up. He put the animal through its paces in the corral, circling both ways and then switching directions. The colt was a dream to work with, following Oscar's cues with his legs, the reins and verbally. Oscar sincerely hoped Allen wouldn't ruin the colt with bad habits after he left. The animal was a fine specimen and deserved better.

Oscar dismounted and was moving toward the gate when movement from the house caught his eye. Sarah. Wrapped in a calf-length coat and scarf against the chill in the air. He'd been thinking all morning it smelled like snow.

His heart thumped—the way it did now every time she was near—as she moved toward the corral. Toward him?

She propped her arms on the railing, not flinching when he led the colt by the reins a few feet away and braced his boot on the lower railing.

"Morning," he greeted her.

"Good morning."

"You all ready for tonight? Need anything?" Was it his imagination, or were her hands shaking? Was she scared of the horse? She seemed calm, but she might've been pretending for the animal's sake.

"I think the children are as prepared as they are going to be. I'm certain there will be forgotten lines and probably some stumbles, but the parents never really seem to notice."

She still seemed on edge. Almost like a jumpy filly. What could he say to reassure her? "Well, I'll be there early to help you move those extra benches in place and in case you need anything."

She looked down. "Thank you. Were the girls excited about their new dresses? They didn't refuse them?"

"They didn't. I told them Saint Nick dropped off their gifts a couple days early."

She squinted up at him. "And they believed you?"

"Susie did, and Cecilia didn't have the heart to disagree with her. The three of them sure were cute trying on their matching fancy duds. Even their pa couldn't help but smile. He promised to have them at the school on time tonight. Everything will be fine." He closed his fingers over her nearest hand in hopes of comforting her.

Her eyes remained on his, almost as if a question deep within them, for the longest moment. She smiled.

"You're right. Everything will be fine."

That night, the schoolhouse was packed full, parents and families taking up places on the benches that had been squeezed close together to make space for the small raised platform at the front of the room, just in front of the blackboard. Sequestered behind a small curtained area, the children fidgeted and vacillated from shaking with nerves to nervous giggling.

Sarah left one of the older girls in charge and threaded her way to the back of the room, exchanging greetings with parents. There was a knot of fathers in the vestibule and she excused herself, pushing through to stand on the top step.

Where were Cecilia and Susie? Oscar had said their father had promised to deliver them on time. It was now past the hour the pageant was to have started.

She wrung her hands. Cold air bit her cheeks as she scanned the forest and fields around the schoolhouse, straining her eyes in the dusk to spot an approach that she couldn't see. Where were they?

She'd imagined this night multiple times. Wanted the girls to have a fun time and be able to show off their new dresses, to be a part of the class. Fully. Had even imagined their father watching them say their lines, proud of the girls' accomplishments.

But they weren't here.

"What's the matter?" a familiar voice drawled at her elbow. Warmth enclosed her as Oscar draped her shawl—left behind in the melee inside—over her shoulders. "Saw you come out here."

Warmth from more than just the shawl overtook her.

"Cecilia and Susie aren't here."

Oscar's brows drew together. But he didn't question her, didn't ask if she was sure. Only said, "You want me to go after them?"

"I don't know if I can stall much longer."

He swept a hand across her bangs. That corner of his mouth tilted up. "Snow. Tiny little flakes, sticking in your hair."

He leaned in toward her and for one heart-stopping moment, she thought he would kiss her. But he only swept his thumb across her cheek, beneath her eye. "Get back inside, Miss Schoolteacher. You stall as long as you can, and I'll see if I can find them."

He shrugged into his coat that she hadn't noticed he'd held in his other hand, and stuffed his hat on his head, giving her that irrepressible smile.

Inside, she fought her way back toward the students, determined to keep them calm and ready to go.

She hadn't made it far before Mr. Allen grasped her arm, tugging her to one side. "Miss Hansen, everyone's ready to go. What are you waiting for?"

He knew exactly what the delay was. She didn't know how he knew that Cecilia and Susie weren't present, but the red in his cheeks and the set of his jaw told her his temper was high.

A glance around revealed several other parents watching their interaction.

She infused as much patience as possible into her voice. "I'm sure you remember from last year, Mr. Allen, that these productions always have little problems." She exchanged a smile with his wife, sitting slightly behind him. Last year, the problem had been his son Ham's total disregard of the lines he'd learned as he played up to the crowd, who had roared with laughter.

"Miss Hansen, I demand you get this show on the road—"

"Certainly. As soon as we're ready," she interrupted him coolly.

Almost before the words were out of her mouth, the door opened, letting a cold blast of air in that raised the small hairs on the back of Sarah's neck. Oscar ushered in two girls, one holding the baby, with snow-capped hair. Cecilia clutched Velma to her chest, eyes panicked.

Oscar kept his hands reassuringly on each girl's shoulder as he guided them through the crush of people to Sarah.

"Didn't have to go far," he murmured, leaning close so no one else could hear. "They were all three riding bareback—almost made it the whole way by themselves in the dark."

"S-sorry, Miss Sarah," Susie whispered, looking close to tears.

Oscar raised his brows at her above the their heads. Taking in his protective manner and the girls' serious faces, Sarah dared not express any emotion—she didn't want to embarrass the girls in front of the parents.

"It's no matter," she said clearly, so that anyone who was trying to listen could hear. "I've been readjusting the backdrop so it won't fall over since Miles accidentally tripped on it yesterday at recess." It was true. She'd adjusted it just before she'd pushed through the crowd looking for the girls.

Those near her chuckled, no doubt familiar with the boy's dreamy ways and clumsiness.

Cecilia looked at Sarah speculatively as she shepherded the girls through the crowd to the partition where the other children were.

After a short introduction, Sarah directed the younger children on to the makeshift stage and they began to recite their lines. Then she quickly turned to Cecilia and Susie and took the baby and helped the girls brush the snow from their hair, kneeling behind the partition and balancing the baby on her hip. Susie's hands were like ice, chapped and red, as Sarah took the girl's shawl. She wrapped it around Velma, who surprisingly felt the warmest of all. No doubt she'd been bundled between her sisters. They always took such good care of her. But all three of them needed a mother's touch. How well Sarah knew that.

Sarah couldn't blink away the image of the three girls clinging bareback to a horse's back. How dangerous! What if they'd fallen off the animal? What if they'd gotten lost? It was getting colder, what if they'd frozen to death?

"Where's your father?" Sarah mouthed, not wanting the other children or nearby parents to overhear.

Cecilia shook her head, her wide eyes showing her upset.

Sarah brushed a hand against the older girl's cheek and then must've shocked her, because Cecilia froze as Sarah embraced her thin shoulders. When Sarah released her and turned to Susie, the half-frozen girl burrowed into Sarah's hug.

"I'm glad you both made it," she whispered.

It was clear by their gawking stares that some of the other children were curious. Or maybe they just noticed Cecilia and Susie's new dresses. Whatever the cause, when it was their turn up on the improvised stage, the Caldwell girls did remarkably well, with Susie making only one small stumble over her lines.

After the initial delay, the entire event went off remarkably well, and Sarah fielded congratulations and praises from the parents about their children's success.

From the corner of her eye, she watched as Cecilia and Susie were surrounded by a gaggle of other girls, clearly admiring their new dresses and making rapid-fire conversation.

"Watch them," she mouthed to Oscar, who stood near the door. She cut her eyes to Cecilia and Susie and Velma so he would know who she was talking about. "They can't leave by themselves."

He grinned his understanding.

"Miss Sarah." One of the mothers, a woman who lived outside of town, pulled her aside. "I just want to say that I'm glad for what you're trying to do for those little girls." She was almost whispering the words and Sarah leaned closer to hear. "Our son came home telling us what happened in the classroom a couple of weeks ago. I wish there was something more we could do, but we're barely eking out a living this winter as it is."

Sarah was familiar with the family's circumstances, and couldn't begrudge the woman for wanting to help but not being able to. If only more of the people in town had the same attitude. She squeezed the woman's hand and moved away.

The crowd had thinned by the time she was able to approach the Caldwell girls, now standing with the horseman, faces shining as he told about how they'd helped him with a project at their stepfather's homestead.

"Goodbye," Sarah called over her shoulder to a student, and when she turned back, the horseman and the Caldwell girls were alone.

"Girls. You did wonderfully tonight. I am so proud of you."

Her words brought pink to both their cheeks, but their chests seemed to puff even more, if it was possible. Velma reached for her, and Sarah took the tot into her arms, settling her on one hip.

"However, you gave us a fright when you weren't here on time. What happened to your father?"

Cecilia's smile faded. She crossed her arms over her stomach. "He couldn't bring us."

"Well, what happened? He should have sent word to me this afternoon, and not sent you out all by yourselves. I could've made other arrangements…"

"We made it here, didn't we?" Cecilia's belligerence stung, especially in the face of Sarah's worry and the stark fear that had hit her when she'd realized the full danger the girls had been in while out on their own.

Oscar put one hand on Cecilia's shoulder. "Cecilia, Miss Sarah is just worried about you. And I am, too."

Grateful for his support, Sarah opened her mouth to continue, but an ominous voice from behind her interrupted.

"Sarah, the room's about cleared. We'll wait in the wagon for you to close up. Hurry, though."

Sarah wheeled to face Mr. Allen, who'd spoken loud enough for the few families lingering and talking to start picking up their coats and wraps. Had he forgotten she'd promised to visit the Caldwells' home this evening after the pageant? She'd told him about it several days before.

"I'll see her home, Mr. Allen," said Oscar, stepping beside Sarah. "I've got the sleigh hitched and ready."

"After we settle the girls at home," Sarah put in firmly, on hand clasping Susie's arm so the girl wouldn't try to go out the door behind her. Susie's face shone with hope up at Sarah. Velma gurgled from her hip.

"It's already dark and the snow's coming down. Best you ride home with us, Sarah." His words were friendly, but his tone made it a command.

"I've promised to see the girls' Christmas socks," she argued. Although Cecilia remained distant, Susie had asked her to come and see the Christmas socks that Oscar had helped them hang and she *had* given her word.

Mr. Allen's lips twisted in an ugly sneer. "Leave those ones to the horseman." He turned his narrowed gaze to Oscar. "We're about due to settle up, aren't we?"

Sarah stifled as gasp as the man's meaning became clear. Oscar was through with Mr. Allen's colt, whether he was done training it or not.

"If that's the way you want it, sir," Oscar responded coolly.

But Sarah couldn't just leave the girls to Oscar's care, not without seeing what was going on at home. Perhaps it would take both of them to dry out Mr. Caldwell if he'd gone on a binge, or at least she could settle the girls while Oscar took care of their stepfather.

"I have a duty to my students," she said softly, still with as much firmness as she could muster.

"You have a duty to the school board," he trumpeted. "If you go with them—if you sully your reputation— you will be finished in Lost Hollow."

He slammed out of the schoolhouse, leaving a ringing silence behind him. A soft panting sound came from Susie, and Sarah realized the girl was terrified into crying. She slung her arm around the girl's shoulders, hugging both girl and infant.

"Wh-wh-why does he have to be so mean?" Susie mumbled into her shoulder.

"Some people are just cruel, honey." Sarah met eyes with Oscar above Susie's head. His face was more serious than she'd ever seen him.

From outside, the sound of wheels creaking and hoof-beats seemed overly loud in the silence.

"You can still catch him if you run," said Cecilia with forced casualness from closer to the door. She had her back turned and was absently kicking the corner of one desk.

"I'm determined to see these Christmas socks you've spent all week telling me about," Sarah said with a lift of her chin. She'd been bullied by Paul Allen for too long. She wouldn't let him ruin Christmas for these three precious girls. Not when their stepfather was doing a good enough job of it.

Oscar moved to the potbellied stove to bank the fire while Sarah moved around the room, snuffing the borrowed lamps that had lit the room.

When he stood, there were two wrapped bundles in his arms. "Well, let's get loaded up, then. It's a good thing I brought extra blankets, it feels colder already."

After they'd wrapped up as best they could, their little troupe followed him outside, Sarah securing the door behind them. As she settled the girls in the sleigh—it was going to be an incredibly tight fit—he tied their bareback horse to the side and snugged two large blankets around Sarah before coming around to his side and adjusting something in the floorboards.

"I warmed some bricks in the stove," he explained when he looked up to find her watching. "Don't want our feet to freeze."

It was a thoughtful gesture. He'd been more than helpful the entire evening. Almost as if he'd done it for her.

The sleigh rocked when he stepped into it. "You're gonna have to scoot—"

"Oomph!" Sarah was shoved almost off her side of the sleigh as Oscar settled himself into the seat.

Both girls giggled. "Miss Sarah, don't fall!"

Somehow they managed to fit all five of them on the single bench seat. With Susie half seated on top of Sarah's lap, and Cecilia no doubt the same on Oscar's, and Velma sandwiched in the middle.

"Hyah!" Oscar snapped the reins and they began to

slide across the snowy landscape. Mr. Caldwell's horse trailed behind.

With snow falling faster now, it formed a blanket of silence around them, insulating them from seeing houses that Sarah knew weren't far off the road. It was as if they were the only ones out.

"It's kinda spooky," Cecilia said softly.

"Too quiet," Oscar agreed. He winked at Sarah over the top of the girls' heads. Even with three girls between them, his look was pure male appreciation. Just that look could keep Sarah warm for the entire ride.

"You know what we need?"

"I'm afraid to guess," Sarah teased him.

"What? What?" the girls chorused.

"Christmas carols." He didn't wait for agreement, just began belting out "Jingle Bells" in his strong baritone.

The girls looked at each other, looked at Sarah and dissolved into giggles. But soon they were singing along with him with abandon, voices high and not quite in tune. Velma giggled and clapped along.

When he changed to "The Holly and the Ivy," he nodded at Sarah to join in. She did, though quietly, because she didn't have a strong voice, not like his.

She admired him. He'd distracted the girls almost immediately so they wouldn't dwell on Paul Allen and the man's explosion of temper. Unfortunately, Sarah was not so easily sidetracked.

She would do her best to see the girls settled, and quickly, and then have Oscar return her home to the Allens' ranch. She couldn't afford to lose her job. But she wouldn't consider herself much of a teacher if she put her own needs above those of her students. If only

Mr. Allen could understand her need to care for her students. She couldn't understand why he held such a grudge against two little girls, no matter their heritage or family situation. They were children and deserved to be cared for.

But what about Sarah? Who would care for her if she lost her job? She'd been taking care of herself for so long and wanted a husband to partner with. Would she ever receive what she longed for so desperately?

Oscar could see Sarah's mind working even as she sang along with them. Worrying about Paul Allen's threat?

Oscar didn't believe the man would go through with firing her. It was the middle of the year—where would he find another teacher? Surely the parents could be rallied based on Sarah's performance. *If* they could be brought together to stand up to the man. They had showed a surprising lack of backbone when it came to helping the Caldwell girls. Perhaps it was a bluff to keep Sarah under his thumb. One could hope.

In all of Oscar's dealings around town and with the cowboys on Allen's ranch, he hadn't been able to discover what Allen had against the Caldwell family. He didn't know if it was the dead mother, the stepfather or the girls' Indian heritage that made the man dislike them, but it sure didn't seem fair.

And he'd do what he could to keep Sarah from getting punished for something that wasn't a punishable offense.

But he was getting a little worried about this snow. It was coming down even harder now, in huge, fluffy flakes and clumps. The breeze was picking up, too, and if it got any worse, he might even call it a blizzard.

It could be difficult to get Sarah home after they got the girls settled. But his pa would say there was no sense worrying about it now—he'd wait until he knew for sure.

He held the reins loosely in his left hand and reached out of the blankets and over to Sarah's shoulder with his right. His gentle clasp of her shoulder shook her out of her thoughts and he grinned, bringing that color he loved into her cheeks. Yes, she was fun to rile, and if it brought her out of her worries, even better.

He guided the horses into the Caldwells' yard and all the way to the barn. "It's really coming down, gals. Let's let this boy warm up a little in here and go check on your stepfather."

Instantly subdued, the girls obediently clambered down from the sleigh. He followed them to the cabin, glad he'd spent one evening earlier in the month repairing the chinks and roof with pitch, making the little cabin snug enough to survive this storm.

As they moved inside, Caldwell roused from the sofa, where he'd apparently been in a drunken doze—he stank like a distillery.

"Where you been?" the man lisped, pointing a shaking finger at the girls.

"They came to the school pageant," Sarah said, more patiently than Oscar expected her to be. "Alone. On your horse."

"Stole my horse?" he rasped, stumbling across the floor to grab Cecilia's arm. "I told ya we wasn't goin'. Refuse to be humiliated in front of the whole town.

Charity cases…." His mumbling wound down as he seemed to lose his train of thought.

"Mr. Caldwell, your daughters performed exceptionally well tonight. It's a shame you weren't there to watch them."

"She's right," Oscar said. He moved to the man and gently encouraged him to release Cecilia's arm, which the man did, but backed away, face coloring. "You were doing better with your drinking. What happened tonight?"

"Couldn't face them all," the man muttered, rubbing one hand over his face. "Self-righteous…" His words faded behind his hand.

"But the girls needed you," Sarah pleaded.

"They ain't my brats!" he hissed.

Susie gasped. Tears streamed down her face. Oscar tried to reach for her, but she ducked past his outstretched hand and ran into the bedroom.

Red-faced, Cecilia scooped Velma off of the floor where Sarah had set her down. "You are…are…a horrible man." She followed her sister into the bedroom and slammed the door closed.

"Cain't do this anymore," Caldwell muttered. "Interfering busybody, and…" He pointed at Oscar. "You with your sanctimonious ideals trying to sober me up. This ain't my place—can't make nuthin' grow, can't make a living. And those ain't my kids!"

He slammed outside, letting in a flurry of snow and leaving a wake of bitter cold behind.

Chapter Eleven

Oscar watched Sarah wilt onto the edge of the sofa Caldwell had vacated upon their entrance. "That didn't go so well."

"No," he agreed.

She covered her face with her hands and for a moment he thought she might be crying, but when she looked up at him a moment later, her eyes were dry.

"I just…" She paused. Swallowed. "I can't believe he could say that he doesn't want them. They're bright girls. Adorable and friendly. How could anyone—" Her voice broke and he found himself moving toward her.

He knelt at her feet, gathering her hands in his. He remembered her words from their late fall picnic, knew she must be remembering the sense of abandonment she'd felt after her father's injury. "I know how you feel," he whispered.

She startled and their eyes met and held. "What do you mean?"

He hesitated. Could he really tell her this? The only person who knew all of it was his brother Maxwell. But she'd trusted him with her past….

"My parents died when I was ten. There was no one else but an uncle to take me in. He didn't really want me. Didn't like me at all. I stayed as long as I could, but I ran away when I was twelve. That's when I met my pa—Jonas. He took me in and I helped him and Breanna get the homestead up and running. And then the other brothers came along and then Penny, too." He hid his face in her hands, unable to watch her expression change if she felt sorry for him. "My uncle might not have abandoned me in the same way your father did you, but I know what it feels like to be with someone who isn't there emotionally. No kid should have to feel like that."

She untangled one of her hands from his grasp, but when he thought she would push him away, her fingers threaded through his hair, her palm resting against the exposed nape of his neck.

They remained like that for several minutes, silent. Sharing and empathizing together about parents and caregivers who had let them down.

"You and your brothers seemed so close," she finally commented softly. "I'm surprised you can be away from home for so long without missing them and your father like crazy."

He turned his head, still pillowed on her knees, to stare at the fire crackling in the hearth, enjoying their closeness.

"It's different now," he said quietly. "My brother Maxwell—he and I are the closest in age—has left home for medical school, and now that I've got my own place…"

He could've left it at that, but he'd told her all of the

rest of it. He might as well say the words, reveal what was really eating at him. "And my pa has his own kids now," he whispered. "It's not the same between us."

She nearly dumped him off her lap as she stood and moved away, facing him with hands parked on her hips. "You mean to tell me the reason you've been gallivanting around Wyoming on your adventures is because you think your father doesn't love you anymore now that he's got his own children? That is the most absurd thing I've ever heard."

He had to smile at her impassioned speech and that just seemed to rile her up even more. She scoffed at him. "Your father cared enough about you to take you in and give you a place to stay, give you his love for all those years and you think he just stopped loving you? Are you daft? Have you even talked to him about it?"

Oscar looked at her askance, as if asking if he'd talked to his father about his mistaken feelings was crazy.

"He's been busy with the little tykes. No, I haven't talked to him."

She glared at him. How could he be so cavalier about something so important? "Babies take time. There's feeding and diapering and cleaning up after them and their messes." She gestured to the supper table, where dishes had been left, including those from little Velma's dinner. "Or haven't you noticed?"

He grinned again. "I've noticed."

"That doesn't mean you stop loving the older children. They still have a place in your heart."

He shook his head. "It's not the same. They're his kids. His *real* kids."

She'd seen the way his brothers had acted when they'd been in town. Family members didn't share that closeness without a strong foundation. She sincerely doubted that his father had stopped caring about Oscar just because he'd had more children.

"Will you talk to your father when you get home? Just talk to him about what you've said to me?"

His face changed. It was imperceptible, but it was there. Some of the spark behind his eyes had died. "I'll think about it."

He stood up. "I'd better go check on Caldwell. Hopefully he's warm in the barn. And sleeping off the liquor." He turned for the door, picking up his coat on the way.

A cold blast of air hit her ankles, and then another as Oscar scooted right back inside, muttering.

"What's wrong?"

"It's snowing even harder, and the wind's picked up. Just want to make sure I can get back to the cabin once I'm out there."

A nervous thrill went through her stomach. "Will we be able to get back to the Allens' place?"

"I'll let you know when I get back." He unhooked the thin cord she'd seen clean diapers hanging on that first day, then followed it to a second hook on the opposite wall where the coil of cord rested. He took it out with him.

She should probably be concerned about the state of her job, but right now her worry was for the girls. She went to the bedroom door and knocked softly.

"What?" came Cecilia's voice. Sarah was prepared

for the girl's belligerence, but the vulnerable note in her voice made Sarah's throat prickly and hot.

She pushed open the door gently. "It's Sarah."

"What do you want?" The wobble was still there in Cecilia's voice, but she had her back to the door, and her arms crossed.

Susie sat on the floor, tears tracking down her face.

Only Velma was peaceful, curled up in a nest of blankets in the middle of the bed.

"I want to make sure you and Susie are all right."

"We're fine." But the words were punctuated with a sniffle.

Sarah moved into the small room and sat on the floor next to Susie, her back against the wall and knees pressed against the bed. All three of them slept in here, in that bed barely big enough for one adult?

"I know it's hard—" Sarah murmured.

"What do you care, anyway?" Cecilia blurted out, whirling. Her face was as tearstained as her sister's, but her eyes were full of fire.

Velma murmured in her sleep, stirred, but didn't wake.

"I care." Sarah reached for the older girl, but Cecilia slipped away from her. "I care, because I know what you're going through. And I want you to know you're not alone."

"What do you mean?" Susie sniffled.

Sarah took a breath and started her story. "My mother died when I was young. A little older than Cecilia. I had two younger sisters, too," she said, trying to engage the other girl in the story, but Cecilia remained aloof. "I wasn't very good at taking care of the household chores—not like you girls are—but we muddled through. Then when I was fifteen, my father decided there was money in mining. I guess some men make a living at it, but my father's choice was disastrous. He was gravely injured in a mining accident and could no longer work."

Susie moved to sit cross-legged on the end of the bed, paying avid attention. Cecilia absently flicked the curtain at the dirty window, but even though she pretended to ignore them, Sarah had the sense she was listening.

"I was really angry with my father for a long time," Sarah admitted. "He had three daughters. I thought he should have chosen a less risky job so that he could better take care of us. When he was hurt, there was a little savings, but after it was gone, we were basically destitute."

There. A flicker of interest from Cecilia, whose chin turned minutely in Sarah's direction.

"No one in town seemed to know or care that we were poor—barely making it. We never had new things. My poor sisters wore hand-me-downs until they were worn through, underthings and everything."

Susie giggled.

"I even…" This part was hard for Sarah to tell. "I even had to have a friend cut down my mother's dresses, because I didn't have anything to wear and no money to purchase material—not that I could've sewn a dress, anyway. Many times the children in school made fun of me. Not so much my sisters, but all the children thought I was bossy and too strict." Oscar had been the start of those jokes, but now that she knew him better, the memory was less painful. "None of them knew that we were just trying to survive."

Now Cecilia joined her sister on the end of the bed. Though she didn't look at Sarah but stared down at the worn quilt covering it, Sarah knew she had the girl's attention.

"And do you know what I wished almost every day?"

"What?" breathed Susie.

"I wished for one person in town—one adult—to really see what was going on in our family. See that we needed help. But no one ever did."

"So what did you do?" Ah! A quiet question from Cecilia.

Sarah held back her smile, but hope soared through her. *Please God, let me be getting through to the girl.* "I left my schooling early and went to the Normal School in Cheyenne. When I wasn't in class learning how to be a teacher, I washed dishes and did laundry for the house where I boarded. I hoarded every penny to send back to my sisters. Then, after I got my first teaching job, things got a little easier."

"Did—did your papa die?" asked Susie softly.

"Yes. Just after my first months at the Normal School. I had to miss classes to see to the funeral arrangements." And had nearly starved herself in the months after trying to pay for the resulting expenses and keep her sisters fed.

"I don't want things to be hard for you girls." Sarah reached out and took Susie's hand. She awkwardly patted Cecilia's shoulder, and for once the girl didn't lean away. "That's why I've been trying to help, even though I've botched things part of the time. I don't want you to have to suffer like I did."

Inside his gloves, Oscar's hands were numb by the time he reached the barn and tied off the end of his cord to the door handle.

The barn was blessedly warm compared to the gusting wind and swirling snow. Between the couple of cows and Caldwell's horses along with Oscar's own animals, there was enough heat from the animals to warm the area enough to sleep. He hoped.

"Caldwell?"

No answer. Oscar scoured the barn, beginning to worry when he didn't find the man. Perhaps he'd visited the privy?

After fighting the storm to reach the barn, Oscar knew it would be impossible to get Sarah home tonight. It would risk both of their lives to try it. He started unharnessing the horse from the sleigh, giving it a brisk rubdown before putting it in its stall. Hopefully Sarah wouldn't be too upset. And hopefully her boss would see that she'd had no choice but to stay in a safe place during a snowstorm. But that was a worry for tomorrow.

By the time Oscar had the horse comfortable in its stall, Caldwell still hadn't shown his face.

Oscar began to really worry.

If the man was out in the building blizzard, he could get lost or disoriented. Oscar had had the wash line to guide him, and had still been unsure of his course before he'd knocked into the side of the barn. What if the man got injured? Or had just found a hole to burrow in somewhere until the storm passed?

Should Oscar risk going after him?

Chapter Twelve

By the time Oscar banged inside, shaking a thick layer of snow from his person, Sarah had Cecilia and Susie somewhat calmed and sitting on the sofa. Their eyes were red-rimmed, but they'd retained a sparkle that even their cruel stepfather couldn't dim. Once Sarah had shared her story about her past and that she wouldn't let Mr. Caldwell bring harm to the girls, Susie had thrown herself into her teacher's arms. Cecilia's reception had been cool, but there had been a new trust in her eyes. At least Sarah hoped that's what it was.

Sarah was determined to settle things with Mr. Caldwell tonight, whatever she had to do.

Except the girls' stepfather did not follow Oscar inside. The younger man's mouth was set and expression grim as he took off his hat and coat and spread them on a chair near the fire.

Sarah went to him in the kitchen area, where she'd started a pot of coffee—that much she could do in the kitchen without burning it. "Are you all right? Where's Mr. Caldwell?" she asked in a low voice.

"He's gone. Not in the barn. I checked the privy, too."

"What?" She glanced over her shoulders to the pair on the sofa. They were whispering to each other and didn't appear to have heard.

The horseman's fingers were like blocks of ice when she pressed a mug of the hot beverage into his hands. "Thanks."

"But he can't be gone," she whispered. "This is his place."

"He leaves sometimes when he's drunk." Cecilia's sudden words fell loud into the silence.

"But, honey, it's snowing." Sarah tried to reason with the girl, tried to understand what would make a man go out in this weather.

"It's not just snowing." Oscar ran a hand through his dark hair. "It's a blizzard. Practically a whiteout." He turned to Sarah, frowning. "I'm sorry. I won't be able to get you home like I promised."

She froze momentarily, mind spinning with all the repercussions of his words, then a look over his shoulder to the two urchins huddled on the sofa steadied her. If she couldn't get home, she couldn't. The girls needed her now.

She went to them, perching on the couch next to Susie, who leaned into her side naturally, as if Sarah was her older sister. Oscar pulled one of the kitchen chairs close and sat in it, propping his elbows on his bent knees.

"I thought about going out after him," Oscar said.

"You can't!" Sarah admonished. "What if you get lost? Or can't find him? Or get hurt? You'll freeze."

His eyes stayed steady on hers and his ever-present

grin was nowhere to be seen. "It is dangerous. Do you girls know where he might've tried to go?"

Cecilia shook her head, little face set but fear deep in her eyes. "Sometimes the next morning we find him in the wheat field. Once down by the creek. Sometimes he makes it into town and stays at the saloon."

Oscar shook his head. "Even if I went looking, I couldn't get far from the cabin for fear of getting disoriented and losing my way. Let's pray for him."

The girls looked skeptical, but Oscar bowed his head and led them in a sincere prayer for Mr. Caldwell's safety.

After his "amen," Susie looked up at Sarah and asked, "What if…what if he doesn't come back?"

"It's best not to think like that." She squeezed the girl's shoulders.

"Good riddance," muttered Cecilia, but before the girl turned her face toward the fire, Sarah saw her lower lip tremble.

"But who will take care of us?" Susie asked, still shivering against Sarah's side.

"Whether your stepfather comes back tonight or in the morning—" Sarah refused to say aloud the other option "—I'm still your friend. I still want to help you, whatever comes."

"But what if you get fired from bein' the school-teacher?" Cecilia demanded.

"I won't get fired." Sarah hoped she was telling the truth.

"Girls, it's late," Oscar said. "We'll get everything figured out in the morning. Hopefully your stepfather is holed up somewhere warm for the night."

"Fine." Cecilia gathered up her sister and they moved toward the bedroom where Velma still slept.

"I'm going to talk to Miss Sarah for a minute and then I'll be in the barn, as usual."

Sarah watched the girls as they disappeared into the room, closing the door with a soft click behind them. She would open it once they'd dozed off, so the fire's warmth would reach in there, as well.

Oscar motioned her up off the sofa as he moved back into the small kitchen and reached for his hat. He didn't put it on, just knocked it against his thigh a couple of times—a sign he was nervous.

"I'm sorry I can't get you home," he said softly.

"It isn't your fault." The sense of panic that had started in her belly when she'd heard the word "blizzard" went spiraling out of control now that the girls had left the room. "It's mine. I'm the one who challenged Mr. Allen and dared come here in a snowstorm."

She turned away, afraid he would see the rising anxiety in her face. She was the one who'd made the decision and she was the one who would pay—possibly with her job. Would she be able to get employment elsewhere if Mr. Allen refused her a letter of recommendation? Her savings were negligible, more so now that she'd spent money on the girls' pageant dresses.

She did have one other option. The man who'd answered her mail-order bride letter from Montana. But there was a risk in that decision. What if the banker wasn't the right man for her—what if he turned out to be as reckless as her father had been?

"Sarah. Sarah! Quit worrying so much."

Oscar touched her shoulder and she turned to him,

surprising them both by burrowing into his chest. His arms came around her shoulders; she heard a soft sound as his hat fell to the floor.

"What am I going to do?" she asked, the words muffled in his chest.

"What you've been doing." His reply rumbled in her ear. "Comforting those little girls. I expect they'll have more to worry about tomorrow. And right before Christmas, too."

The thud of his heart was steady in her ear. A comforting sound. His flannel shirt soft against her cheek.

Even with the very male distraction, she couldn't stop her mind from whirling. "But, what—"

"You leave Allen to me. If I have to go to every school board member's home and explain that I slept in the barn and everything was proper, I will."

She suspected he might have to follow through on that. "But you're leaving. Aren't you? Now that your job is finished?" She pushed away from his chest slightly, the better to see his face.

"Sarah—" His voice sounded strangled and he reached up to touch her cheek with one calloused hand. When he drew away, she saw the sparkle of tears on his fingers. Her tears. She hadn't even realized she was crying.

"Darlin'—" He cupped her cheek again, this time drawing her face up toward his.

He was going to kiss her.

She saw it coming—he even paused just before their lips brushed. He held her so gently, she could draw away if she wanted to.

But she wanted his kiss. Raised up on tiptoe to meet his lips.

And it was everything she'd expected.

Oscar lay awake in his straw cradle, wrapped in his bedroll in the pitch-black barn, listening to the wind buffet the walls outside. He was warm enough, not uncomfortable. And he'd grown used to the animals' soft nighttime sounds over the past few weeks sleeping out here.

No, what kept him from sleep was Sarah's kiss.

First, she'd gone into his arms as if she'd *needed* his comfort. She'd trembled against him, and when he'd seen her tears, he'd been undone. Hadn't been able to stop himself from taking her mouth with his.

And she'd kissed him back. She'd curled her arms around his neck and responded to his touch and it had completely surprised him.

Her eyes had been luminous when he'd said goodnight a few moments later and rushed into the cold night.

What had she thought about his kiss? He'd been afraid to stick around and find out if she was angry or regretted it.

He'd thought they were friends, enjoyed spending time with her. When his brothers had visited and she'd first shown her playful side, he'd realized how much he enjoyed being with her.

But now he wondered if he might be falling in love with her.

He loved spending time with her, was impressed with her compassion toward not only Susie and Cecilia and Velma but toward all her students. Didn't even mind any more when she was bossy. Actually found it kind of cute.

But when you loved someone, it made you vulnerable to them. They could leave you.

Just like his parents had left when they'd died. And his uncle had abandoned him. Even Maxwell had gone, moving on with his life, and then Jonas got busy with the kids....

Oscar didn't know if he dared to love her. And she'd made it very clear before that she wasn't interested in marrying a cowboy.

His gut churned. Had he done the wrong thing by kissing her? It sure hadn't felt wrong.

Tucked beneath a blanket and her shawl on the uncomfortable sofa, Sarah stared into the fire, unable to sleep. Replaying Oscar's kiss in her mind.

His lips had been warm and firm. He'd held her so carefully, as if she was precious to him.

She'd wondered briefly if he'd thought of Sally, but other than the occasional mention in casual conversation, Sarah's younger sister didn't seem to cross his mind. True, they'd both been young when they'd been sweet on each other, and Sally now considered him a friend. And his passionate kiss certainly didn't seem to indicate he was thinking of her sister in any fashion.

But could she really trust a man like him, a man who made his living working with dangerous animals?

She was afraid she'd already trusted him too much. He hadn't answered her whether he was leaving immediately. He'd often said how much he wanted to return to his cabin and get started on his herd. With his job finished, what was keeping him here in Lost Hollow?

Insecurities flooded her. She hadn't been enough for the man who'd courted her while she'd been at the Normal School. In the beginning, Oscar had found her bossy and independent. Had his feelings really changed?

She didn't know.

It was a long time before she was able to fall asleep.

Morning brought a decrease of dimness and more snow, but no Mr. Caldwell. After fighting his way through the gusting wind to the snug cabin, Oscar remained concerned about going out to find the man. Could Caldwell have even survived the night?

He burst into the cabin, startling Sarah, who stood near the stove, staring out the window into the white morass.

He sniffed appreciatively. "Coffee's on, I guess?"

"Yes. Let me get you some." Her cheeks were that interesting shake of pink as she rushed to get a mug from the sideboard and fill it.

But he couldn't tell if she was regretful about their kiss, or not. She could just be embarrassed to face him.

When she pressed the mug into his cold hands, he intended to link his fingers with hers and make her look at him, but the girls tumbled out of their room, hair in crooked braids, wearing the dresses his ma had sent down for them.

Any important conversation with Sarah would have to wait.

"Is our stepfather back?" Cecilia asked.

"No. Visibility is a little better this morning, so I

thought after breakfast I'd see if I can do a little searching in the yard. It's still coming down pretty bad out
there," he said as an aside to Sarah. "It'd be risking the
horse to try and get you home."

She shrugged, not fully looking at him. "I suppose
the damage is done already. Perhaps it will let up later
this afternoon."

"What's for breakfast?" Susie asked.

Now Sarah did look at him with a slightly panicked
look on her face. "I didn't attempt anything. I was afraid
I'd ruin it…."

The girls dissolved into peals of laughter and he
couldn't help but chuckle.

"I think she was asking me," he informed Sarah,
who blushed rosy pink. "I fed and watered the animals
in the barn. They're comfortable, at least. Why don't I
escort you ladies to the privy—make sure you don't get
lost—and then we'll start on breakfast?"

The girls bundled up, even Sarah, and followed him
out into the blowing snow toward the privy. He'd insisted they link hands, and he was glad he'd done so.
The outline of the small building was visible, but that
was about it. And the girls were so slight, it was easier
to navigate the yard as one group.

Not wanting to embarrass them while they took care
of their needs, he shuffled off behind the nearby barn,
looking out past the corral into what he could see of
the woods behind.

His eyes scanned the area, mostly by rote, but he
froze when he saw a dark shape at the base of one of
the trees.

The wind changed and snow blew and he squinted,

trying to get another glimpse of the thing he thought he'd seen. The dark shape could've been a man, lying on the ground. Or it could've been a downed tree. An injured—if large—sort of wildlife.

But what if it was Caldwell? He couldn't just leave the man out there.

Oscar poked his head out from behind the barn to see Sarah still standing beside the privy with one of the girls. He waved his hat at her and she returned the wave, raising one mittened hand.

It took him several labor-intensive minutes to skirt the corral in the high snowdrifts. Longer to cross the open space between corral and woods, with the wind shoving him until he was bent like an old woman.

The closer the got, the lower his spirits sank. And when he knelt next to the man's frozen body, Oscar's heart pinched for the girls, who now had no one to take care of them.

Chapter Thirteen

When Oscar didn't return for them and the girls were shivering beside her, Sarah ushered them back to the cabin, of which she could only see a faint outline. It seemed the sky had darkened further in their few minutes outside. Could the storm be worsening again?

Inside, it seemed blessedly quiet after the roar of the wind in their ears. She helped the girls take off their outer garments and shake free of the snow. The trio immediately went to the fire in the hearth and sank down beside it.

Sarah returned to the window, relieved when Oscar's bulky form could be seen crossing the yard toward the cabin.

But when he came inside, she immediately knew something was wrong. His face was drawn and tight—even worse than it had been last night after Mr. Caldwell's disappearance.

He took off his gloves, but not his coat, and motioned her to the doorway. She didn't even have a thought of not going to him.

She clutched his cold hands between hers. "More coffee?"

"No. I found the stepfather," he muttered, pulling her closer to speak in her ear.

But it was too late. Cecilia popped up off the floor. "Is he alive?" Her voice shook.

Oscar's shoulders slumped. He released Sarah's hands and went to the girls, kneeling on the floor next to them. "I'm sorry. He's not."

Susie dissolved into tears and Sarah moved to gather the girl into her arms.

Cecilia remained standing, a defiant tilt to her chin, until Oscar put his arm around her shoulders, and then she, too, starting crying. Soft, almost-silent tears like the ones Sarah had often shed at night, not wanting her sisters to hear.

Velma looked between her sisters then started bawling. The tot likely had no idea what was going on, but could read her sisters' emotions well enough. Sarah scooped up the baby and held both her and Susie close. Remembered many nights where she herself had wanted a comforting embrace.

She would be that for these girls. No matter what.

"We'll get things figured out," she said. "But I want you to know that I'm here with you."

"Will you stay with us, Miss Sarah?" asked Susie, voice quivering.

Cecilia pierced Sarah with her eyes, daring her to answer. Maybe daring her to follow through on the promises Sarah had made last night.

Oscar watched her, too. Sarah could feel his eyes on her but couldn't look at him. Would his expression tell her not to make a promise like that? But with her past, how could she not?

"We'll stay together," Sarah promised. "I'll take care of you girls."

Cecilia's eyes darkened and her lips tightened, but she didn't protest Sarah's words.

Susie clung to Sarah's neck, and Velma finally calmed.

After several emotional minutes, they finally got the girls calm enough to settle on the couch and Oscar went to the kitchen. He pulled a tin from one of the high shelves and showed it to Sarah. Baker's chocolate.

"To make a hot chocolate drink. I was saving this for a treat for tomorrow," he said.

He went and scooped a pot of snow from outside the door and then put it on the stove to boil into water. Into a second pan went the chocolate, pushed farther back on the stove where it wouldn't be quite so hot.

"What do we do now?" Sarah asked, voice low. The girls talked among themselves, and played with Velma, trying to cheer their little sister.

"Try to make the best of things today and tomorrow. I imagine this will stain their Christmases for some time to come."

Sarah felt stubbornness rise within her. "Not if I can help it. We'll still celebrate. The girls deserve that much. I suppose funeral arrangements can wait until after the holiday."

That one corner of his mouth lifted briefly before he returned to the task of mixing the chocolate. "I've also got to figure a way to get the body moved. There's a chance wild animals could get to it and maul it. Need to bring it to the barn lean-to."

Her heart beat faster at the morbid thought. "Weren't you able to…carry him?"

He shook his head. "His clothes were soaked through and refrozen. He was too heavy for me to lift alone. I thought about going for help, but the nearest neighbor isn't close and I wouldn't be much use to you if I got lost in the storm."

"What about a sled? Do the girls have one? Or you could hitch up the sleigh for a bit?"

"Couldn't reach him with the woods and trail's too thin. But you're onto something with the sled idea. There's some poles in the barn and I can fix a travois, take one of the horses with me to do the real work."

She remembered the way the sky had darkened just while they'd been visiting the privy. "Isn't the storm getting worse? Should you really be out there in it?"

"Don't have a choice," he said matter-of-factly.

She helped him serve the hot chocolate to the girls and then explain that they needed to move the stepfather's frozen body. The girls worried about Oscar and his safety, and he promised them he'd be careful.

At the door, Sarah held his hat while he shrugged into his coat. Worry niggled at her, but she bit her lip to keep from asking him to stay. If he thought it was important to retrieve the man, then it must be.

"Be careful," she whispered. "Don't get lost."

"The horses know their way around here by now," he said with one of those cocky grins. "They'll want to get back to the warm barn, so as long as I stay with Pharaoh, I'll be fine."

Sarah had been right. The storm had worsened noticeably by the time Oscar got the travois lashed together and Pharaoh convinced to go out in the blowing wind. Leading the horse by its reins, he was able to follow the corral to where he thought he should veer off to the woods.

It was sheer chance that he stumbled onto the body. By then, Oscar's extremities were going numb and it was difficult to maneuver the body onto the travois, but finally he had it strapped into place good enough that he thought he could make it back to the barn.

He'd gotten the horse turned back—hopefully—toward the corral, though he couldn't make out the fence through the blowing snow, but they'd only gone a few steps when Oscar's foot sank deep into the snow—too deep. The ankle wrenched and he was thrown off balance, losing his grasp on Pharaoh's reins. He cried out, pain searing through the coldness and up his leg.

The horse whinnied at the sudden movement, but Oscar could only pray the animal wouldn't bolt as he struggled to fight off the pain causing black spots to dance before his eyes.

He'd been out too long.

Sarah couldn't fight the worry churning in her gut. What if Oscar was hurt and needed help? Did she dare leave the girls to go to him? Would she be able to find her way back if she did?

"D'you think the horseman needs help?" asked Cecilia. She was concerned about the man but had hardly responded to Sarah's overtures since last night. It stung a little.

The sound of a horse's whinny cut above the screaming wind.

Cecilia and Susie exchanged a wide-eyed glance even as Sarah reached for her coat.

"Wait!" Cecilia cried. She rushed into the bedroom and came back with a thick woolen sweater that had seen its share of wear. "It was our mother's. It's plenty cold outside but maybe an extra layer will keep you warm."

Touched by the girl's surprising show of kindness, Sarah shrugged on the sweater, which was a tad too large, and then her coat. Finally winding her scarf around her neck and donning her mittens, she took a deep breath with her hand on the latch.

"Here." Susie handed her a knitted cap.

"Thank you. Girls, you'd better pray. And stay inside. No matter what." The worried expressions on their faces did not reassure her as she stepped out into the blustery, driven snow.

She was able to find the cord Oscar had tied to the back of the cabin. Her skirt pressed into her legs, tangled with her feet. She fought the wind as it burned her cheeks and whipped her hair out from under the cap. By the time she reached the barn, her legs felt like lead and she was exhausted. And Oscar had been out in this for much longer than she had.

She followed the barn, keeping one hand on it at all times, until she'd reached its back side, then stood with her back to the wooden wall, attempting to peer into the swirling white for the broad-shouldered man she'd come to care about.

By herself in the whistling, disorienting wind, she admitted it. She was falling in love with the horseman. It had been building for a while now, with his jovial nature and compassion for three hurting girls. But seeing him comfort the girls and his bravery in fighting the storm to bring back a man he didn't even like had sealed it for her.

"Oscar!" she tried calling his name, but the wind snatched her voice.

The blowing snow made it impossible to see anything. She couldn't even glimpse the corral. What if he'd misjudged the distance and gotten lost in the woods?

What should she do? If she got lost in the blizzard, too, who would care for the girls?

But she couldn't just leave him out in this....

"Please, God," she begged, voice erased by the wind again.

Another whinny.

For a moment, a lull in the wind allowed her to see the corral, twenty feet in front of her, and farther around its contour, the hulking figure of a horse. Oscar's horse.

She ran forward, toward the corral, and when the wind came again it nearly blasted her off her feet. Instantly, she was blinded by the snow and tears the wind brought to her eyes. She struggled on, and after a moment, rammed into the corral fence, letting out an unexpected "oomph!"

She used the top railing to guide herself around the corral. "Oscar!" she yelled again.

She thought she heard a groan, and she definitely heard a sound like a horse stomping its feet. But she still couldn't see anything.

Breathing hard, she releasing the railing and strode out into the wall of snow, heart pounding frantically at her daring.

She tripped over him, sprawling facedown in the

soft snow, then sitting up and spluttering, attempting to brush her face clear with snow-covered mittens.

"Sarah?" He gripped her shoulders almost painfully. "What're you doing out here?" he demanded.

"Coming after you, you foolish man." Silly tears filled her eyes, but she blinked them back. No doubt the moisture would freeze to her face if she let them fall.

"I should be angry, but I'm just glad to see you. I've managed to turn my ankle. I don't think it's bad, but I can't put my full weight on it. I tried to get up on Pharaoh's back, but the wind caught my coat or scarf or something and it flapped and frightened him. If you can hold his head, I think I can manage to mount up."

Sarah gulped. He wanted her to approach a dangerous animal—and hold on to it?

Oscar caught her face in his gloved hands. The fact that she couldn't tell a difference between his hands and the air temperature worried her. He had been out here for too long. They both needed to get back inside.

"Trust me. Trust the horse. We need him to get back to the barn. I know you can do this." Oscar's steady voice and gaze reassured her, right until after she'd helped him stand and the moment she was to approach the beast.

"H-hi, boy. Remember me?" she asked, trembling voice betraying her.

The horse only looked at her with those large brown eyes.

"He's a little out of sorts from being out in the wind. Just be firm with him, hold him steady while I hop on his back."

Oscar's words rang in her ears as she reached out—

taking her life in her own hands—and grabbed the animal's halter. The small piece of leather didn't feel as if it could control the animal. It only felt as if her arm could be ripped off if the horse decided to rear its head.

Oscar huffed and hopped awkwardly, swinging one leg over the horse's back.

The animal didn't move, didn't blink.

"All—all right," said Sarah. "Let's go."

The horse still didn't move. Then Oscar clucked from the animal's back and it began slowly trodding through the drifting snow. Hopefully toward the barn.

She'd done it. Faced her fear. She was still holding the animal's halter, half guiding and half being led toward safety.

Oscar was elated at Sarah's victory with the horse. He really was. But by the time they'd reached the barn, unloaded Caldwell's body into the lean-to and unattached the travois from Pharaoh—with Oscar awkwardly hopping on one foot the entire time—he'd gone past cold, past numb, to drowsy.

Which a faraway part of his brain knew was dangerous, but he couldn't seem to rouse himself to care.

"Need to get back to the house," he slurred, propping himself upright near the barn door.

Sarah's worried face swam in front of his vision. He fought the urge to close his eyes. Just for a second, it would be such a relief.

"C'mon," she said, very close to his ear. She put one arm around his waist and tugged him until his feet started moving. At least he thought they did.

He felt the cold envelop them again, but this time it

didn't sting as it had before. He could barely feel the wind even though Sarah seemed to be struggling to follow the cord across the small yard to the cabin.

And then she pushed him inside and it felt as if a furnace blasted across his face. Unwelcome, tingly prickles crawled across his exposed skin.

"Miss Sarah!"

"You found him!"

Two young voices chorused, sounding loud in the sudden quiet of being out of the wind.

"Yes, I found him, but I think he's half-frozen."

She pushed and prodded him forward until he toppled onto the sofa, closer to the fire and the overbearing heat.

He allowed his eyes to fall half closed, but still saw her struggling to take off her mittens and unwind her scarf from her neck. He wasn't the only one half-frozen.

Little Velma came up to him and pounded on his knees. He saw it, but couldn't feel it. Was he suffering from frostbite? Hypothermia?

He struggled to sit up, knowing that he needed to keep his blood flowing, no matter how painful this was going to be.

Cecilia reached for one of his gloved hands and Susie the other.

"Careful," Sarah cautioned as the girls helped pry the gloves off his numb fingers.

His hands emerged chapped and red, but not white like they might've been if they were frostbitten. Just half-frozen, like Sarah had said.

In the warmth of the room, he could feel heat creeping back into his skin, back into his limbs. It felt like little ants, stinging him all over.

"Is there any of that chocolate left?" Sarah asked.

"We made coffee." One set of footsteps retreated to the kitchen. Cecilia.

"Make sure it's not too hot—more like lukewarm," Sarah called after her. She knelt at his feet and started taking off his boots. "Did your stepfather leave any socks behind?" she asked Susie, and that girl left, too, disappearing into the bedroom.

"Are you in pain?" she asked softly. "You've gone all quiet and your mouth is pinched."

"Yeah," he gritted out. "Yeah, but at least I'm alive. Thanks to you."

Her golden lashes fanned her face as she lowered her eyes, but a small smile played around her lips.

He was proud of his schoolteacher gal. Thankful to be alive. And he'd prove it to her, as soon as he could get his limbs working right again.

"It smells burnt," called Cecilia from the floor where she and Susie played pat-a-cake with Velma.

Sarah fought the urge to turn away from the stove, where she stood with a spoon in hand. The girl was right. Sarah had let water in the pot of potatoes boil over.

"Give her a chance, Cecilia," defended Susie. "Her potatoes will be as good as yours were. They can't be any worse."

So far the overboiled water had been the only disaster.

Sarah was supremely conscious of Oscar, wrapped in a blanket and sitting at the kitchen table, instructing her. She desperately didn't want to mess up their late lunch. And she was ravenous after fighting through the storm to get to him.

He still shivered violently, which was why she'd suggested he let her make lunch. The fact that he'd agreed easily worried her. Perhaps he felt worse than he let on.

"You'll want to move that grease pan to the middle of the stovetop," he said now. "Get it nice and hot before you fry the ham."

"You want more coffee?" she asked, doing as he suggested, careful to use a towel to guard her hand from the pan.

"I'm already sloshing around from what you've already got in me."

She'd followed his directions and remarkably, the biscuits were only a little on the brown side of golden, not burnt. The potatoes were mashed and only slightly lumpy, and the ham was crisp. Everything appeared edible. She hadn't botched it too badly.

She was reaching for plates to set the table on a high shelf when her hand bumped a small wooden box. A glance inside revealed several handwritten recipe cards, stained and spotted, the recipes written in faded pencil. Sarah absently flipped through them, until the last item in the box. It wasn't a card, but a torn piece of paper. And on it was a name and address for someone in Green River, down in Sweetwater County.

Had Mrs. Caldwell hidden this address for a reason? Could this be a relation that the girls didn't know they had? Sarah tucked it into her dress pocket, determined to send a wire when the snow stopped and she could get to town. Certainly, she wouldn't abandon the girls, but a relative would likely want to help, as well.

But Sarah had been the one to promise she would take care of them. Would they see it as a betrayal if someone else came for them? And how would she survive, now that she'd opened her heart to the girls?

And what of her job? She couldn't even think about what would happen if Mr. Allen followed through and fired her. She had enough to worry about with a half-frozen man to tend and trying to make Christmas a joyful occasion for three little girls who deserved it.

Chapter Fourteen

That night, Oscar snuck back in the cabin, taking care to close the door softly behind him. He set down the brown paper-wrapped gifts he'd brought in from the barn on the kitchen table, and began shrugging off his coat.

He could hear the murmur of Sarah's voice as she tucked the girls into bed and his heart swelled.

During the afternoon, they'd strung popcorn and dried cranberries on the small tree he'd cut yesterday morning and stored in the barn. She'd seemed to know when the girls needed a reassuring touch or hug, been sensitive when the girls dissolved into tears or just needed quiet time. She would be a great mother.

And he knew he was falling in love with her. Couldn't help it.

The small gift he'd stowed for Sarah in his pocket burned against his skin. He wanted to give it to her tonight, in private. It wasn't much to look at, but it was one of the last things he had from his mother, a silver locket. He hoped, after telling her the story of his past and his parents' death, that Sarah would understand its significance. He thought she would.

What was taking her so long? He staunched the desire to pace, instead looking for anything in the kitchen that hadn't been cleaned up earlier.

His eyes fell on something on the floor. A folded piece of paper? He knelt to pick it up. A letter.

Thick, masculine handwriting addressed the letter to Sarah. From someone in Montana.

A suitor?

He shouldn't read it. He really shouldn't, but Oscar couldn't help himself from taking out the sheet of paper and unfolding it.

Dear Miss Hansen,
Thank you for your letter in response to my ad. I am a prosperous banker in a small town in western Montana, unfortunately unlucky in love, which is why I placed the ad.

Your letter was particularly well-versed, I assume because of your vocation. I believe an intelligent woman would be a good match for myself as a future mate.

I am interested in meeting and moving forward with a courtship. When will your school term be up? If it pleases you, we should continue our correspondence until that time and then be married.

I would love to hear more about your family history when you next write.
Sincerely,

The man had signed his name with a flourish.
Oscar sat in one of the kitchen chairs, heart pound-

ing in his ears. Was Sarah going to marry this Montana man? Was she already planning to leave?

Cold and then heat rushed over him, making him feel much like he had earlier when he'd been warming up after being outside for so long.

It was the same way he'd felt when he'd learned his parents had died. The same way he'd felt the night he'd realized his uncle would never really love him.

A banker. She'd chosen a banker.

How many times had she told him she wasn't interested in marrying a cowboy? And here was the proof.

She might've kissed him last night, but if she was leaving, she couldn't truly have feelings for him. Maybe she'd been caught up in the moment, in her emotions.

The sense of abandonment weighed him down more than his limbs had been sluggish that afternoon.

He'd given her a piece of his heart before he'd really been ready or even known that he'd done it. And she was leaving.

The door clicked closed and he looked up to see her coming toward him with a tired smile.

"They're subdued, but resilient. They've been through a lot this year."

She joined him at the table, motioning to the wrapped items strewn across its surface. "What's all this?"

He cleared his throat, tried to unstick his tongue from the roof of his mouth. "Gifts for the girls. Just trinkets, really."

"Are you all right? Chills all gone? Will the barn be warm enough for you tonight?"

She sounded as if she really cared, but could he

trust her words now that he knew she had another plan in mind?

"I'm fine," he said stiffly. "The barn's a little cool, but it will be fine."

Her brow furrowed. "What's wrong?"

He pushed the letter across the table to her, around the edges of the girls' Christmas gifts. It was halfway out of its envelope, there was no use hiding he'd read it. He didn't offer an apology, only said, "It must've fallen out of your pocket."

She looked down at it and a flush immediately rose in her face. "This is private correspondence."

That didn't sound promising, and he found himself on his feet, turning away and rubbing the back of his neck, trying to ease the muscles that had frozen up.

"Perhaps you're surprised someone would be interested in marrying me."

"I'm not surprised, Sarah." He blew out a frustrated breath. "You're a beautiful woman. You're smart and capable, and—" *I want to marry you.*

The statement he couldn't say surprised him into silence. He'd been moving toward a declaration until tonight, until just a few moments ago when he'd found that letter.

"Any man would be lucky to marry you," he finished lamely.

Her soft gasp made him turn, reluctantly, to face her. Her eyes were luminous, though her face was pale.

"Well, it isn't as if I have been offered a reason…a reason not to continue corresponding with this man."

Her words seemed to hang in the air between them, waiting for a response. One that Oscar couldn't give.

Not when he was afraid that she would decide he wasn't good enough for her.

"Of course you've got the right to do whatever you want," he said. "It's your life. If you want to marry a banker, you go right ahead." He swallowed. "It's not like I'll be here to see it, anyway. I'll be leaving as soon as I collect my pay from Mr. Allen." He strode for the door, almost forgetting his coat and hat in his hurry to get somewhere private. "It's been a long day. I'm gonna get some rest. You mind putting those gifts beneath the tree?"

He didn't wait for an answer, just went out into the cold.

Sarah knelt beside the tree after placing the girls' gifts under the spindly pine, shaken and trembling.

She had the sense that her answer about the suitor letter had not satisfied Oscar, that something irreparable had changed between them.

If he'd given her any indication that he cared about her, that his kiss last night had meant something more than comfort, she would've told him that she wasn't interested in marrying the other man.

But he hadn't. He'd reminded her that he was leaving, and soon.

Leaving her with no choice but to continue the correspondence. The banker might prove her only chance for marriage, if they got along well enough.

Her thoughts went to her young charges. Hopefully the man liked children, because she had no plans to leave the girls behind, not without anyone to care for them.

What if…what if the man didn't want a ready-made

family? It was a lot to take on, Sarah well knew. She'd had enough trouble even finding a candidate for a husband in the first place, without having three young charges to look after. Would taking on the girls hinder her chances for marriage?

But that wasn't really what bothered her. Sometime in the past several weeks, she'd started imagining herself with Oscar. Seeing their family, starting with Cecilia and Susie and Velma. And growing with their own children, in the future.

Obviously, he didn't see things the same way, or he would've declared himself when they'd spoken about the letter.

She told herself it was disappointment that churned in her stomach as she curled up on the sofa with her shawl and the tattered blanket around her shoulders. But it felt more like the loss of the hope she'd been unaware had started growing.

In the barn, Oscar paced between the front and back walls, frustration steaming.

Finally reaching the boiling point, he slammed both fists on the doorway to an empty stall.

Nearby, Pharaoh snorted and Oscar's mare shrieked.

Breathing hard, Oscar pressed his balled hands against the stall, hanging his head between them.

He didn't want Sarah to go off and marry a banker from Montana. He wanted her for himself.

Shaking, he turned his back to the stall door and slid to the ground.

Should he have told Sarah what he felt? Could it have changed her answer?

What if he did tell her that he wanted to marry her? And then after a few years, she died, just like his parents had?

The thought of losing her, losing something they'd built together was like a bullet in his gut, a fiery brand. He had to rub his hands over his eyes.

Wasn't it better to let her go on with her life? Marry someone safe, someone who she would be happy with?

It would be less risky for him…wouldn't it?

Then why did he feel so lost and alone?

Chapter Fifteen

It was the silence that woke Sarah in the dark stillness of morning. No wind blew.

She stood stiffly and moved to the window. It was quiet, no snow falling. A thin line of gray lit the horizon.

A dark shape left the outline of the barn, moving toward the water trough Sarah knew was nearby. Oscar, doing the morning chores. Taking care of things. Steady, reliable. Those weren't words she would have used to describe him weeks ago when he'd first come to Lost Hollow.

But she'd been wrong.

And now that she knew, it was too late to change things between them. He was going to leave. And she was going to move forward, most likely caring for three little girls. Could she find purpose and happiness in that?

She would have to. She refused to let Cecilia, Susie and Velma fend for themselves the way she and her sisters had had to.

She freshened up with the cold water in the bowl near the door and ducked outside to visit the privy, passing

Oscar with a brimming bucket of milk as she did so. He didn't say a word, only tapped his hat brim in greeting.

Her heart clenched, but she determined to put on a smile for the girls this morning.

When she snuck back inside, he was standing in the kitchen with his sleeves rolled up, holding two pots and wearing a sheepish grin.

The girls tumbled out of the bedroom, wearing their nightgowns and hair all tangled.

"Sorry," Oscar said in apology. "I dropped one of the pans. I meant to let you girls sleep awhile while I start the turkey."

Sarah took off her coat and pushed up her sleeves, as well. "I can start the coffee."

She took the coffeepot and went outdoors to fill it with snow, shivering when she came back in.

As she began the task, she was almost shoulder-to-shoulder with Oscar.

"Snow's stopped," he said as he plopped the plucked turkey into a large pan. Had he hunted the animal for the girls' Christmas dinner? "Figured we'd let everyone celebrate their Christmas morning before we try to take care of things." He cleared his throat with a glance at the girls, and Sarah realized he meant the girls' stepfather. "Then I'll take you back to the Allens' place."

She nodded her acceptance. She would have until the afternoon to figure out how to explain things to her boss. Surely he could understand the plight of three little girls whose lives had changed so suddenly. Who needed help.

At least Oscar was talking to her this morning, after the abrupt end to their conversation last night. Maybe she could find a way to bring up the letter again, tell him she wasn't *confirmed* in her decision to continue the correspondence. Maybe it wouldn't matter, anyway.

"What's all this?" asked Cecilia from beside the tree.

Sarah finished preparing the coffee and left it to heat and turned to the girls with a smile. "Christmas gifts, what else?"

"For us?" asked Susie, voice hushed with excitement. "But we already got the fancy dresses."

"Yes, for you." She couldn't imagine what Oscar had bought for the girls. Before yesterday, when Sarah had been only the girls' teacher, she hadn't wanted to show favoritism to any students. And so, she hadn't gotten them any gifts.

Next year, as their guardian, she would do differently.

Baby Velma picked up one of the brown-wrapped packages and waved it in the air with a squeal.

"Can we open them?" Susie asked. "Now?"

Oscar continued to wrestle with the turkey and his pan, but answered her. "Let me get this bird in the oven and then you can. I suppose, just this once, breakfast can wait."

Susie cheered and Velma squealed again, but Cecilia remained quiet, perched on the edge of the sofa near the tree.

Sarah poured herself and Oscar a mug of coffee and left his on the kitchen table, briefly reminded of the moments they'd sat across from each other last night. She brought her mug to the sofa and sat next to Cecilia.

"Are you all right this morning?" she asked in a low voice. "I know you must still be sad about your stepfather and worried about what's going to happen now.

But it's okay to be happy with your sisters. At least a little bit."

The girl shrugged, keeping her face downturned. "He was a mean drunk. Never did like us much. Maybe it's better he's gone."

"You won't be alone," Sarah said, placing a comforting hand on the girl's arm. Cecilia pulled away, still not really looking at Sarah and not accepting her touch. Sarah hid her disappointment by sipping her coffee.

Oscar joined them and sat with the girls on the floor in a semicircle around the tree, plopping Velma on his lap. It left Sarah on the sofa, somewhat apart from them all. She knew Susie was excited about the gifts and Velma didn't really know what was going on. But Oscar's distance bothered her, and Cecilia still continued to be detached, even when Sarah was reaching out to the girl.

Oscar handed each girl a small package and then pointed to the larger one still beneath the tree. "That one and what's outside are for all three of you to share."

"There's something outside?" Susie asked, jumping up from the floor.

Oscar laughed. "Just wait, Firecracker. I'll bring it in momentarily. Sit back down."

She did with a giggle. Sarah watched Cecilia consider her sister, a more serious look on the older girl's face.

Was she worrying about her younger sibling, as Sarah had on many an occasion? Planning ways to make things the best for her younger sisters? It was a big responsibility, too large for a little girl.

But how could Sarah convince Cecilia to trust her? That Sarah's intentions were good?

She blinked aside the thoughts as the girls ripped into their packages. Susie shrieked when she pulled out a doll with a porcelain face. Cecilia's reaction was quieter, but the soft gasp when the paper fell away to reveal a set of paints said more than words.

Oscar glanced at the older girl even as he helped Velma tear the paper from the small gift he held for her to reveal a soft cloth doll. She immediately stuck it in her mouth, all grins.

"Can I?" Susie reached for the one wrapped package left beneath the tree. She looked to Cecilia for approval and the other girl nodded.

The paper fell away to reveal a basket of treats. Oranges, candies and peppermint sticks. Both girls exclaimed.

"Only one before breakfast," Sarah warned.

"Aw," the girls complained in near chorus, but neither seemed to really mind as they returned to examine their other gifts again.

As they did, Oscar played with Velma, teasing her with the doll, playing peekaboo and sending her into fits of giggles.

Sarah observed all over again how good he was with both the older girls and the tot. He'd chosen gifts that meant something to each girl—paints for Cecilia, who often drew fanciful portraits on her school assignments, and a doll for Susie, who mothered Velma with such love.

Another raspberry against Velma's chubby neck sent a pang of remorse straight to Sarah's heart. She wanted marriage and a family of her own. With the girls, she had the family, but it wasn't just any man she wanted for a husband. Not anymore.

No matter if he was safe. Or a cowboy.

She wanted to marry Oscar White, the horseman.

But he didn't want to marry her.

Oscar pretended joviality for the girls' sake, but it was harder than he'd thought it would be.

Last night, he'd wanted to gift Sarah with his mother's locket. Wanted to see it around her neck this morning and know that she felt something for him, too.

But instead, she was going to pursue marriage with a safe banker from Montana. Someone better than Oscar, a cowboy.

Just the thought of it made him feel sick.

She seemed content to focus on the girls this morning, barely speaking to him at all. Part of him just wanted to shake her like he would one of his little brothers. Shake her until she realized that *he* was right in front of her and he was good for her. Could be a good father to the girls, too.

He imagined what his family back home was doing this morning. Knowing his pa, Jonas had probably made a huge spread for breakfast, but it would be untouched until the little kids had opened their gifts from beneath the tree that Penny would've spent days decorating. No doubt the older boys had pooled their funds to purchase gifts Penny wouldn't approve of—possibly a slingshot, or a BB gun.

Part of him wished he could be there, but part of him struggled with the fact that everything was different now.

To hide his emotions, he got up and went to the back

door, pulling in the gift he'd left just outside when he'd
come inside this morning.

"A sled!" Susie cried.

He couldn't help grinning at her excitement. "It's
for you all three to share. You'll have to hold Velma for
now and then teach her how to do it when she's bigger."

A pang hit his gut. He wanted to be the one to teach
the little girl how to sled. Wanted to bring the same
kind of joy to Susie every day, not just on Christmas.

When he'd come to Lost Hollow, he never would have
thought he'd want a ready-made family, but Sarah and
the girls had crept into his heart—and just in time for
him to lose them.

The afternoon was bitter cold, but with no wind,
which was a blessing. They'd visited the parsonage
first, where they'd received a cool reception. Oscar
hadn't been able to determine if it was because of Mr.
Caldwell's reputation in town or something else.

At least the preacher and his wife had agreed to keep
the girls while Oscar and Sarah visited the undertaker.
They didn't need to be involved in this discussion, not
as young as they were.

Oscar pulled the makeshift sleigh—Caldwell's
wagon attached to long runners—up to the boardwalk
near the storefront that doubled as a furniture maker
and undertaker. Oscar had been in town several times
during his stay in Lost Hollow, but he'd never seen the
streets this deserted.

"Everyone must be inside because of the holiday,"
Sarah murmured. It was the first thing she'd said to him
since they'd left the parsonage. He disliked the distance

between them. Wanted things back to where they'd been before.

"And the weather," he agreed.

"I just remembered I need to send a telegraph," she said as he assisted her from the sleigh. "Do you mind if I run down to the telegraph office quickly? I'll meet you right back here."

"Fine."

She'd told him the undertaker lived above his shop. Oscar figured he'd have to pound on the door to get a response since it was Christmas, but to his surprise, a thin man opened the door fairly quickly. He eyed Oscar and reluctantly invited him in to the darkened storefront out of the cold.

After Oscar had explained who he was and about Mr. Caldwell's demise, the man moved to a desk in the corner and began writing something on a piece of paper.

"I'll have you bring him around back, if you don't mind. Don't like the other customers to see, you understand."

Oscar nodded.

"You payin' cash?" the man asked.

Oscar paused on his way to the door. "I'm not family. Caldwell claimed he didn't have any money, and he's left behind three little girls."

The man shrugged. "Not surprised, but I can't do it for free, I'm sure you understand."

Oscar frowned. "What about a collection from the church?"

Now the man wouldn't meet his gaze. "Doubt you'd get the funds there, either, son."

Frustrated, Oscar scratched the back of his neck. "Then what am I supposed to do?"

"I'll take a trade. The man had a horse last I knew."

He was right. Caldwell's one horse was a decent animal. Not great, but decent. Oscar doubted Sarah would want her around. And they couldn't just leave the man's body without a proper burial.

"Fine," Oscar agreed. "I'll bring the wagon around back."

He maneuvered the conveyance down the snow-covered street and around to the alley behind the row of shops, just as the undertaker had instructed him, mind racing all the while. Was Sarah planning to stay on at the Caldwell place? He knew there wasn't room for her and the girls at the Allens' place, but would the school board frown upon her living alone? Would it even count as "alone," with her caring for three little girls?

Regardless, the spread was too much for her to handle by herself. If she could find someone to lease the land and farm it, she could bring in a small income from that. Not enough to live on, but with her schoolteacher salary, it should help. At least until she left with the girls to marry her Montana banker.

She'd do well with a milk cow and a few chickens, maybe a small garden plot.

But would she know how to take care of any of that? And the other animals would need to be sold off.

He'd planned to return to his cabin and his life after he'd made sure she'd settled in with the girls. But now it looked the process of settling in would take longer. A few days at least.

Could he continue on here without going crazy, wanting what he couldn't have? Did he have any choice? After the fuss the townspeople had made before the pageant, he doubted anyone would be willing to help Sarah now. And he had to admire that she was willing to help the girls. How could he do any less, especially when he knew what it meant to be abandoned?

Sarah carefully navigated the icy boardwalk to the telegraph office and the little house behind it.

Bert, one of her older students, answered her knock with a look of surprise. "Miss Sarah! What are you doing out and about?"

He quickly ushered her inside the small home. His father looked up from the kitchen table nearby.

"Miss Hansen," he greeted.

"Hello, Bert. Mr. Cooper. I've got a telegraph I need to send." She fished in her pocket for the small stash of coins she'd put there.

"Won't go out today," the older man said. "It'll be tomorrow."

"That's all right. I'm afraid it's bad news." She explained the situation to the two of them, and that she'd found an address for what she suspected was a relative of the girls and wanted to send a notice.

"I'm sorry to hear that." Bert's father pulled a sheet of paper from a nearby drawer before returning to the table. "Let's compose something."

She paid him, but hesitated before getting up, fingering the letter from her Montana suitor in her pocket. "Perhaps I should send another, as well."

She'd been thinking about it the entire trip into town. When she wasn't dwelling on how she wished things with Oscar were different. Now that the girls were going to be her responsibility, she should really let the banker know. She could only hope that he would understand that things had changed, and welcome the girls as she did.

Perhaps a letter would be better, but as the circumstances had changed very quickly, she thought he had a right to know now.

She made a decision. "Will you help me compose something else?" she said, settling back at the table with Mr. Cooper.

Chapter Sixteen

After they'd picked up the girls from the parsonage, the only destination left was the Allens' ranch.

Sarah's stomach clutched the closer they got. No doubt Mr. Allen would be angry, especially after his threats at the pageant. Could she salvage her job by explaining the situation? And surely the man would be more compassionate when faced with the fact of Mr. Caldwell's demise. She hoped.

She needed to make sure Clara was there. Mr. Allen's wife was much more understanding. She might be able to calm his temper and help him see reason.

But what if he refused to come around? Sarah had been trying not to think about the possible ramifications of directly disobeying her boss for the past two days. But now that her reckoning was here, she couldn't stop wondering what she would do if he did fire her.

She couldn't have done anything differently. Her conviction wouldn't have stood for it. No matter who the girls' parents were, no matter what their situation. They were just little girls and deserved to be taken care of.

They turned into the Allens' yard before she was really prepared.

Oscar met her eyes as he reined in the horses. His steady look at once asked if she was ready to face this and told her he would stand beside her.

For now, until he left for his life back in Bear Creek.

She hiked her chin. She'd made her own decision to visit the Caldwell place the night of the storm. She'd decided she couldn't leave the girls without a home. She would find a way to take care of them, same as she'd taken care of her own sisters.

Clara answered the door at their knock. Her eyes widened when she saw Sarah, then her mouth dropped open when she saw the girls clustered around and Oscar standing a half step behind.

"Where have you been?" she barked.

Sarah moved into the kitchen, motioning the girls inside with her. "Is Barbara in her room? I thought the girls might like to visit."

Clara's brows gathered, but she ushered the girls toward the bedroom.

"Clara—" Mr. Allen's voice preceded him, but not by much. He filled the doorway, his face reddening almost immediately in a show of temper.

"Where have you been?" he boomed.

Clara hurried back into the room, standing half-hidden in her husband's shadow.

Oscar moved to Sarah's elbow, a silent show of support.

"You know that I went to the Caldwells' place, and then the blizzard hit." Sarah did her best to make her voice confident, but not confrontational.

"We would've been risking our lives if we would've tried to make it here through that blizzard." Oscar joined the conversation.

"You should've come home with us in the first place," the older man said. Something was wrong. Though the set of his features showed anger, his words were too calm.

"Mr. Allen, I can promise you that nothing untoward happened." Oscar stood stoic and tall beside her. "I slept in the barn and Sarah stayed in the cabin with the girls."

"Unfortunately, it isn't only what actually happened—which is only your word to go on—but what this looks like to the town, the county. The school board has to ensure appearances are kept up, you understand."

"There were other circumstances, as well," Sarah said. "Something that I hope you'll listen to with an open heart. The girls' stepfather went out in the storm and…froze to death."

Mr. Allen's face whitened for one moment. Behind him, Clara sank into a chair at the table.

"I've told the girls that I would care for them." Sarah refused to make it a question.

"Sarah, you can't," breathed Clara. "You're a single woman."

"She's right," Mr. Allen blurted out. "Leave them to someone else."

"Who else?" asked Sarah. "Is there anyone in this town who would take them in, other than me?"

"Let their family come and get them."

"They are convinced they have no family." Sarah spared one thought for the telegraph she'd sent. But she didn't even know if that person was still alive, let alone if they were relatives.

"There's Indians aplenty a couple towns over," he said with a shrug. "Take them over there."

"I won't," she said firmly. "They were my students first, my responsibility. And I've grown quite fond of them." And she refused to let them end up on their own, like she and her sisters had.

"How are you going to support yourself and three little girls without a job?" asked Mr. Allen.

Sarah swallowed hard. "Sir, we explained that nothing untoward happened."

"But that's not what it looks like."

Her heart sank. He wasn't listening.

"Mr. Allen," Oscar offered, "if I have to, I'll go visit the other school board members and every single household in Lost Hollow to explain what happened. Sarah didn't do anything wrong."

The older man sneered at him. "She chose to associate with the wrong people."

Sarah turned her gaze on the rancher's wife. Her last chance at saving her job. "Clara, you know me. You know my character, and you have since I arrived in Lost Hollow."

The other woman lowered her eyes to her hands clasped on the table in front of her. Sarah's heart plummeted. The other woman wouldn't even say one word on Sarah's behalf.

"Even if folks in town believe you, they aren't going to go against my wishes," Mr. Allen said. "I bring in the most cash to this town. No one wants me to take my business elsewhere."

Sarah knew he was right. Knew he wouldn't bend. Her knees were weak, and only Oscar's supporting hand beneath her elbow kept her upright.

"I can't believe you would be so cruel because of some bias you have or had against their parents." Oscar remained strong and resilient beside her. Unflinching, a man as immoveable as a mountain.

"One has nothing to do with the other," refuted Mr. Allen. "As school board chair, I can't countenance even a hint of immoral behavior."

"You and I both know Sarah would never do anything immoral," Oscar spat back. "So you're firing her because of her compassionate heart and the fact that she wants to help three little girls who have no one else."

A small gasp drew Sarah's attention to the hallway that led to the bedrooms, and the short shadow that ducked away. One of the girls. Most likely Cecilia.

Well, it couldn't be helped if she'd overheard part of their conversation. It wasn't as if Sarah losing her job was going to be a secret once they returned to the Caldwells' place. Plans would have to be made.

Beside her, Oscar took a deep breath and Sarah knew he would keep fighting—fighting for her—but she also knew it was no use. Once Mr. Allen had his mind made up, there was no changing it.

She placed a hand on the horseman's arm. "Leave it," she said softly. "He won't change his mind. And I can no longer continue working for someone like him."

She looked to Clara, whose eyes were red-rimmed but remained silent. That wasn't the kind of wife Sarah wanted to be—not ever. Someone who couldn't stand up for right, whose husband refused to listen to reason.

"I'll gather my things," she said to Clara, not asking permission from Mr. Allen. "Do you have a crate I might use?"

"And you and I can settle up." Oscar directed his words to Mr. Allen. "Unless you need my help," he turned to say to Sarah before she moved away.

His eyes met hers and promised that whatever she needed, he would do.

She was able to give him a trembling smile and a small shake of her head.

Somehow she made it to the bedroom she'd shared with Barbara. Inside, Barbara played with Susie and Velma on her bed, wrinkling the quilt with their antics. Cecilia stood with crossed arms in the middle of the room, jaw set and with a half-wild look in her eyes.

Sarah locked eyes with the girl and didn't hold back her disappointment or the slight fear that sickened her stomach. But she tried to convey that somehow, they'd get through this together.

Sarah moved to the bed and untucked her mother's quilt, folding it into a neat square. Barbara looked on with wide eyes, but said nothing as she played with Velma. She was a smart girl. Perhaps she'd overheard her parents speaking of plans for Sarah after the Christmas pageant.

"Miss Sarah, what're you doing?" asked Susie, coming to stand at the side of the bed.

"I'm packing my things," she said, surprised at how even her voice sounded. "Barbara won't have room for the four of us—the three of you girls and myself—to stay. I'll be moving into your cabin until we make further plans."

"Oh," was the only response, but it was a quiet word from the usually exuberant Susie. Had she picked up on Sarah's despondence?

The two drawers with Sarah's underthings were next, and her three dresses removed from the pegs on the wall and folded. She only had the plain bonnet and the fancy one she'd worn to the picnic. Those went in the pile on the bare bed, as well.

She had a small bundle of letters kept from her sisters, the few books from her childhood she'd been able to keep and her school things. Her meager savings were kept at the bank; she would have to face town at least once more to obtain them and close her account.

All of her things together would barely reach halfway to the top in a standard-size crate.

It wasn't much to represent her life up to now. She'd hoped to begin building a life together with someone, a husband, to share memories with. Would that dream ever come to fruition?

Oscar followed Allen into the man's study, feeling itchy and hot all over. He couldn't believe that the man had no sense of honor, that he would make a woman and three little girls' lives miserable because of his own prejudice.

"Looked at the colt with my brother-in-law Ty this morning, saddled him up and took him around the ring. Seems you did a decent job," the older man said grudgingly.

Oscar didn't reply, only crossed his arms over his chest. He knew the job he'd done—the man wouldn't find a better trained horse on his spread.

"I'll honor our agreement," continued Allen as he bent over the desk and began writing out a bank check.

Oscar couldn't leave without fighting for Sarah one more time. "You're making a mistake," he said. "Sarah has the biggest heart of anyone I know. She honestly cares about not only those three little girls, but every kid in that class. I heard the parents saying nothing but good things about her the night of the pageant. You're not going to find another teacher like her, no matter how far and wide you look."

The older man's face turned beet-red. He ripped the check from its holder on the desk and thrust it at Oscar, looking as if he wanted to rip up the check, too.

"My mind is made up."

Angry on Sarah's behalf—he refused to examine the fury searing through him too deeply—Oscar wheeled and walked out. He met Sarah in the front hall, carrying a half-full crate. The girls were slightly behind her, all bundled against the cold already.

"Let me get that," Oscar insisted, taking Sarah's burden for himself. It wasn't heavy in the least. "This it? Nothing in the barn? A trunk stored somewhere?"

She shook her head slightly, eyes shiny. Was she close to tears? Oscar's heart rocketed and he headed for the front door. No sniffles sounded behind him. Maybe she was all right.

He kept thinking that all the way home, though she was quiet, and all the way through supper. Right up until Cecilia burst up from the table with its emptied dishes, shaking and red-faced.

"You can't really be this peaceful," she accused

Sarah, pointing a shaking finger at her. "Just say it. Say that we're the reason you got fired."

"Miss Sarah, you're not gonna be our teacher anymore?" asked Susie, now with a wobbly lower lip.

Sarah's face went white, and Oscar had to stop himself from reaching out to her. It wasn't his place. No matter how brave she'd been this afternoon and no matter how badly he wanted to.

"No, dear. I'm going to be your guardian. And you don't have to call me 'Miss Sarah' anymore. It's just Sarah."

"You got fired because of us," Cecilia said, voice thin. "Why aren't you mad?"

"I was let go from my position because of the choices *I* made, Cecilia. I already told you girls about my mother dying and my father's bad accident and how I had to take care of my sisters. My father chose to do a dangerous job—mining. He chose it because he thought he would be able to find gold and get rich. But it was a dangerous choice and he lost the ability to work and take care of his family, and he never got rich.

"My choice wasn't dangerous, but it was life-altering, too. I saw the way people from town treated you and your sisters and I didn't like it. I tried to help you while your stepfather was alive and now that he's gone, I still want to help you."

"Why?" Cecilia demanded. "Why do you care? Why don't you leave us alone like everyone else? Send us away?"

"Because I care about you," Sarah said quietly. "All three of you have snuck into my heart. If you can't think of me as your mother, think of me as your older sister, because in my heart you are my sisters."

Cecilia looked at her for a long moment and Oscar thought the girl would relent from holding on to the reserve she used to protect herself, but she finally just turned and swept into the bedroom, closing the door quietly.

Susie came around the table to embrace Sarah while Oscar helped Velma out of the towel they'd tucked around her middle to keep her upright in the kitchen chair.

"I'm glad you're not gonna leave us," murmured Susie into the shoulder of Sarah's dress. "I love you, Miss Sarah. I mean—just Sarah."

Sarah smoothed the girl's hair. Watching her, Oscar couldn't help but admire her courage in the face of the security she'd just lost when she'd lost her job. She was good for the girls, and he doubted it would take long for her to win Cecilia over.

They would be a fine little family.

But didn't a family need a father figure, as well?

When Oscar insisted on cleaning up the supper table, Sarah escaped to the barn. It was too cold to stay outside, and since her adventure with Oscar's horse in the snow, she wasn't quite so afraid to venture inside.

She needed a place to hide before she burst.

It was so hard, being strong for the girls when she was just as scared as they were. What would they do if she couldn't find another job? Her savings wouldn't last long, and if they had to move to another town, or even another state for her to obtain a new teacher job, the money would be used up that much faster.

Sarah stalked through the barn until she found an empty stall where she likely wouldn't be found for the moment. She didn't want any of the girls to come looking for her and see her in distress. She snuck inside and put her back to the side of the stall, hiding her face in her hands.

Thanks to the generosity of Oscar's adoptive mother and the mysterious benefactor from Lost Hollow, the girls were outfitted for winter, but Sarah knew how fast they could grow—they would need new things by springtime, even if Susie could wear some of Cecilia's hand-me-downs.

And what would they do about meals? The girls had teased her at that first picnic with Oscar, but their words had had the ring of truth—she couldn't cook at all.

"What am I going to do?" she breathed. She had no plan, no prospects. She couldn't even really count on the Montana banker—his offer of correspondence had been made before she'd had three mouths to feed.

"I'm so frightened."

Too frightened even to pray. The words stalled in her throat and she could only hope the Father above understood the very moanings of her heart.

Motion near her ear startled her, and Sarah opened her eyes, two tears burning hot trails down her cheeks.

And froze.

The mare had stuck her head over the half wall between the stalls and her jaw was inches from Sarah's cheek. She let out a low neigh. Almost as if she was checking on Sarah, asking "what's wrong?"

Emotion overflowed and Sarah laughed even as she let out a soft sob. She reached out tentatively and touched the horse's nose with her palm. It was so soft—like velvet. The horse remained still, her breath hot against the cool air of the barn on Sarah's skin. Then the animal bobbed her head down, in effect rubbing Sarah's palm against the bridge of her nose.

Breath filled Sarah's lungs, expanding within her. "You want me to pet you?"

The horse neighed softly again. As if communicating with Sarah.

Sarah curled her fingers to scratch beneath the horse's forelock. "You aren't so scary, are you?"

The horse remained still under her ministrations. Sarah carefully watched its ears, remembering what Oscar had said before about gauging the horse's mood.

"Just like your owner, hmm? A little frightening in the beginning, but not so bad, after all...."

"Are you talking to my horse?"

Oscar's voice from outside the stall startled Sarah and she jumped, quickly wiping her face with her sleeve. The last thing she needed was his pity.

The horse snorted and Sarah blinked and looked up at it. Its ears were still forward—had it been trying to respond to Oscar, as well?

"I can't believe you still haven't named her." There. Her voice had sounded somewhat hoarse but perhaps he would attribute it to the cold.

"I still maintain she isn't mine to name," he said softly, leaning one arm and his chin on top of the stall door. "You okay?"

"Why wouldn't I be?" She avoided the question,

humming a little to disguise a sniffle. She kept her focus on the horse, turning her shoulder to Oscar but still feeling his gaze on her. She reached out to scratch the horse's nose again.

And then he pushed into the stall beside her, close but not touching. Except then his hand closed over her elbow, and curled around to follow the line of her forearm to where she petted the horse, fingers threading between hers so they both touched the horse at once.

Everything within Sarah froze, then seemed to expand at his touch.

"What is she saying to you?" His voice was so low and close that it sent tremors down Sarah's spine.

"She's...she's comforting me," Sarah said.

"That's what I want to do, too." His fingers clasped her wrist and he turned her toward him, releasing her hand only to close both of his arms around her.

With her nose buried in his neck, she was surrounded by his warmth and the smells of leather and man. And everything she'd been holding back tumbled out. She let her tears fall, her fears flow as she quivered in his arms.

He didn't speak, only brushed one hand up and down her spine. His breath warmed her temple, the day's whiskers on his jaw rasping against the fine hairs there, as well.

He held her until her emotion had run its course. As she pushed away, keeping her face low so he wouldn't see the tears and redness, he wouldn't allow her escape. With one hand, he captured her wrist; the other slid along her jaw, raising her face to his scrutiny.

He brushed her cheek with his thumb; his eyes glittered down at her and then he leaned closer and his lips slanted over hers.

She clutched his shoulders, holding tightly to his strength, his steadiness.

The horse blew directly behind her, startling them apart. Oscar's hands on her shoulders steadied her and they laughed together softly.

"We should get back to the cabin," she murmured, and he let her go.

She kept her face averted—afraid he would read the raw emotion there. He saw too much already, and his kiss only confused her.

Stepping outside into the cold air was like waking from a dream to reality.

She should have pushed him away, not returned his kiss. He was leaving, after all. Perhaps he'd only meant to comfort her, but her emotions were entangled now and the kiss had only made things worse.

What was she going to do now?

Chapter Seventeen

Oscar knew he shouldn't have kissed Sarah again. Inside the cabin, busying his hands with pouring a cup of coffee, he was far too aware of her. But he couldn't retire to the barn yet. He had things to discuss with her—important things.

Bringing their emotions into this discussion wasn't the best strategy. Not when what he felt for her was too frightening. Things were already muddled enough.

But when he'd had her in his arms, he couldn't help himself. He'd started out the embrace wanting only to comfort her, but when it had ended, he'd wanted so much more.…

He pushed away from the dry sink as she turned from peeking into the darkened bedroom doorway. They met at the table, her face pink and eyes tentative.

He motioned her into the chair across from him and sat down himself. "You're determined to keep the girls?"

She nodded, not quite meeting his gaze. "I suppose we should get through the funeral first. I found—I found a name and address in some of their mother's things.

It could be a family member, or a friend who knows of some family."

He was confused. "I thought the girls said they didn't have any family."

"So they did. But perhaps the mother was estranged, or perhaps she simply told them there was no one else. I have to—I have to check. Family is important." She glanced up at him and he remembered her urging him to speak to his father.

"If there really is no one, then I intend for the four of us to stay together."

He cleared his throat. "I've been making a list of the things around the place that can be sold. I already told the undertaker we'd trade the Caldwells' horse for the casket and burial, but this is the rest. I want to help you and the girls make a good start of it." He pushed the half sheet of paper he'd filled up toward her, hoping she could read his handwriting. He hadn't exactly honed the skill since his school days, and she *was* a teacher.

Her brow furrowed as she looked down at the list. "And the items with the marks?"

"If you wanted to, those are things you could keep. For the household." He swallowed. He was nervous about what was coming, but tried to focus on getting the conversation there.

"Now that you've got the girls, you'll want to set up a household. Won't you? If you've got a place of your own, having a cow to give milk and a coupla chickens to provide eggs could be a blessing."

She glanced up at him briefly and then back at the list. "Yes, but I don't know how to care for those animals."

He shrugged. "You're smart enough. You can learn."

"I suppose…" Her voice faltered and she looked away. "I suppose it will depend on where I—where the girls and I settle. Most schools will take a winter break. Perhaps some of the teachers won't return for the spring term. I'm just not sure…without a reference—"

Her voice caught and she stopped talking, biting her lower lip.

This was his moment. Heat scorched his cheeks and he sucked in a deep breath. "Sarah—" His voice cracked like one of his younger brothers and he had to clear his throat and start over. "I know you've got your banker-suitor waiting in the wings, but…"

Her cheeks pinked to an even deeper rose. Interesting. Was something going on with the banker he didn't know about? But he couldn't focus on that now. He took a deep breath and just blurted it out, heart thundering.

"What if you married me?"

She sat in stunned silence, her eyes wide and focused on his face. "What?" she whispered.

"What if— Why don't you marry me, instead?"

Sarah stared at the man across from her, part of her wondering if she possibly could've heard him correctly. Another part of her trembled with anticipation, waiting for the assertion that his feelings had grown to match hers. Had his kiss been intended for more than comfort, perhaps as a declaration?

Her heartbeat thudded in her ears so loudly that she almost missed the beginning of his next words.

"You've got the girls to take care of now, and no job,

and we get along all right." He fidgeted in the chair before rushing on. "You said before that you didn't want to marry a cowboy, but I've got some land near my pa and a plan for the future." He spread his hands as if beseeching her.

"Is that…is that all?" she asked after a moment that stretched interminably long.

"What do you mean?" His forehead creased and he genuinely looked confused.

And Sarah's heart dipped. He didn't love her. He'd said they *got along all right,* but he'd made no mention of tender feelings toward her.

"I'm partly responsible for you losing your job—"

"So this is about your sense of duty, then?" She hadn't meant her voice to emerge that sharp, but the hurt prickling her skin like tiny needles infused her voice. She worked to steady her words. "What about your cabin? And your horses?"

He looked at her with his brow furrowed as if he didn't understand her questions.

"You've talked about going home, getting back to your cabin all by yourself. If you bring home a new wife and three children, you won't have a moment's peace."

And she knew what it was like for a person to have a responsibility like that thrust upon them. Knew how it could wear on a body, could wear you down because you wanted something else from your life.

She couldn't bear it if she became a burden to him, not when she loved him so deeply.

His face smoothed and he looked down to where his long square fingers played with a chip in the corner of the table.

"I don't think that would be a good solution for us," she said softy. "We'll figure something out. It isn't as if we don't have some options." She tried to smile, but the effect was pretty wobbly. But he didn't look up to see it, anyway.

"I understand."

Oscar kept his eyes on his hands, on the little chip of wood beneath his thumbnail.

She didn't want him.

It was that simple.

If he'd thought his cheeks were on fire before his proposal, it was nothing compared to now.

He wanted to howl at the unfairness of it—of being in love with someone who didn't love you back.

He wanted to get up and run out of the room, and just keep going until he got home to Bear Creek. Except it didn't really feel like home anymore, either. And he'd just promised Sarah—and himself—that he'd help her get things in order here before he left Lost Hollow.

So he just sat there, trembling inside, and tried not to remember what it felt like the day his parents had died.

"Maybe you're right and we should keep the cow. I'm not certain about the chickens. They seem like a lot of trouble…."

She peered down at the list as if it was intensely interesting and he suspected she was waiting for him to excuse himself.

There was a soft noise, a cry, from the small bedroom and she stood.

Grateful for the reprieve, he pushed up from the

table, as well. "We can work it out in the morning. I'll be in the barn."

And he turned tail and galloped out of there, leaving his heart behind.

Chapter Eighteen

Early the next morning as she sat at the same little kitchen table, Sarah still couldn't breathe properly. It felt as if a heavy weight sat on her chest.

Saying no to Oscar's duty-bound proposal last night had been terribly hard. She had tossed and turned on the narrow, uncomfortable sofa most of the night, replaying their conversation and asking herself if she could've done anything differently.

She wondered if she should have accepted regardless of his lack of feelings for her. After all, she was nearly a spinster with only the hope of another prospect through her correspondence with the Montana banker. And that was no guarantee—they hadn't even met in person yet, and he hadn't yet responded to her telegram about the girls.

She'd gotten this far in life with no other proposals—no one who had even come close. Maybe this was her only chance at marriage and she'd said no.

But there was still a part of her that wanted to be loved—not to be someone's duty. She knew better than anyone what it felt like to be responsible for people, even people you loved, and how that could eat at you. And if you were responsible for someone you didn't love… how much more would the responsibility rankle, like a burr under a saddle?

She couldn't do that to Oscar. And somehow, she still had a little pride left. She couldn't do it to herself.

She considered the two blank pieces of paper before her on the table. She needed to write to her sisters and tell of the adversity that had befallen her, but the letters were hard to begin. Her sisters had looked up to her, admired her, while she'd cared for them and worked hard to support them. What would they think now that she'd lost her job and had three mouths to feed besides?

Somehow, she made herself sound calm and rational while she wrote the letters, when what she really wanted to do was pour out her feelings. Her sisters both loved the men they'd married. Surely they would understand her feelings for Oscar. But she resisted. She wrote only the bare facts and told her sisters she would write again when she knew where she'd be settling.

She'd just signed the second letter when the back door opened, spilling gray morning light inside to compete with her candle.

"Something burning? I smell smoke."

Then the acrid odor registered and she jumped up from the table with a cry. "The biscuits!"

She rushed to the stove, where smoke poured out from the seams around the door. Using a dishtowel to pry it open, more smoke poured into the room. She waved the towel to clear it a bit until she could see the edge of the pan, then grabbed that.

What emerged was a pan of black, charred lumps. Still smoldering.

"Toss them out here," Oscar ordered, holding the door wide.

Sarah took a step in that direction and let the pan go. It went sailing past him and landed in the yard with a clatter.

He coughed.

Behind her, the two older girls dissolved in giggles. She whirled, the dishtowel swinging from her hand. "What?"

Oscar stepped inside, looking as if he was biting his lip to keep from joining the girls' laughter. "I meant, 'toss the biscuits outside,' not the whole pan. Oh, well. I suppose it will wash."

The girls bent over double from laughing and he smiled, that crooked funny smile that she loved. She found herself responding, drawn closer to his humor and smiling herself when he seemed to remember that things were different this morning. His face closed and that smile disappeared.

Sarah turned toward the counter, not wanting him to see her hurt at his withdrawal. "I was trying to prepare breakfast, but I guess time got away from me," she explained. She lifted the two letters from the table and slipped them in her pocket. His face darkened. What did it matter to him if she wrote to her sisters?

"I can show you how to make flapjacks real quick," Cecilia offered shyly. It was the first overture the girl had made toward Sarah. Was the girl finally opening up?

* * *

"And I can scramble some eggs!" Susie was quick to jump in.

Oscar was left to hold little Velma. He bounced her on his knee as Cecilia instructed Sarah on the best way to stir the batter with a fork, and watched Susie cracking brown eggs into one side of the cast-iron skillet.

Velma's attention kept returning to her sisters and the schoolteacher, those chubby arms reaching out for them.

She wanted to be part of their group, be with them.

Oscar knew exactly how she felt. He couldn't quit thinking that this might be his last morning with them like this, together almost like a family. He wanted to see Sarah settled, wanted to be at the girls' side for the funeral, but it was too hard. Sarah was their family now. It would be better to leave before they got too comfortable with him around.

Was he destined to forever be denied the one thing he wanted most?

"You seem sad this morning," Susie said, surprising him when she came close and touched his cheek lightly.

"Who, me?" he asked, reaching out to poke her side.

She darted away, but didn't giggle like he'd hoped she would.

"I know what it is," she said.

Sarah glanced over her shoulder at Oscar and their eyes met for just a moment—just long enough for it to hurt. He blinked and looked away.

"I think you miss your family."

Susie couldn't know how close her words were to the truth. He did miss his pa and the whole clan. But worse than that was the ache in his bones for *this family,* for Sarah and his girls.

He had to clear his throat to speak. "Well, I'll be home in a coupla days. Just got to make sure you gals and Miss Sarah have everything you need before I go."

Sarah moved to the table and put a steaming bowl of golden eggs in the center. Behind her, he could see Cecilia carefully scooping a flapjack out of the pan and onto a waiting platter. They made a good team. He didn't need to worry so much. Between the girls, who were much more self-sufficient than they should be, and Sarah, who carried so much responsibility, they would be fine.

It was him who was going to have a hole in his heart for the foreseeable future.

"I'm sure your father will be glad to have you back," Sarah said softly. Her words threw him back to a previous conversation, one in which she'd encouraged him to tell his pa that he'd been having trouble with loneliness ever since Maxwell had left for college and Jonas and Penny's children had started arriving.

Maybe she was right. Because right now, he sure could use some advice from his pa on how to get rid of these softer feelings for this particular woman.

In town later that morning, Sarah posted the letters to her sisters and then stopped by the bank.

When she arrived, there were two people, a man and a woman, in the teller line. Both glanced over their shoulders when Sarah came through the doors, then quickly turned forward without so much as a nod of acknowledgement or a smile.

The manager stepped out of the small partitioned area where his desk was located and approached Sarah. "Miss Hansen. Can I help you this morning?" His smile appeared stilted.

She followed him to the desk overrun with papers and perched on the edge of the chair. "I need to withdraw my savings."

The man nodded and pulled a form from one of the desk drawers. He didn't look at Sarah as he scrawled on it, then pushed it across the desk to her. "I have to say this is probably the best decision. Our customers wouldn't appreciate it if we continued doing business with you."

"Excuse me?" she asked, her words betraying her surprise.

"Someone with your…questionable morals won't be looked upon favorably by our other clients. I'm sure you understand."

She was so stunned she couldn't speak for a moment. He nodded to the paper and she signed, although her hands were shaking badly. Had Paul Allen been circulating rumors about her stay at the Caldwell place? She was well aware how quickly news traveled in Lost Hollow—especially after how eagerly her students had spread the word that she and the horseman were courting, But this…the banker's disregard for the truth and callous manner surprised and hurt her.

Had the two customers in line thought the same about Sarah? Was that why they'd ignored common courtesy and turned their backs on her upon her entrance?

Was there no one in Lost Hollow with any sense? Was everyone under Paul Allen's thumb?

Numbly, Sarah tucked her savings into her small purse and left, her last hopes of receiving some help from the people in Lost Hollow gone.

Her mind reeled. She knew she needed to find a new job and a place for her newly acquired family. And quickly. The bank check in her purse wouldn't stretch nearly far enough.

She should telegraph her professor from the Normal School in Cheyenne. Often the professors knew of open positions and perhaps taking action would be better than waiting to hear back from her sisters or swimming in this mire of uncertainty.

But her plan was derailed when she arrived at the telegraph office and found a short note waiting for her from Mr. Butler, the Montana banker. It was only one line, and the message was unmistakable.

Not interested in children. Stop.

Her heart plummeted and the last of her hopes faded. She ducked into the narrow alley between the telegraph office and the next building over, holding one hand over her mouth to stem her emotions.

She hadn't known if she would really marry the banker, not without meeting the man to determine his true character, but at least she'd held out hope that she *could* marry him and have a nice future ahead of her. Until now.

Now her future looked like hard work in whatever job she could find. Just like when she'd had care of her sisters, she wouldn't likely have time to court. And who would want to marry a woman with so much responsibility besides?

For a moment she reconsidered Oscar's marriage proposal. Perhaps she could beg, tell him she'd made a mistake and did want to marry him.

But the prospect of a loveless marriage with the man she'd grown to love seemed too much to bear.

She would have to find a way to muddle through.

Chapter Nineteen

That night after supper, Oscar stood at the corral in the twilight, watching the mare circle, her breath puffing out in white clouds in the cold air.

He'd spent all afternoon selling and trading old man Caldwell's junk and things Sarah wouldn't use, to give her and the girls a good start. They now had plenty of supplies and Sarah could get rid of the chickens later if she wanted.

She was going to have to hire a wagon to take her to her next destination, once she figured out where that was going to be. Oscar couldn't stay. It hurt too much to interact with Sarah's new family and not be a real part of it.

He was leaving in the morning. Now he just had to tell her, and the girls. And hope that they weren't too disappointed that he wouldn't be around for the funeral. They seemed to be getting along better with Sarah, although Cecilia was still reserved. Wasn't it better to make a clean break now?

The cabin door closed behind him, but in the twilight stillness, he heard it. Boots crunched in the crusty snow and then he felt it deep inside when she joined him at the railing.

"She's yours," he said with a nod at the horse. Hoping his Stetson hid the squint of his eyes. He didn't want her to know how hurt he was by her rejection.

"What?" She half laughed the question. Then she seemed to realize he was serious, because she said, "Oscar, I can't."

The horse rounded the pen and approached Sarah, slowly but surely. When the animal was close enough, she nudged Sarah's mittened hand until the woman gently patted her nose.

"I don't know enough to take care of her. I can't ride her—"

He cut off her protest when he bent and ducked between the corral railings, joining the horse inside. "We can solve that one right now." He held up the bridle he'd had in his opposite hand as he approached the horse.

The mare didn't back away, but it did bob its head, neighing quietly as if to warn him off.

"Easy, girl. It's all right." Sarah was a natural, and her touch calmed the horse as she stroked its neck with her mittened hand.

Oscar approached and the horse stood for him to put the bridle on.

"Get in here," he ordered Sarah gruffly.

"I—" Her breath caught on her own protest and she sighed lightly, and then moved farther down the railing to join him and the horse inside.

"There's not a saddle," she said softly. She approached his shoulder, still showing wariness of the horse.

"Don't need one, not for this. C'mere." He brought her in front of him, right alongside the horse's middle and then spread her hands on its side. He rubbed her hands over the horse so it got more used to her touch, but it wasn't nervous at all—no quivering, no ear flicking, no stomping. The mare was ready. Was Sarah?

"I'm going to give you a boost. You swing your leg over and just settle. Try not to tense up."

He boosted her onto the horse's bare back, looking away when he might've seen a flash of petticoat. He helped her adjust her skirt around her legs and felt her muscles tighten when she looked down. Probably looked far when one was afraid of falling, but Oscar knew better.

"Look right over the horse's ears," he instructed. "Keep your eyes in front of you." She still didn't relax and he didn't want the horse to respond to Sarah's anxiety. "You won't hurt yourself, even if you do fall off. Besides, I'll catch you."

He didn't mention he could only catch her if she fell to his side, but his words seemed to comfort her somewhat. Her posture eased a bit.

"All right. Just feel the horse beneath you. She's not tense. You'll feel it if she starts to tighten up. Remember to watch her ears, that'll also tell you how she's feeling."

Sarah managed to unclench her grip on the base of the horse's mane. She smoothed out her fingers inside the mittens to the horse's shoulder in more of a pat.

"O-okay." Her voice was shaky. Maybe he shouldn't make her do this.

But he wanted to leave her with something tangible

to remember him by. And the horse had taken to Sarah when she hadn't responded to him in weeks of trying.

"I'm going to guide her forward. Don't clench up your legs. Think of it more like an embrace than a grip."

She wobbled and nearly fell off when the mare took its first step.

"You've got to balance!" Oscar cautioned in as calm a voice as he could muster. She'd never forgive him if she fell off, even if they weren't moving fast enough for her to be hurt. He needed to distract her.

"You never did tell me how you came to be so scared of horses."

She took a deep breath, glanced at him briefly. "We lived on a homestead when I was very small. I don't think my youngest sister was even born yet. I had a friend from one of the nearby spreads who liked to come over and play. We were playing hide-and-seek one afternoon and I hid in the barn. I don't think she ever did find me that day...."

They'd reached almost halfway around the corral and Sarah had finally started to relax, and when her thoughts and voice trailed off, he wanted to keep her distracted. "And...?"

"My father brought in his horse, a mean-spirited thing that didn't like anyone, but especially not him. Somehow it got loose and when I tried to escape the corner of the stall it saw me and reared. I can still hear it screaming...."

She began to tense, in reaction to her memory no doubt, but he didn't want this horse reacting to Sarah's body language. "Were you hurt?"

"Yes," she said, shaking her head and coming out of

the memory. "One of its hooves landed on my foot before my father pulled me out. The doctor didn't think any bones were broken, but I was bruised and could barely walk for weeks. I got the brunt of my father's belt, as well, for hiding in the barn."

"And the horse?" Oscar asked, wondering if her father had known the fear that the animal had sparked in Sarah and gotten rid of it.

"He had it for years and it never got any nicer."

And most likely being around the horse that had scared and hurt her had made Sarah's fears worse.

"Look at you now. You're riding," Oscar said softly.

Sarah looked up, and gasped softly. They had already traversed the entire corral's circumference once and were almost halfway around again.

"But you're doing most of the work," she argued quietly.

"You're the one keeping the horse calm. Telling her everything is okay."

She shook her head. "But what about a saddle? And feeding her? Don't horses need to be brushed and cleaned?"

They reached the corral side closest to the barn and he slowed and stopped the horse with gentle pressure on the reins. He'd been right about the animal. She was a steady ride, and would be a good horse for Sarah. The mare had just needed the right owner.

He'd been right about Sarah, too. She was brave enough to overcome her fear. She'd just needed a little impetus.

He reached for Sarah's waist, but released her quickly once her feet were on the ground. He made a big deal out of taking the bridle off the horse, so he didn't have to face her.

"Good girl. What a good girl," Sarah said, rubbing the horse's nose when he released the animal. It neighed softly, almost seeming to communicate with Sarah.

Sarah glanced at him as they ducked out of the corral. "But what happens if she gets spooked?"

"Then you do the same thing you would if one of the girls gets spooked. Calm them down. I've seen you do it. The rest of it, you can learn."

"But she's…" She turned back and put her elbows on the corral's top railing, watching the horse. "Beautiful. Big, but beautiful."

He couldn't help himself from one last long look at Sarah's profile as the sunlight faded. The sweep of her lashes, that pert nose with its sprinkling of freckles. Her mouth that could sting a man with her words or spread in a sweet smile. "Beautiful," he echoed.

"What about Belle? For her name?"

Sarah looked at him now and he forced his head to turn to the corral and the animal it contained. Hoped she couldn't see his face in the shadows beneath his hat. "It suits her."

He shoved his hands into the pockets of his coat. "I'm leaving in the morning. I'll go inside in a minute and say my goodbyes to the girls, but I'll probably be gone before sunrise."

She was silent. For a moment, he couldn't even hear her breathing. And then she said, "I understand. You've got things to get back to." She took another breath and it almost sounded as shaky as when she'd been on top of the horse moments ago. "Thank you for all you've done for the girls—and for me."

She turned to him and he couldn't be rude enough to give her his shoulder, even if he didn't want her to see his face. He faced her, hoping his hat and the growing shadows hid his expression.

"I'm glad—I'm glad I got to know the real Oscar. Not the reckless, arrogant cowboy I thought you were."

She was near tears and he wanted to ask her to reconsider. He knew he wasn't good enough for her, but he'd worked hard all his life to get to this point, and he could work hard to provide for her.

But he was too scared to put himself on the line again. She'd said no; she didn't want him.

So he stayed silent.

When she stretched out her hand, he shook it, thankful that they both wore gloves and he couldn't feel her skin against his.

That was it.

"Goodbye," he said.

Sarah was awake before dawn, lying on the couch in the dark, when she heard hoofbeats in the yard. She couldn't help herself—and went to the window to watch Oscar lead his horse into the yard and check its tack.

Thanks to the clear night and half-full moon, she could make out his silhouette and that of the animal. Only one horse, so he'd gone through with his threat of leaving Belle for her. What would she do with a horse?

She desperately wanted to run out into the yard, to ask him to stay, but she had some pride left. She didn't want to burden him.

So she remained where she was and let the silent tears slip down her cheeks as he mounted up and rode off without looking back. Taking her heart with him.

Chapter Twenty

Sarah had been so upset about the Montana suitor's telegram yesterday that she'd forgotten to send her wire to the Normal School in Cheyenne. It was for that reason that she and the girls had walked into town the next morning—she wasn't quite ready to saddle up Belle and attempt to ride on her own.

The girls had been quiet, almost withdrawn, all morning. Sarah suspected they missed the horseman, as she did. His sense of humor would've lightened things up when she'd scorched the bottom of the eggs this morning. Knowing he was there to assist them had made things seem so much brighter.

Sarah closed one hand around the pennies she'd stashed in her pocket. She would let the girls choose a piece of candy, even though they had some left from Oscar's Christmas party. Hopefully that would brighten their moods, at least for a bit. She suspected they would all have some adjusting to do without Oscar around. And they still had the funeral to get through tomorrow.

They'd nearly passed the train station when someone hailed her.

Sarah turned, raising one hand to shield her eyes from the winter sun's glare, to see one of the shopkeepers pointing, directing a strange, dark-haired man toward her.

Susie scooted a little closer to Sarah's side as the stranger approached. "Who is that?"

"I don't know, honey." Sarah placed a comforting hand on the girl's shoulder.

As the man neared and his dark skin and razor-sharp features registered with Sarah, a sense of foreboding shook her. Though he was dressed in trousers and a woolen shirt, boots and a leather coat, his braided hair hung down his back and marked him an Indian.

"Are you Cecilia and Susie Caldwell?" he demanded.

Beside her, Cecilia gasped and clutched Velma closer, making the little girl cry out.

Perturbed that he'd addressed the girls first, Sarah extended her hand. "I'm Sarah Hansen. I have charge of the girls."

"Not anymore," the man said with no responding smile creasing his face. "I am Sitting Dog Smith. I am the girls' uncle."

The name she'd telegraphed. Between being fired, making funeral arrangements and Oscar's departure, she'd completely forgotten about it.

Susie squeezed close to Sarah's side and even Cecilia took a step closer.

"We ain't got no relations," the older girl stated. The same thing she'd told Sarah before.

"Mr., ah…Smith, the girls' mother told them they didn't have any family."

"It was a lie," came his words, in a bitter tone.

Sarah became aware of the curious looks from pass-ersby and didn't want the girls' family business spread all over town—any more than it already was.

"Are you staying in town, Mr. Smith? Perhaps a hotel room would be a more private place to talk?"

He crossed his arms, not seeming to care that they were drawing attention. "I will stay at the homestead. You can return to your own home."

Except she didn't have a home anymore. Patience fraying, Sarah forced her voice to be calm and even. "Perhaps we could talk while we walk?"

She turned around and headed back out of town, ush-ering the girls along with her.

"But Sarah, your telegraph," Cecilia reminded her.

"It will keep," she murmured to the girl. Getting this situation settled took precedence over Sarah's search for a job, at least for the moment.

Mr. Smith followed them, walking alongside Ceci-lia. Sarah noticed he didn't offer to carry the toddler, leaving it to the girl.

"Let me take her for a bit," Sarah insisted, trading the small basket she carried over her arm for the sleepy tot, who promptly laid her head on Sarah's shoulder and stuck her thumb in her mouth.

"Mr. Smith, since I had no idea the girls had any family, all my things are at the homestead. You are certainly welcome to stay in the barn overnight." She would have to find a way to bar the door—after all, she didn't know the man. "I'll depart after the funeral for the girls' stepfather tomorrow."

Susie tugged on Sarah's elbow, nearly dislodging

her grip on the baby. "But Sarah, you said you'd stay with us!"

Cecilia's dull look seemed to echo Susie's distress in a different way, almost as if she had expected Sarah to fail them.

Sarah felt as if she was drowning in a sea of failures. She'd lost her job, lost her chance with Oscar and now was losing the girls.

"Let's get back home where it is warm and we'll talk things through. After Mr. Smith proves he is your uncle." She raised her eyebrows at the man in her best stern teacher expression, so he would know she had the girls' best interests at heart. "Well, family should be together, don't you think so?"

"But we want to be with you! We know you!" Susie cried, tears falling down her cheeks.

"Like I said, we ain't got no family," Cecilia spat. She ran off ahead, alone. At least she'd headed in the direction of the homestead. Sarah knew she probably needed an outlet for her emotions, now that things were changing once again. She also knew that Cecilia wouldn't leave her sisters without her care. It was what Sarah would've done.

Sarah looked over to the man beside her, smiling wanly and prepared to dismiss the girls' behavior. He only stared straight ahead with a frown marring his countenance.

"We'll get things figured out," she encouraged Susie instead, drawing the girl close with her free arm as Velma dozed off against her shoulder.

But things weren't clearer the next morning. The girls' uncle had proved his relationship to their father through several letters and a faded photograph. He had scoured the homestead, looking displeased when Sarah showed him the small amount of money she'd set aside from the trades Oscar had made.

He didn't seem happy with anything, and had hardly interacted with the girls yesterday afternoon, only ordered them to be ready to pack their things within the next two days. He'd been preoccupied with something else. He asked her about several people in town, including her old boss, Paul Allen. She was disappointed that the man didn't seem more interested in getting to know the girls.

Sarah worried about how the children would adjust. Cecilia would barely look at Sarah as it was, and when she did, disgust was clear on her features. Sarah didn't know how to make things better.

The uncle had refused to attend the funeral for the girls' stepfather. Sarah knew that even though the stepfather hadn't been good to the girls, they needed a sense of closure. She stood with them near the open grave and listened to the preacher, not surprised when the discourse was short—there hadn't been a lot of good to say about Mr. Caldwell. Only a few had come to pay their respects.

And now she had to let the girls go, so they could begin building a new family with their uncle. Even though it felt as if it would break her heart.

Susie had been teary and almost inconsolable last night, while Cecilia had done her best to completely ignore Sarah. She'd tried to explain to both of the girls that staying with family was the best thing, but her words had fallen on deaf ears.

And she knew her pleas must have been halfhearted, because she loved the girls. Taking on their care wasn't going to be a burden for her, but a joy. Even though she had no job and no prospects—yet—she wanted them, wanted to be the family she'd thought they could be for the few days they'd been together.

And now she was on the verge of losing everything.

The train whistled its arrival, punctuating the end of the preacher's words. Sarah wrapped her arm around Susie's shoulders and reached for Cecilia but was met with a glare.

Not knowing what else to do, Sarah took the girls into the mercantile to warm up for a bit before they trudged home. She had her things packed—the small amount of items she'd taken from the Allens' bedroom was barely enough to fill the saddlebags Oscar had left with Belle and her saddle. Without any idea where she was going, Sarah was rudderless, but she needed to be strong for the girls today.

She settled them near the potbellied stove with a piece of candy each, and asked Cecilia to keep a special eye on Velma. She went to the front of the store to try and compose herself.

Outside the window, she saw Mr. Smith confront someone on the opposite boardwalk. Was that…? It appeared to be Mr. Allen.

Sarah slipped out of the store and crossed the street, intending to find out what was going on. She didn't think Mr. Smith knew her former boss, but she didn't know anything about the man who'd just arrived in town.

"You caused my brother's death!" Mr. Smith yelled at the slightly larger rancher.

"I don't even know who you are." Mr. Allen's face turned an ominous red.

"He's the girls' uncle," offered Sarah, coming near. "Please, can we go somewhere more private?"

Mr. Allen's face went white.

"You see, he cannot even look me in the eye," Smith crowed, looking to Sarah for support.

She was surprised and disgusted by the light of anger in Mr. Smith's eyes and stepped back. What was his motive in attacking the other man as he had?

"I don't know what you're talking about, but—" Mr. Allen tried to back away, but the Indian followed him step for step.

"You killed my brother and I'll have justice!"

"What's going on here?" asked a passerby. He came even with Sarah, still well back from the two men. She recognized him as the circuit judge. She hadn't seen him in town the past few days during her business, but perhaps he'd arrived on the train.

"Mr. Smith has just arrived in town," she tried to explain, "to take charge of his three nieces after their stepfather died. I don't know about this accusation—"

"I don't care about the brats," Smith shouted. "I want restitution for my brother's death!"

"Well, I do!" Sarah said. "I want to raise them as my own."

The circuit judge now turned to her. "Are you family?"

"No," she whispered.

"You married? You look young."

"No."

"Well, I can't say that I'd grant custody to a young, unmarried woman."

The hopes that had risen in Sarah upon Mr. Smith's words began to shrivel. "I've been their teacher," she reasoned. "This man might be blood, but you just heard him admit he doesn't want them."

"Miss, the courts try not to interfere if there is family to take custody—"

"Please." She blinked to stay her tears but couldn't keep her voice steady.

"All right. We can have a hearing, but I can't guarantee I can do anything for you. Unless your circumstances were to change."

Mr. Allen began shouting again, but the judge waved him down.

"We'll meet to talk about both of these matters on Friday morning. I'll use the sheriff's office as my chambers."

At his dismissal, Sarah turned around, mind reeling. Friday. Two days away.

She immediately spotted Cecilia, holding Velma, and Susie across the street on the boardwalk in front of the mercantile. Susie was crying again, and Sarah could only imagine they'd heard their uncle shouting. *I don't care about the brats!*

With the judge's words, *unless your circumstances were to change,* ringing in her ears, Sarah's mind settled on the perfect solution. And she immediately knew what she had to do. Because she did want the girls to stay with her. She loved them.

She strode across the street, leaning down to speak directly to them. She grasped Susie's hand first, and

Cecilia's shoulder. Surprisingly, the usually prickly girl didn't shrug away.

"I'm going to have to leave, but I'll be back for the hearing. I promise. I'm going to figure out a way to make this work."

Susie's dark eyes grew hopeful and she sniffled. Cecilia looked skeptical, but remained silent.

"I'll be back. I promise."

But would she be able to convince the judge to let her keep the girls?

Chapter Twenty-One

Only an hour home and Oscar itched to be away again. But not for the same reasons he'd wanted to go before.

He wanted to rush right back to Sarah and beg her to change her mind. Wanted to see Cecilia and Susie and Velma and hug them. Yep, he was a lovesick fool, for all four women.

He'd arrived just in time for lunch and shared a hearty meal with the family at his pa's long table. He supposed he should be anxious to ride across the valley to his own place, but he was dragging his feet, leaning on the post holding up his pa's porch roof and staring across the space instead.

He'd wanted someone to show it *to*. Sarah.

"Something eating you, son?"

He turned just as his pa clapped a hand on Oscar's shoulder. The man used to be a head taller than Oscar, but now had to reach up an inch or two. Although Jonas wasn't even a decade older than Oscar, he admired the older man and respected his advice. Oscar just didn't know if he could voice his feelings about Sarah.

So he just shook his head in response to Jonas's question.

"Penny's been telling me for a while now that you and I need to sit down and have a talk, one-to-one."

That sounded like Sarah's unsolicited advice.

Oscar followed his pa out to the closer corral, next to the barn. Now that Jonas had been increasing his spread when each son turned eighteen, they needed more horses and had a second corral in the western-most field.

Pa cleared his throat. It wasn't easy for them to talk about this serious stuff. "New babies take a lot of time and attention. I didn't remember it so much from Breanna. Guess I was so overwhelmed with life back then that having a baby around just seemed like part of what I was going through."

"It's understandable." Oscar did understand. He saw how hard Penny and Jonas worked to spend time with the kids and keep the spread running. And he couldn't begrudge his pa wanting to spend time with the little tykes while they were small.

"It's not understandable if I made you feel like you weren't welcome in your own home. I think you and Maxwell offered to bunk down in the barn, and then the bunkhouse, so we'd have a little more room in the house—"

"And so we could sleep through the night," Oscar joked. "The horses are a lot quieter than babies."

Jonas smiled, but shook his head at his son's attempt to redirect the conversation. "I never wanted you to feel like you weren't wanted."

A hot ache began behind Oscar's throat when his pa drew his shoulders into an embrace. "I love you, Oscar."

He slapped his pa on the back. "I love you, too."

They stepped apart, both clearing their throats, and looked out to the couple of young fillies roaming the corral. Oscar found the courage to say, "I was the one who started telling myself I wasn't wanted. After what happened with my uncle…" He had to stop to clear his throat again. "I thought it would be easier if I distanced myself, if I was the one who was moving on, instead of waiting for you and Penny to tell me it was time to get on with my life."

His pa slapped his shoulder. "Are you kidding me? She's been nagging me every day to get you back here. We've missed you. The only reason I resisted was because I thought you were getting some adventures out of your system. Besides, every time you sent home a horse for your herd, I'd think about how you'd have to come home soon for good. And now here you are."

Oscar nodded, squinting as he looked to the far horizon. "Now here I am."

His pa remained at his shoulder, neither one talking, just looking out over the land. Oscar *had* missed this. The sense of family, of camaraderie that he felt just being with his pa or his brothers. Sarah had been right.

Finally, Jonas spoke. "Seems you've got the same look about you that I kept seeing in the mirror those few weeks I thought I couldn't marry Penny."

Oscar darted his eyes toward his pa. "And?"

"And it seems like it might be time for me to return the favor you and your brothers did for me when you told me to quit being afraid and get my hide down to town and ask her to marry me."

Oscar sighed. "I already asked her. She said no."

A glance at Jonas revealed the slightly stunned look on his face. "This the same gal Davy and Seb met when they came up to visit you? They sure seemed to think she was taken with you."

"I thought she might be, but…" He told his father the situation, how he'd tried to explain things to Sarah, the reasons why they should be together.

"And then you told her that you loved her?" Jonas asked.

"Well…no."

His pa snorted. "I guess I'm not surprised that she said 'no' then."

"But it made sense for us to marry."

Jonas chuckled. "If there's one thing I've learned since Penny came into our lives, it's that a woman needs to know how you feel. If she thought you *didn't* love her, she might've said no because she didn't want to be a burden on you." The older man shrugged as if the workings of a woman's mind were a mystery. Which they were.

Oscar considered it. Considered those kisses they'd shared. He didn't think Sarah would've kissed him if she didn't have some sort of feelings for him. Then he remembered how she'd argued back about him talking about returning to his cabin and horses. As if she was worried about his happiness, that he wouldn't be happy with her and the girls.

"How come you didn't tell her?"

Oscar flushed. "It was all tied up with my past, and what was going on with you and I. I guess I thought if I explained that we made sense to be together, then she'd understand what I wasn't saying." He paused. "I guess I got scared that she'd…she'd leave me, too. And if I put my heart out there…"

"She might reject it?"

Oscar swallowed, the reality of what he'd left behind hitting him square in the chest. It was not a comfortable feeling.

"So I guess you're heading back to Lost Hollow?" Jonas asked.

Oscar's heart thudded in his ears. "I guess I am." The moment the words left his lips, it felt right.

Renewed energy flowed through him, making him jittery and anxious to get on the road.

"Go ahead and saddle up," his pa said with a chuckle. "I'll go explain things to Penny and load up some provisions."

Oscar met her in the middle—about halfway between Bear Creek and Lost Hollow. He would've known it was Sarah by the crown of golden hair, but the way she sat her saddle was also a dead giveaway.

She was trotting the horse, but instead of posting and saving her backside from bouncing against the saddle, she wobbled and flopped all over the place. But the horse was allowing it, looking loose and relaxed as if they were just out for a jaunt.

He approached carefully, not wanting to spook the mare and either have her race off or buck Sarah off. He needn't have worried. Sarah reigned in—she wasn't as awful at that part—before he got close and waited for his approach.

The mare whickered to Oscar's horse, obviously recognizing him. Oscar drew up close so that he and Sarah faced each other, knees brushing.

"What are you doing out here?" he asked, eyes glued to her wind-burned cheeks and hair rioting around her face. Her coat was drawn up as tightly as she could make it and she wore a scarf, but it was obvious she shivered with cold.

"Coming after you," she gasped. "I've been riding since this morning. I thought I'd be farther, but I'm not."

"Not riding like that," he agreed. Grinned.

His heart felt so much lighter just being near her. His spirits were restored. She looked somewhat happy to see him—if cold. Maybe he still had a chance. Then he realized she was alone.

"Where are the girls?"

"That's why I was coming to find you," she said, teeth chattering.

He dismounted, quickly reaching out for her. "C'mere. You're freezing." He took off his own gloves and then hers, not surprised to find her fingers felt like blocks of ice. They hadn't turned white from frostbite, though. He rubbed them between his palms, looking around them to the landscape.

"Let me see what I can find to get a fire started. I don't remember passing any houses, and we need to get you warmed up."

She shook her head. They were standing so close that her hair brushed his chin. "There's not time. We've got to get back to Lost Hollow tonight."

Her voice shook with urgency—and probably cold, too. She looked as if she was about ready to jump back on her horse regardless of what he said. Maybe she was so cold she was on the verge of hypothermia? He needed to calm her down, warm her up.

"All right." He unfastened the front of his coat, a much heavier buffalo hide than her woolen garment, and drew her into his arms, tucking the coat around her as best he could, sharing his own warmth.

He chafed his hands up and down her back, across her shoulders, trying to bring back some circulation. "Whatever it is, you're not going to do anyone any good if you're frozen. Don't you know if you're riding all day, you're supposed to get off the horse every once in a while and walk around? Restore the blood flow and warm yourself up? Or you could've found a ranch house to rest for a bit."

He supposed the horse hadn't really been moving fast enough to work up a lather and get herself good and worn out. He glanced at the animal as he held Sarah close, noting she was greeting Pharaoh with noses touching. She seemed fine.

"No t-time to stop." Sarah pressed her icy face into his neck and it was his turn to gasp at the sensation. "Had to get to you."

"Well, now you have," he said, savoring the feeling that expanded his chest as her words sank in. "What do you need me to do?"

"Marry me."

Sarah's head spun as she burrowed into the warmth of Oscar's embrace. His heart beat steadily beneath her cheek, reassuring her of his solid presence. He would help. He had to.

"Excuse me?" Although his voice did sound a little strangled.

"The morning after you left, the girls' uncle—their real father's brother—arrived in town."

She felt him tense up, she was bundled so close.

"What did he want?" he asked.

"I thought he came for the girls, but then after Caldwell's funeral, he started accusing Mr. Allen of things—and he blurted out that he has no interest in caring for the girls."

"Well, that's good, right? So you can still be their guardian?"

She shook her head. Tears filled her eyes as emotion overcame her, now that she didn't have to fight this alone. Now that he would stand with her. "I was standing next to the circuit judge when he said it. I told the judge I wanted to take the girls and he looked at me—" She took a shuddering breath. "He said I was too young, and single besides."

Now Oscar went silent. He was a smart man. No doubt his mind was coming to the same conclusion she had just before she'd left Lost Hollow.

He hesitated and her heart thundered.

"So I thought—I thought if we got married, well, I won't be single any more and the judge will let me—will let us take the girls."

"What about your Montana banker?"

"I didn't even know the man, we only corresponded the once."

"But you know me?" Oscar prodded.

She did, and she loved him. But based on his previous proposal, she couldn't find the courage to say the words. "I know enough," she said instead. "You're a man of honor. You put aside your own wishes and plans to take care of Susie and Cecilia and Velma. You had enough integrity to stand up for me—"

He kissed her, interrupting whatever else she would've said. She melted against him, drinking in his warmth, his scent, the man himself.

Someone nudged her back, and Sarah drew away from Oscar. Reluctantly.

She looked over her shoulder. Make that something. Belle eyed her almost disapprovingly.

Oscar chuckled and drew her in close again for a hug, brushing another kiss to her forehead. "I see you two are getting along fine."

"So will you do it? Marry me?" Pushing back inches from his chest and looking up into his face was one of the hardest things she'd ever had to do.

He wore a funny expression on his face. Surprised, and joyful, and something else besides. "Yes."

He tugged her close again, this time just embracing her and surrounding her with his warmth.

"Hmm. We should go," she said, reluctant to leave his embrace. She felt safe with him.

"You still need to warm up." It was gratifying that he didn't seem to want to let her go, either.

"I'm much warmer than I was a moment ago," she admitted, blushing. His kiss had nudged everything else out of her brain.

He chuckled again, the sound vibrating against her cheek. "All right. But this time, we'll be stopping to warm up—" he gave her a searing look "—when I say so."

He boosted her up into Belle's saddle, and she immediately shivered against the wind. Instead of mounting his own horse, he surprised her by untying a blanket from behind his saddle.

"Here," he murmured, wrapping it around her shoulders and tucking it beneath her legs and the saddle, providing her a little more protection from the wind.

He tapped her booted toe. "It'll be faster riding separately, but if you start feeling sleepy I want you to tell me right away."

She nodded. It was wonderful, having someone care for her for a change. Nice to not be alone anymore. Even if he didn't love her and was marrying her for the sake of the girls.

Hours later, Oscar glanced over his shoulder again to check on Sarah. The tip of her nose was bright-red, her eyes glistening, probably tearing from the wind and their fast pace.

She'd insisted they gallop and hadn't argued when Oscar had taken the reins for her horse. It kept the animal close enough that they could talk, if need be, and that if the animal spooked he might be able to do something about it. After the time spent in hard riding, he and the mare were getting along all right.

He couldn't quit thinking that he should've told her he loved her right away. She'd seemed so relieved when he'd agreed to marry her—and he'd been so shocked by her proposal that he'd agreed. Marrying Sarah was what he wanted. Mostly.

He also wanted her love.

Her words described admiration and he believed she had some feelings for him. She wouldn't have kissed him if she didn't. But had her proposal been made out of desperation to help the girls?

Once they got this mess with the judge and the uncle sorted out, the first thing he intended to do was sit down with Sarah privately and set things straight. He didn't want to go into a marriage with secrets between them, and he had a big one. He was in love with the fiery schoolteacher.

Another glance at her and this time he caught Sarah wincing as she adjusted the blanket around her shoulders.

"We're stopping!" he called out, and began reining the horses in. "Whoa!"

Both Pharaoh and the mare stood, breaths puffing out in white clouds, as he dismounted and walked around to fetch Sarah.

"We don't have time to stop," she protested, with a pointed glance at the waning afternoon sun. "The trial is in the morning and the girls need us there."

He ignored her push against his shoulders and lifted her down from the horse.

"Oscar, no!" She struggled against him, but didn't stand a chance against his greater strength. Plus, her struggling would get her blood flowing and help warm her up. He set her feet on the ground.

"We can't stop," she half sobbed, knocking her fists against his shoulders.

"Sarah. Sarah!" She went still at the sharpness of his voice.

"Do you remember that night I went out in the snow and you came and rescued me?"

Her eyes were wild, looking over his shoulder, at the horses, anywhere but at him.

He grasped and shook her shoulders, just a little. "Do you remember?"

"Yes."

"If you get too cold, what's going to happen?"

"H-hypothermia." Her teeth chattered even as she said the word.

"That's right. And if that happens?"

"C-can't get to the girls."

He smiled at her, even as she narrowed her eyes at him.

He gently disengaged her hands from the blanket and took it off her shoulders. "I want you to march around in a circle until I tell you to stop."

She looked at him askance until he gave her a little push away from the horses. "Do it, Sarah."

Finally, she did, with a grudging mumble, "I'm not a child."

Oscar stifled his chuckle. She was certainly acting like one of her more recalcitrant students. "Swing your arms!" he called out to her, turning away when he heard her muttering.

He went back to the horses, first to Sarah's mare. There was nothing helpful in the saddlebags—their very bareness showed how quickly she'd left Lost Hollow to find him.

Inside his saddlebags, he pulled out the spare flannel shirt he always carried, along with an extra pair of socks. He probably should have done this earlier, but she'd been in such a hurry and his brain had been muddled by her proposal.

"When's the last time you ate something?" he called back to Sarah. A glance above the saddle showed she was still marching, just as he'd told her to.

"This morning!" she called back, sounding none too happy with him. But at least if she was finding her fire, that was a good thing.

"This morning," he repeated, frowning as he dug farther into the pack.

Finally he called her over to him. Her pert chin was high and her blue eyes narrowed suspiciously when he said, "Take off your coat."

He held up the extra shirt and was gratified when she listened to him and shrugged out of the coat, shivering against the wind. He threw the shirt around her shoulders and she stuffed her arms inside.

"Eat this." He handed her a piece of jerky, which she took with a glare. His lips twitched but he managed to keep a smile from emerging as he buttoned up the shirt while she chewed off the tough meat.

"I's fwozen through," she complained with her mouth full.

"That's all right." He kept his focus on the buttons. "Digesting it will keep you warm, too."

He raised his brows as he helped her back into her coat. She handed him the rest of the piece of jerky that she hadn't been able to eat and he chucked it away for some animal to find.

He insisted she put the extra socks over her mittens to give her hands an extra layer of protection. When she was finally bundled to his satisfaction, the blanket over her shoulders again, he stepped back to look her over.

"Happy now?" She glared at him.

"Mmm, not quite." He grinned at her. "We're doing this my way now, got it, Miss Schoolteacher? You ride with me."

He mounted up, gathering the reins for both horses in his gloved hand. Then he reached down his opposite hand for her. Thankfully, she didn't protest.

"Step on my boot, there." He guided her, grasping her elbow and helping her sit in the saddle facing him. It would be easier to have her clinging to him from behind, but he was worried about her getting too cold, and she'd stay warmer this way.

Pharaoh shifted beneath them and Sarah let out a quiet, "Eep!"

"It's all right. He's just getting used to the weight."

She elbowed him in the ribs, a nudge really, but his heavy coat shielded him from the brunt of the blow.

Finally, she settled against his chest, her head tucked beneath his chin and her arms sliding around his waist.

"How come you're not cold?" she said against his neck.

"I am." Although he was certainly warming up now. "But I'm used to being out in the elements, to a point. Seems like my pa always has some cows get too far out and have to be brought back to the nearer pasture. And the ornery animals always pick the nastiest weather to go out in."

He nudged Pharaoh into a fast walk, making sure the animal was going to accept their weight. Sarah didn't add much, but Oscar wanted to be sure the animal was all right before taking him to a faster pace.

She hummed against his neck, sending a thrum of

energy down his spine. "Did you make things up with your pa?"

His lips twitched as he remembered Jonas's advice to woo Sarah. "You could say that. You getting any warmer?"

"Mmm-hmm."

Looking down at the woman in his arms, his heart was full. He loved her. He couldn't wait to get things resolved so he could tell her.

Then he frowned as another thought crowded in. They were still miles from Lost Hollow. If Sarah got any colder, he would have to insist on finding a farmhouse to stop for a while. He couldn't risk her life.

But if they didn't make it back to Lost Hollow to meet with the judge, and they lost the girls, would Sarah ever forgive him?

Chapter Twenty-Two

"Wake up, sweetheart. We're here."

The low rumble against Sarah's ear nudged her from her doze into wakefulness, but it was so hard to want to leave the warm cocoon that held her securely. She could feel winter's bite teasing the periphery of her senses, and she was so tired of being cold.

"I know you're tired, but you've gotta wake up."

She pried one eye open and was met with an expanse of dark material. A coat. Remembrance jolted her fully awake and she pushed away from Oscar's chest, where she'd burrowed her face and fallen asleep.

They'd ridden all night, stopping once at his insistence in a wooded area to build a fire and warm up. Sheltered in his arms, she'd drifted off numerous times, while he'd brought them safely to their destination.

And none too soon. As Sarah turned her face into the cold air, she saw the first orange crescent of the rising sun cresting the horizon. She noted their surroundings— they were just outside town.

She glanced up at Oscar, noting the tired lines around

his eyes and exhaustion in the set of his shoulders. Somehow, he still managed to grin at her.

"I thought we'd see about getting you a room at the hotel so you can freshen up a bit, if you'd like. We've still got plenty of time to get over to the sheriff's office. And I didn't think you'd want to ride into town all snuggled up to me. No matter how much I like it."

The man was incorrigible! And yet, she still found herself returning his smile even as she accepted his hand down off of his horse.

She stretched her arms above her head, noting sore muscles that she wasn't used to at all.

Oscar watched her, making a blush rise to her cheeks. "Not used to riding yet. But you'll get there. I knew you and the mare would be a good match."

She huffed. Arrogant cowboy. Even if he was right. She approached the horse carefully, the way he'd taught her to. "Good morning, Belle. Going to let me ride you into town?"

The mare stood docile while Sarah mounted up, muscles complaining.

"What about you?" she asked. "Don't you want to freshen up? You let me rest, but you haven't even closed your eyes all night."

He raised one brow at her. "How do you know, Sleeping Beauty?"

She gave him her best teacher's expression and he laughed. "Does that actually work on your students?"

She shrugged. "Sometimes."

Still chuckling, he handed her the reins and they guided their horses into a walk toward town. "I thought I'd splash my face over at the livery while I get these two settled." He patted his horse's neck. "No telling how long the judge will want to talk to us, and that way they'll be nice and comfortable and can get a bite to eat."

She wrinkled her nose. "Do you think Belle will be all right? I'd hate for her to get frightened and injure herself."

"I've met the livery owner. He's an old hand and knows what he's doing. She'll be all right for the day. Then after we get things settled with the girls, we'll get her out to my spread pretty soon and she can settle down some more."

She glanced at him from the corner of her eye. She'd been so cold and desperate when she'd asked him to marry her for the girls that it was all a blur to her. He'd said yes, which was the most important part. And he didn't seem to be concerned that he'd be taking on four females.

She was still a bit worried that he would eventually feel burdened by having them around. But between her flight to find Oscar yesterday and the careful way he'd cared for her and got her back to Lost Hollow on time, she'd made herself a promise. He might not love her, but she'd be a good wife, and take as much burden away from him as possible.

She didn't know exactly how that was going to work, since her culinary skills were still questionable, and she didn't know anything about milking cows or anything that went into keeping a homestead running. But she knew his adoptive parents lived nearby and had small children. Perhaps she could help with caring for the small children in return for lessons on how to be a proper horseman's wife.

She was determined to make a success of it. And maybe…maybe Oscar would eventually learn to love her.

Shortly before nine, Oscar met Sarah on the board-walk outside the hotel, and they quickly linked arms. He just about couldn't stand being away from her.

"You look beautiful," he murmured, turning her toward the sheriff's office down the street.

She blushed. It was true. Her cheeks were still pink, likely from all the wind she'd gotten yesterday riding in the elements. Her hair was coifed prettily behind her head and she was smiling.

But her hand on his arm was shaking. He covered her fingers with his own. "Don't be nervous. We'll get all this ironed out."

When they got to the sheriff's office, it was empty. Oscar wheeled around, looking for anyone on the streets, but they were virtually empty, as well.

"Where is everyone?" Sarah wondered aloud.

"They're all over at the church!" came a voice from the back room, where Oscar knew the jail cells were.

"Stay here." Oscar left her on the front step momen-tarily.

A toothless old man who smelled ripe with whis-key cackled from inside the cell. "Too many folks was standing around outside, trying to hear what was goin' on, so they's moved the hearings over to the church, so it's more organized-like."

"Thanks," Oscar muttered, returning to Sarah. "The church," he told her.

The worried lines on her face didn't lift as they hightailed it down the street in the opposite direction. He could only pray things would go their way. If Sarah couldn't keep the girls with her, he knew she would be heartbroken.

And if they didn't need to get married to keep the girls, would she still have him? He hadn't told her he loved her yet. And even if he did tell her, would it really matter? She'd told him all along that she didn't want a cowboy....

He did his best to silence the doubts inside him, the voice that wanted to bring back all his childhood fears.

Someone hailed them from a shop door halfway down the street. Oscar paused, but Sarah kept going. He released her hand momentarily as the shopkeeper waved something—a letter—frantically in their direction. Oscar grabbed the missive from the man and then caught up to Sarah, boots pounding on the boardwalk. He pressed the letter into her hand, noting with relief Sarah's name penned in a feminine scrawl and not a masculine hand. The last thing he needed was her Montana banker changing his mind and ruining Oscar's chances—again.

They slipped into the back of the church, but it was packed with people and they began pushing their way through.

"Do you see the girls?" Sarah asked over the murmuring voices surrounding them.

He stretched his neck, but couldn't get a glimpse of anything other than more bodies.

Someone banged a gavel and Oscar felt Sarah jump—her hand clutched his arm tighter for a brief instant.

Finally, the crowd parted and they were thrust into

the aisle between two rows of seats, at the same moment that the room went silent. The pews before them were filled with townspeople—probably more than the church had seen in its entire history. Were they all here to see what would happen with the Caldwell girls, or for another reason?

"Ah," said a dry voice. "So the young lady has decided to grace us with her presence." Oscar looked to the front of the sanctuary, where a man in a fine black suit stood behind the lectern, wooden mallet in hand. He did not smile.

"Sarah!" Susie slipped out of the first pew on the left and raced back to them, throwing herself into Sarah's arms, making her stumble back. Oscar caught her shoulders, steadying the both of them.

Cecilia stood where she was, holding on to Velma just as he'd expected, face carefully blank, but her eyes were just a bit wide. Looking like the little girl she really was, in need of someone to support her.

"Well, sit down so we can get on with this," the judge ordered.

Sarah nudged Susie back toward her seat and when Oscar followed and slid into the pew beside them, this time the judge's expression changed as he raised an eyebrow.

"Let's get the custody issue dealt with—"

"Your Honor," Mr. Allen blustered, and it was the first time Oscar noticed him in the pew across the aisle, his wife at his side. "This man—" he pointed to a dark-skinned, dark-haired man sitting by himself on the very front row "—maligned my character in front of the town and I want this matter taken care of immediately."

The crowd around them murmured. Either people were gossiping about what the girls' uncle had said about Allen, or they were now impressed at his imperious way toward the judge.

Another bang of the gavel silenced the crowd. The judge glared at Allen. "Fine. You want to be first, you can be first. Stand up. What's your complaint?"

Both men stood, talking almost as one, their words overlapping so a body couldn't understand them.

"Silence!" the judge ordered. "You first." He pointed to Allen.

"Aren't you going to have us swear on a Bible or something?" Mr. Allen asked.

The judge crossed his arms, obviously becoming impatient with the man. "I see no need for a formal hearing at this time. We can conduct our business informally unless matters warrant it."

"Fine. Yesterday, I was in town doing business and this man approached me and began spouting unfounded accusations. He made false charges against my character, and I want a public apology. And restitution!"

Of course he did. Because if there was anything Oscar knew about Allen, it was that the man looked out only for himself. He tapped his hat impatiently against his knee, ready to get this show on the road. Ready to get hitched.

Sarah met Oscar's sideways glance and crooked grin without turning in her seat. She didn't want to give the judge any reason to scrutinize them until she absolutely had to face the man. She tapped Oscar's bouncing knee in a silent admonition to sit still. He was as bad as a little child sometimes.

She didn't understand how he could be so jovial, so calm, when she was a mess. Her heart raced and her palms were sweaty as she clasped both hands in her lap. The judge had the power to grant her dearest wish—a husband and family all at once. How could she *not* be nervous?

Susie leaned against her side, pressing close, and Sarah put her arm around the girl's shoulder. She looked to Cecilia and Velma just as the toddler began speaking a garbled nonsense phrase. Cecilia shushed her sister gently, providing her the doll Oscar had given Velma for Christmas as a distraction.

A sense of calm settled over Sarah. This was the reason she was here, and why all her troubles—past and future—would be worth it. These girls.

Sarah shifted her legs and paper crinkled. Brow wrinkling, she reached beneath her skirt. A letter. The mercantile owner and acting postmaster had hailed her on the street, but she'd been in such a rush to get to the church she'd ignored him. Oscar had retrieved the letter and handed it to her, but she'd nearly forgotten about it. Now she slid it into her lap, unobtrusively, and studied the handwriting that made up her address. Sally. Her sister must've written before Sarah had sent her hasty letter the day after Christmas.

The envelope's flap was open. Sarah could slip out the correspondence without making too much noise, and she did. As she opened the folded sheet of paper, several green bills slipped out onto her lap.

Oscar nudged her, a question in his eyes, as she

worked to slide the money back into the envelope. She shrugged at him, not knowing what to say. Why had her sister sent her the cash?

Dearest Sarah,

I've heard some news about you from a friend of a friend who lives close to Lost Hollow. If my suspicions are right, by the time you're reading this letter there's a chance you'll need some cash. If not, you can consider it a loan until we're able to see each other next.

I'm not terribly surprised , except that you haven't mentioned the horseman in any recent letters to me. Or perhaps our letters have just crossed paths. Since we were children, your heart has been bigger than your common sense. I've sent what I can (how could I do less after all you've done for me over the years?), and wired Elsie, as well. No doubt her support will follow.

Please write when you've settled.

With love, your sister,

Sally

Heart beating wildly, Sarah stuffed the letter back into the envelope, and then the envelope into her pocket. Tears of gratefulness clouded her eyes and she had to blink them away. Somehow, Sally had discovered that her job had been in jeopardy and sent money ahead.

Sarah now had funds to supplement her savings. And from the sound of it, her youngest sister was sending a bit more. Even without a marriage to Oscar, she and the girls would be all right.

Sarah forced herself to pay attention to what was happening before her, lest the judge get irritated with her.

"What do you say to this?" the judge directed Mr. Smith to speak.

"My accusations were not unfounded. Years ago, my brother settled in this area, a homestead just outside of town. He married a white woman." He spat the last words and Cecilia drew in a sharp breath.

Sarah reached across Susie to touch the girl's shoulder, offering what comfort she could. Cecilia glanced at her, dark eyes furious, and Sarah shook her head gently. They couldn't afford to make a ruckus, even if they didn't like what they heard.

"Almost immediately, things started happening around my brother's homestead. Sabotage. There is always prejudice against the red man from the whites, but this seemed to be something more. Finally, my brother's wife confessed. She had rejected the advances of a man and married my father instead. The man was crazy with jealousy and she thought perhaps he was the cause of the troubles at their home.

"That man was Paul Allen."

Another murmur rippled through the crowd and the judge quickly banged his gavel for order.

"My brother went to the local sheriff," continued Mr. Smith, "who looked into the matter and the mysterious events stopped happening. For long enough that my brother fathered three children. Those children." He pointed to the Caldwell girls. "But then after the sheriff passed away, mysterious things started happening again around my brother's home."

"That's true," Susie whispered. "Some tools disappeared and one of our milk cows died."

Sarah squeezed her shoulders, saddened that this family had gone through so much. She so desperately wanted to give them a new start. In Bear Creek.

"My brother confronted the man who did these things—Paul Allen—but the man refused to admit it. Later that night, my brother was murdered in cold blood on his own land."

Again, murmurs spread through the crowd. Someone behind Sarah said, "I thought he drowned in a creek."

"I heard he fell and banged his head on a rock—drunk as a skunk."

Beside Sarah, Susie sniffled.

Cecilia turned around in her seat, hissing, "My father—my real father—never drank a day in his life!"

"Cecilia," Sarah cautioned. "Be still."

"You'll want to be respectful of the deceased," Oscar said, turning, as well, to give a stern look to those behind them. The pews behind them went silent, and then the judge banged his gavel again and the room went quiet once more.

"You can't know all of that—you ain't—haven't even lived here. Where's your proof?" Mr. Allen sputtered. His stumbling over his words showed his obvious upset.

"I only came to visit my brother's homestead yesterday, but when scouting around, I found this." Mr. Smith held up a fancy tooled pistol, dirty and rusty as if it had been left outdoors for a long period of time.

Mrs. Allen gasped audibly.

"Do you know what that is?" the judge asked her pointedly. "Stand up."

She stood, her face gone white. She clutched the back of the pew in front of her. "It is—at least, it looks like my husband's prized pistol. It went missing…a while ago."

The judge now turned his gaze to Mr. Allen. "Any idea what it was doing on this other man's homestead?"

Mr. Allen opened his mouth, then closed it. Opened it again, but this time all that escaped was, "I—" He shook his head, features drawn and pale eyes wild. Weaker than Sarah had ever seen him.

Mrs. Allen wilted onto her seat, looking as if she might faint at any moment. "Is that why…why you've stirred up trouble for those poor girls, that poor family all these years? I thought you held a grudge because of their Indian blood, but…you just wanted…you just wanted this other woman?"

The crowd began to murmur in earnest. Mr. Smith began railing at Mr. Allen, who fell onto the pew beside his wife.

"Order!" the judge shouted, banging his gavel repeatedly. "Silence!"

Still, no one seemed to be listening to him. "Sheriff!" he finally shouted, and the room went still.

"It seems," the judge began, "that we have need of a trial, after all. Will you escort this man and keep him contained until the details can be settled and any other witnesses tracked down?"

Mr. Allen went with the sheriff without another word, shoulders hunched and head down. His wife followed a few paces behind, openly weeping into her hands. Sarah's heart ached for the woman. She'd never have guessed her boss was capable of murder. Cruelty yes,

but outright murder? How Clara must be suffering…
Perhaps they would have time for Sarah to check on the
woman before they headed to Bear Creek.

The judge had lost all semblance of order over the
crowd now, and rapped his gavel loudly, then finally let
loose an earsplitting whistle.

"I'll ask the majority of the crowd to leave. Now.
There's nothing more to be seen here today. I'll need
a few witnesses, though. Preacher, you and your family stay. And you—" He pointed to someone else in the
room, Sarah couldn't tell who.

The room emptied with a large amount of shuffling
feet and murmuring.

Finally quiet once again, the judge rubbed his forehead as if he had a headache. "Now for the matter of
these three orphans. Am I to understand that you have
no desire to take care of your nieces?" He directed the
question to Mr. Smith.

"I am a single man. They are half-white. What would
I do with three girls?"

Sarah didn't understand how the man could be so
selfish to come to town for his own gain—hoping to
gain something from his brother's death, but not care
about these three precious girls. Just like Mr. Allen
hadn't cared.

She forced herself to stand on shaking legs. Immediately, Oscar was there beside her, his hand beneath
her elbow. Steadying her.

"Remember your first day of school?" he whispered.
She immediately recalled his horse lesson and his idea
that acting as if she wasn't afraid was the best solution.

Her trembling and her voice steadied. "Your Honor, I would like to take responsibility for the girls."

The judge steepled his hands on the lectern in front of him. "Ah, yes. The young woman. And you are?"

"My name is Sarah Hansen. I have been the schoolteacher here for four years, until…" She faltered. "Until my employment ended recently. I'm twenty-four years old and I assure you I am responsible. I had charge of my two younger sisters until they married. I've known and taught Cecilia and Susie for several years, and recently become much better acquainted with Miss Velma. They deserve better than to become wards of the state or even to be thrust upon a family who doesn't want them."

"And you believe you can give them that, eh? A single woman?"

Sarah glanced at Oscar, who gave her an imperceptible nod and spoke clearly. "Miss Hansen and I are getting married."

Susie gave a soft gasp, but Sarah didn't turn to the girl, only reached out her hand and Susie clasped it tightly.

"Is that so?" The judge stared at them both for a long moment, eyes squinting slightly. "Mighty convenient."

Sarah's heart sank. Her impending marriage to Oscar was the one thing she'd counted on to sway the judge in her favor. But it sounded as if he either didn't believe them or didn't particularly care.

"Miss Hansen, is there anyone here who will vouch for your character? Other than…eh, your fellow?"

Sarah glanced behind her, to see the preacher and his family and the local carpenter—who thought she was a shrew. She swallowed hard. "No, your Honor."

She doubted anyone in Lost Hollow would speak for her, even after the revelations about Mr. Allen and how he'd stirred up trouble.

"Sir, if I might speak," Oscar said. "This woman loves those little girls. When the school board threatened her job if she chose to take care of them, she chose Cecilia and Susie and Velma's best interests, not her own. She was fired because of it. Even though she could've been upset and worried, she worked hard to give these girls a decent Christmas. And then, when she thought they would be taken away from her and her only chance was to marry this cowboy, she rode halfway to Bear Creek— Sir, this is a woman who is deathly afraid of horses. Yet, she rode a far distance to track me down, and proposed to me, just for those little girls. She loves them."

Sarah stared at him as his passionate speech closed, throat clogging with tears. No one had ever stood up for her like that before. Could this really be the same person who had teased her mercilessly back in school?

Then she glanced at the girls. Susie was still clasping her hand, but now Cecilia had stood, Velma on her hip, and was watching Sarah with wide questioning eyes.

"It's true," Sarah said softly, a soft sob escaping her lips, emotion she couldn't contain overwhelming her. "I love all three of you. And I want us to be together, be a family."

For once, Cecilia didn't hold herself distant. She threw herself at Sarah, dislodging her sister's hand as they embraced, baby Velma squished between them. Sarah laughed through her tears. Did the girl finally believe what Sarah had been trying to show her all along?

Susie joined in the embrace, as well, sliding in between Sarah and her older sister. Sarah squeezed them both tightly.

The judge cleared his throat. "This may be a moot question, but what do you girls want to do?"

"We want to stay with Sarah!" the girls chorused, without loosening their arms from hugging their former teacher.

"And do you have the means to support these children?" the judge asked Sarah.

Thinking of the money her sister had sent her, and what savings she had, she now believed it was possible. "Yes, sir."

He banged his gavel on the lectern, startling Sarah. The girls giggled at her.

"Then my ruling is that the girls remain with Sarah Hansen from now on." He pointed at Mr. Smith, who'd been silent and sullen on his pew. "You'll need to stay in town until we can get this other mess sorted out."

Joy flowed through Sarah, expanding in a bubble of laughter. They had done it! Somehow, the judge had been convinced to let Sarah keep custody of the girls.

She shot Oscar a joyful look that was mirrored in his crooked smile.

"We'll be married right away," he said.

"I see no need for that," the judge said. "In your words, Miss Hansen has already been taking care of them alone." He picked up his gavel and moved to one of the front pews where a black case lay open. The preacher moved forward to talk to him and they spoke in hushed voices.

Stunned, Sarah could only look up at Oscar while

the girls crowded around them. "We don't have to get married," she said numbly.

Oscar felt as if someone had cinched his chest cavity far too tightly. He couldn't breathe.

They didn't have to be married. Sarah looked down, embraced the girls with joy. And she didn't seem upset about the judge's last words.

But he wanted to marry her. He loved her. He couldn't go back to the solitary life he'd thought he wanted before, not when he'd felt what it was like to be with someone who lit up his whole life with joy.

Doubts threatened him, crowding in. Had Sarah only wanted to marry him to save the girls? She'd rejected him once before. Would she want to part ways now?

Remembering what his pa had said—was it only yesterday?—he took a deep breath and all the courage he could drum up to blurt out, "I still think we should get married."

Sarah went still and Cecilia and Susie looked up at him with wide eyes. As usual, Velma was too little to realize what was going on and babbled excitedly in her sister's arms. Cecilia seemed to understand the gravity of the situation and pulled Susie back to sit farther down on the pew, giving them a semblance of privacy.

Heart drumming in his ears, face on fire, Oscar confronted the hardest thing he'd ever done. "I'm—I'm in love with you, Sarah."

Now it was her turn for her eyes to widen, blue irises going big and making her face look younger and vulnerable.

He rushed on, hoping he wasn't making the biggest

fool of himself. "I know you've said before you didn't want to marry a cowboy, but this cowboy promises to do anything within my power to take care of you. And our family." He nodded toward the girls, including them. "In the beginning, I thought you were prickly, and bossy, but really you were trying to protect yourself and take care of yourself when no one else had ever done that before. I want to take care of you, Sarah." He took her hands in his shaking ones. "I love you, and I want to marry you for *me,* not because we have to."

She was still and silent, looking up at him with luminous eyes. His heart was in his throat, he was afraid of her rejection—

She squeezed his hands, smiling slightly, and somehow he knew that she was aware of his struggle. His tenderhearted schoolteacher would know that he had been afraid to say the words, though he'd said them, anyway. "I love you, too, Oscar. And yes, I'd love to marry you. Even though I'm still a little afraid of horses. You'll have to teach me they can be trusted."

He reached for her and she came into his embrace. With her head tucked beneath his chin, he finally noticed the girls behind her, whooping and hollering. Baby Velma started fussing at the noise and Susie dissolved into laughter.

He turned, Sarah still in his embrace, and spoke to the judge. "I think we're in need of your services after all, sir."

The man grinned, the first sign of positive emotion he'd shown all day. "It would be my pleasure."

He motioned them forward, calling for the preacher

and his wife to stand as witnesses. Sarah gathered the girls around her, bringing them forward, as well.

"We're a real family now," she murmured as explanation.

He clasped her hands between his and pressed them. It was right, having the girls here with them.

The judge joined them and got right to it, turning to Oscar. "Will you have this woman to be your wedded wife? Will you love her, comfort her, honor and keep her in sickness and in health, so long as you both shall live?"

Oscar couldn't tear his eyes from the woman he loved, the woman God had blessed him with. "I will."

Sarah's eyes filled with joyful tears at the conviction in Oscar's voice.

From the side of her vision, she saw the judge turn to her. "Will you have this man to be your wedded husband? Will you obey him and serve him, love, honor and keep him in sickness and in health, so long as you both shall live?"

After Oscar's declaration, her heart was sure, even if her voice trembled a little. "I will."

She was gratified to see his eyes get a little moist, too. He pressed her hands in his warm wide ones.

"Do you have a ring?" The judge's voice broke their intimate moment, and for a second, Oscar looked panicked.

"I don't." His voice shook. "We'll get you one, I promise." And then his expression brightened. He let go of her hands to reach into the breast pocket of his shirt and pulled out a little pouch. From the little leather pocket, he removed a silver chain and locket.

"This was my mother's. I've been carrying it around since Christmas," he said meaningfully.

She wasn't sure she could take it, not when it must be one of the only things he had left of his mother. And then she realized he meant he'd wanted to give it to her on Christmas…perhaps when they'd shared their first kiss? Had he loved her even then? The thought warmed her.

He swept it around her neck and fastened it.

"I'll treasure it," she whispered.

"You my kiss your bride," the judge intoned.

And Oscar did.

Sarah blushed and broke away when the girls' giggles became a little too loud. Her heart was full.

She'd thought she'd lost the chance of marrying Oscar, the man she loved. She'd thought she might end up a spinster forever. But God had had other plans for her.

Oscar wrapped one arm around Susie's shoulders and extended his other arm for Sarah to take, which she did. She drew Cecilia and Velma close, glad when the girl came easily, with a genuine smile.

"Let's go get some lunch and rest at the hotel for a bit, then we'll collect the girls' things and think about heading home to Bear Creek."

Home to Bear Creek. It sounded wonderful.

They pushed out the door and into the weak winter sunshine, a family unit, but were drawn to a halt by the small knot of people waiting outside.

Sarah's shoulders tensed, but with Oscar at her shoulder, she was confident they could weather whatever would come.

"Miss Hansen—"

"Mrs. White," Oscar corrected the first person to speak, shooting a proud grin in Sarah's direction. A thrill went through her. She was his *wife*.

"Er, Mrs. White," said the mercantile owner, taking off his hat. "And, girls. Well, there's a bunch of us…" He waved his hand at the group behind him. Sarah recognized the dressmaker, several mothers of schoolchildren and the banker. "There's a bunch of us who have realized we've done wrong in listening to—letting ourselves be bullied by one particular person. We should've done the right thing all along, and we didn't."

"We're sorry!" called out one of the mothers, and several others rumbled their agreement.

Sarah looked down at Cecilia squeezed the girl's shoulders, as Cecilia stared at the group with wide eyes.

"We know we can't make it up to you, but we'd like to give you girls some gifts to help you get started at your new home."

Someone pressed a bundle of cloth into Susie's arms. "My girls have outgrown these dresses but they're still in good condition. Should have some more years of wear in them."

One mother handed a cloth-wrapped loaf of soft bread to Sarah. Another brought a basket of eggs and a can of preserves.

When Sarah next looked down, Cecilia had tears in her eyes. "Thank you," the girl whispered.

Sarah hugged her shoulders, looking over at Oscar who wore a proud smile on his face. "Let's go home," she murmured.

Epilogue

Sarah drew up the reins and Belle obeyed, slowing from a walk to a stop at the top of a hill. Oscar reined in beside her, close enough that he reached out for Sarah's gloved hand.

They didn't speak for a moment, looking over the valley between Oscar's small cabin and Jonas and Penny's larger house. Even covered with snow, the winter landscape was breathtaking.

Oscar's herd was bunched up near the forested part of the land, while across the way in a different pasture, cattle moved restlessly. Sarah could see activity around the barn and corral at Jonas's place. Smoke curled from chimneys at both houses.

"A new year. A new start," Oscar said. "Do you think you can be happy here?"

Though he stared out at the land, squinting slightly beneath his Stetson, Sarah heard the gravity of his tone.

Pretending to consider it, Sarah leaned her head to one side. "Hmm. Well, I don't know," she teased. "The cabin *is* small—too small for a family of five, wouldn't you say?"

He cut his eyes to her. "My brothers will help add on a couple of bedrooms in the spring."

"Yes, your brothers. I didn't realize there would be so *many* of them." She wrinkled her nose at him, knowing he understood she was joshing him.

She *had* been a bit overwhelmed upon their arrival, when they'd been besieged by young men—along with a pigtailed girl about Cecilia's age wearing trousers. Sarah had recognized Davy and Seb, and had quickly been introduced to the rest. The girls had taken to the large boisterous group immediately, Susie and Cecilia following Breanna to her room, leaving Velma with Sarah. Her heart warmed when she thought of the trust Cecilia had showed her by relinquishing the tot she held so close to her heart.

Sarah had been relieved when Penny had commandeered her and they'd retired to the kitchen with Velma and Penny's two small children. Penny had told Sarah the story of her first experience—a boisterous meal—with the family, and they'd shared a laugh at the overwhelming nature of it. Sarah felt she could grow to love the family, but had been thankful to retire to Oscar's small cabin and the relative quiet of only the voices of three girls.

A couple of days later, Penny hosted a New Year's party and Sarah had enjoyed herself immensely as she got to know the family more and discovered the personalities of each brother and the firecracker who was Breanna. The only solemn moment of the whole evening had been when Jonas had read a letter from Maxwell, who was away at medical school. Oscar had slipped his hand into Sarah's and she knew he still missed his brother and was sharing the emotion with her, opening up. She'd fallen even more in love with him at that moment.

"And there are the horses," she continued now. "A lot of horses around all the time. In the corral, the barn, all around. What if one of the children were to get stepped on?"

She patted Belle's neck with the hand that Oscar didn't have a hold of.

Now her husband was looking directly at her, frowning.

"You don't like the herd?"

Actually, she'd been impressed by the quality of the animals. She didn't know much about horses at all, but she could tell the animals were fine. And there were so many of them. She had no doubt that Oscar's herd would bring in plenty of profits for their family.

"You know, I'm finding I don't mind them as much as I once would've."

"You've mentioned everything except your new husband," he said, jiggling her hand. "Do you think you can be happy with *me?*"

Her usually jovial husband was still so serious. She knew he must be thinking of the deaths of his parents and the uncle who hadn't wanted anything to do with him. Could he really be worried that she would reject him, even now?

"Yes," she whispered, because she couldn't tease him about something like this. And because she had no doubt of it. He'd proven that he was loyal and trustworthy, proven his love before he'd been able to utter the words.

Her horseman was the perfect man for her.

* * * * *

Dear Reader:

Thanks for reading *Roping the Wrangler.* I really enjoyed writing Oscar and Sarah's story and seeing the two of them grow and ultimately fall in love. Both of these characters had to overcome not only their preconceived notions about each other, but also individual fears to reach their happy ending. It seems that I struggle with fear each time I write a book—fear that I won't be able to finish it, fear that it won't be "good enough," fear that no one will like it. And yet, every time, I've learned to trust God more and that when I let Him be in control (He is, anyway!), the result will be a success.

I hope you'll watch for Maxwell's story coming soon—I can't wait to write about one of my favorite characters from *The Homesteader's Sweetheart,* where we met all of Jonas White's kids for the first time.

Thanks for reading and please let me know what you thought of the book. You can reach me at lacyjwilliams@gmail.com or in care of Love Inspired Books, 233 Broadway, Suite 1001, New York, NY 10279.

Lacy Williams

Questions for Discussion

1. At the beginning of the story, both Sarah and Oscar have preconceived ideas about each other. What were their impressions of each other? Were their ideas right or wrong?

2. Have you ever misjudged someone based on a wrong first impression? What happened? How did you find out you were wrong?

3. At the beginning of the story, what does Sarah want most for herself? Have you ever had something you wanted more than anything? What was it and why did you want it? Did you get it?

4. Sarah tried to be sensitive to the needs of Cecilia, Susie and Velma, but she faced opposition from many people in town. Have you ever fought for something that no one else seemed to care about? What happened?

5. Oscar tried to fill his life with other things to combat his loneliness. Did this work for him? Why or why not?

6. Have you ever tried to keep busy to avoid an emotional issue? What happened?

7. When did Sarah's attitude toward Oscar start to change? When did she start falling in love with him?

8. Sarah had a deep-seated fear of horses. What are you most afraid of? Why?

9. Oscar was scared of revealing his feelings and committing to Sarah because of what had happened to him in the past. Have you ever been afraid to commit to a relationship, friendship or otherwise? Why? Discuss.

10. Sarah ultimately made a difference in the lives of three of her students. Have you ever had a teacher who made a big difference in your life? How did they affect you?

11. Oscar and Sarah try to create a memorable Christmas for the girls in the face of their difficulties. What is your favorite Christmas memory, and why?

12. Sarah was unfairly fired from her job. Have you ever been treated unfairly? What happened?

13. Both Sarah and Oscar have heroic qualities, such as compassion, bravery, humor and tenderness. What is your best quality?

14. Did you enjoy this book? What was your favorite part?

15. Did you relate more to the hero or heroine in this story? Why?

COMING NEXT MONTH
from Love Inspired® Historical
AVAILABLE SEPTEMBER 3, 2013

FALLING FOR THE TEACHER
Pinewood Weddings
Dorothy Clark

Cole Aylward may be helping Sadie Spencer's grandfather, but he's the last man Sadie wants to see when she comes home. He *must* have an ulterior motive. Can Cole convince her that his intentions—and feelings—are genuine?

KEEPING FAITH
Hannah Alexander

After her husband's death, Dr. Victoria Fenway is determined to find his murderer. But could her quest for revenge ruin her second chance at love with wagon-train captain Joseph Rickard?

THE DUTIFUL DAUGHTER
Sanctuary Bay
Jo Ann Brown

Sophia Meriweather knows she's expected to marry her late father's new heir. But when widower Charles Winthrop, Lord Northbridge, and his two young children arrive, Sophie must choose between duty to her family or to her heart.

A PLACE OF REFUGE
Boardinghouse Betrothals
Janet Lee Barton

Kathleen O'Bryan was searching for a safe refuge, and Heaton House boardinghouse gave her the shelter she needed—and reunited her with the man who had rescued her in the past. Can Luke Patterson offer her a safe haven where she can risk opening her heart once more?

REQUEST YOUR FREE BOOKS!

2 FREE INSPIRATIONAL NOVELS
PLUS 2
FREE
MYSTERY GIFTS

Love Inspired.
HISTORICAL
INSPIRATIONAL HISTORICAL ROMANCE

YES! Please send me 2 FREE Love Inspired® Historical novels and my 2 FREE mystery gifts (gifts are worth about $10). After receiving them, if I don't wish to receive any more books, I can return the shipping statement marked "cancel." If I don't cancel, I will receive 4 brand-new novels every month and be billed just $4.74 per book in the U.S. or $5.24 per book in Canada. That's a saving of at least 21% off the cover price. It's quite a bargain! Shipping and handling is just 50¢ per book in the U.S. and 75¢ per book in Canada.* I understand that accepting the 2 free books and gifts places me under no obligation to buy anything. I can always return a shipment and cancel at any time. Even if I never buy another book, the two free books and gifts are mine to keep forever.

102/302 IDN F5CN

Name _____ (PLEASE PRINT) _____

Address _____ Apt. # _____

City _____ State/Prov. _____ Zip/Postal Code _____

Signature (if under 18, a parent or guardian must sign)

Mail to the **Harlequin® Reader Service:**
IN U.S.A.: P.O. Box 1867, Buffalo, NY 14240-1867
IN CANADA: P.O. Box 609, Fort Erie, Ontario L2A 5X3

Want to try two free books from another series?
Call 1-800-873-8635 or visit www.ReaderService.com.

* Terms and prices subject to change without notice. Prices do not include applicable taxes. Sales tax applicable in N.Y. Canadian residents will be charged applicable taxes. Offer not valid in Quebec. This offer is limited to one order per household. Not valid for current subscribers to Love Inspired Historical books. All orders subject to credit approval. Credit or debit balances in a customer's account(s) may be offset by any other outstanding balance owed by or to the customer. Please allow 4 to 6 weeks for delivery. Offer available while quantities last.

Your Privacy—The Harlequin® Reader Service is committed to protecting your privacy. Our Privacy Policy is available online at www.ReaderService.com or upon request from the Harlequin Reader Service.

We make a portion of our mailing list available to reputable third parties that offer products we believe may interest you. If you prefer that we not exchange your name with third parties, or if you wish to clarify or modify your communication preferences, please visit us at www.ReaderService.com/consumerschoice or write to us at Harlequin Reader Service Preference Service, P.O. Box 9062, Buffalo, NY 14269. Include your complete name and address.

LIH13R

SPECIAL EXCERPT FROM

Love Inspired

*Gracie Wilson is about to become the most famous
runaway bride in Bygones, Kansas. Can she find true
happiness? Read on for a preview of
THE BOSS'S BRIDE by Brenda Minton.
Available September 2013.*

Gracie Wilson stood in the center of a Sunday school classroom at the Bygones Community Church. Her friend Janie Lawson adjusted Gracie's veil and again wiped at tears.

"You look beautiful."

"Do I?" Gracie glanced in the full-length mirror that hung on the door of the supply cabinet and suppressed a shudder. The dress was hideous and she hadn't picked it.

"You look beautiful. And you look miserable. It's your wedding day—you should be smiling."

Gracie smiled but she knew it was a poor attempt at best.

"Gracie, what's wrong?"

"Nothing. I'm good." She leaned her cheek against Janie's hand on her shoulder. "Other than the fact that you've moved one hundred miles away and I never get to see you."

What else could she say? Everyone in Bygones, Kansas, thought she'd landed the catch of the century. Trent Morgan was handsome, charming and came from money. She should be thrilled to be marrying him. Six months ago she had been thrilled. But then she'd started to notice little signs. She should have put the wedding on hold the moment she noticed those signs. And when she knew for certain, she should have put a stop to the entire thing. But she hadn't.

"Do you care if I have a few minutes alone?"

"Of course not." Janie gave her another hug. "But not too long. Your dad is outside and when I came in to check on you the seats were filling up out there."

"I just need a minute to catch my breath."

Janie smiled back at her and then the door to the classroom closed. And for the first time in days, Gracie was alone. She looked around the room with the bright yellow walls and posters from Sunday school curriculum. She stopped at the poster of David and Goliath. Her favorite. She'd love to have that kind of faith, the kind that knocked down giants.

"You almost ready, Gracie?" her dad called through the door.

"Almost."

She opened the window, just to let in fresh air. She leaned out, breathing the hint of autumn, enjoying the breeze on her face. She looked across the grassy lawn and saw...

FREEDOM.

To see if Gracie finds her happily-ever-after, pick up
THE BOSS'S BRIDE
wherever Love Inspired books are sold.

Cole Alyward may be helping
Sadie Spencer's grandfather, but he's the last
man Sadie wants to see when she comes home.
He must have an ulterior motive. Can
Cole convince her that his intentions—and
feelings—are genuine?

PINEWOOD
WEDDINGS

Falling for the Teacher
by

DOROTHY CLARK

Available September 2013
wherever Love Inspired Historical books are sold.

A FATHER'S PROMISE

by

CAROLYNE AARSEN

When the child she gave up for adoption shows up in
town with her adoptive father, Renee must overcome
her guilt to find true love.

Available September 2013
wherever Love Inspired books are sold.

www.LoveInspiredBooks.com

LI87836